FORGOTTEN

DJINN DOMINION: BOOK 2

CHRISTINE POPE

DARK VALENTINE PRESS

FORGOTTEN

ISBN: 978-1-946435-14-9

Published by Dark Valentine Press

Cover design by Lou Harper

Book formatting by Indie Author Services

ONE

DEIRDRE GRAVES LOOKED DOWN AT THE nearly melted patch of snow under the spreading pine tree next to the Forest Service lookout building and frowned. The storm that had brought the snow to California's San Bernardino Mountains was already almost three weeks in the past, and, according the calendar that hung on the wall of the wildlife research station that had become her home, it was now December first. The warm sun beating down on her head gave a lie to the date, but that was Southern California for you. It might be comfortable and mild now, but more storms were sure to come eventually…which meant Deirdre had a decision to make, one she really couldn't avoid for much longer. Should she stay here in her mountain refuge, or head for the lowlands to look for survivors?

That same question had passed through her thoughts dozens of times already. It had been easy to push the decision aside as late summer gradually shifted into autumn, because the mild weather had held and she had no real place to go. Surely she was better off staying where she was.

More than two months in, and no djinn had found her yet. Deirdre didn't know whether those murderous elementals had decided there were no humans left in these mountains, or whether they were busy exterminating the rest of humanity and would get around to the few stragglers in outlying areas when they felt like it. Neither prospect was very reassuring.

Even though she'd seen no sign of any activity —animal, djinn, or otherwise—on her hike up to the lookout, she still held a shotgun in one hand, both chambers loaded. It could probably knock down a bear, and maybe make a djinn think twice about coming after her.

Could you even kill a djinn? Deirdre had no idea…and really didn't want to find out.

A cool wind blew down from San Gorgonio Peak, fresh and clean and scented with pine. If she had to spend the rest of her life alone, she supposed she could have ended up in a much worse place—like her university's desert research station out near Borrego Springs. Temperatures over a hundred degrees nearly year-'round and no air conditioning?

No, thanks.

Now that she was safely among the trees once again, the tension that took hold whenever she went to the lookout—which was quite exposed, sitting on the edge of an open, rocky stretch of land—began to leave her body. It was one thing to tell herself that there wasn't anyone or anything around to give her trouble, and quite another to feel comfortable with being so exposed. This had been her third trip to the fire lookout post; she was probably tempting fate by going up there so many times, but she kept hoping against hope that she might find some evidence to prove she wasn't the only human being left in the world. The horrible fever known as the Heat had killed almost everyone, and those few who were left had been systematically hunted down by the djinn. She didn't consider it outside the bounds of possibility that she might very well be humanity's sole survivor.

It was very quiet in the woods today. Usually she could hear birds twittering on the branches above her, sharing their gossip, only going quiet when a hawk circled far overhead. Now, though, as Deirdre made her careful way between the pines and the fir trees, the only sound that came to her ears was the soughing of the wind in the pine branches. She'd always thought it a beautiful sound, but now it seemed mournful to her, as if the wind itself wept for the world's losses.

Halfway back to the research station was a spot she'd found some weeks earlier, a secluded pond in its own little hollow, with a small sandy beach and the forest clustering around on all sides. She liked to go there and watch the clouds drift overhead as they reflected in the water, to see the wind ripple over the surface of the pond. Why there weren't any houses near that secluded meadow, she wasn't sure. It seemed like an ideal spot, especially since having a pond or a creek or a stream on your property generally increased its value.

Deirdre had thought it would be good to stop by the pond today, to try to find some solace in the beauty of the quiet, out-of-the-way spot. Just a few minutes to breathe deeply and do her best to forget the empty world she'd seen once again from the fire lookout station, a world that no longer had any place for her in it.

Not for the first time, she reflected how appropriate her name had turned out to be. The cause of her sorrows might be very different from that of her Irish namesake, but it seemed her destiny had proved to be just as unhappy. No, she hadn't caused a war or been caught in a conflict between a mighty warrior and a jealous king, and yet she had to wonder if that long-ago Deirdre's losses could ever measure up to her own.

Doing her best to push that gloomy thought aside, Deirdre came down out of the woods and began to walk toward the water's edge. Before she'd taken more than a couple of steps, however, she spotted something very out of place in the green landscape. A few yards from the pond was a splash of bright, gaudy color, what looked like several yards of discarded silk fabric in a bold scarlet shade.

A curtain from someone's house, one that had somehow been blown here by the wind? That was the only explanation she could think of for why something so out of place would be lying by the pond. Possibly, but how could it have come here? The weather had been strangely mild lately, with hardly any wind.

She took several cautious steps toward the shimmering red cloth, then a few more. Now she stood only a few feet away. Her heart leapt into her throat when the bundle of fabric moved, rolled over. Staring up at her was a man. Bright blue eyes caught hers.

"Help me," he whispered.

Amaal al-Tariq had done his best to make good use of his exile in the mountains. He'd left the furnishings in the house he had been given alone for the most part, since the place had been decorated with a thoughtfulness he was not sure he could match. However, he had amused himself by creating a wine cellar in the basement and stocking it with the vintages he most enjoyed. He had explored the woods around his new home, and had even—shudder—taught himself to fish, although he threw all of those he caught immediately back in the water. Boning and gutting fish was not high on his list of enjoyable pastimes, especially when he could conjure any fully prepared meal he wanted with a snap of his fingers. Such things came easily to his kind.

However, these activities had begun to pall as the days and then weeks passed, a situation of some concern. After all, if he was already tired of these simple pastimes and bored with himself in so short a span of time, what on earth was he supposed to do with the endless centuries of his future existence?

It had been so much better in the penthouse he had taken for his use in downtown Los Angeles. From there, he could see a vast swath of Southern California—all the way to the shimmering Pacific Ocean from one side of the rooftop apartment, and out to the snow-capped mountains of the San Bernardino range from the other.

Now those very mountains were more like his prison. One could not complain about the beauty of the place, he supposed, but there was also nothing here to entertain himself. In Los Angeles, he could explore the empty museums and decide which of those priceless works of art might look better on his own walls, or wander through the once-bustling stores and help himself to any items he thought might be useful or amusing. But there was certainly nothing like that in the closest town to the house he must now call home. That town was once called Running Springs, and while the setting was picturesque enough, it did not offer much in the way of Picassos or hundred-year-old wine.

Why the elders had even decreed that this must be his home, Amaal was still not certain. He had been given this property long before his brother Omar stirred up all that trouble by kidnapping Malik al-Mazin's Chosen, so Amaal was fairly certain the elders hadn't selected this secluded mountain spot as any kind of punishment for his participation in that particular debacle. Besides, Malik had gotten his revenge, killing Omar in a battle fought with their elemental powers, so one would think everyone should consider the matter settled.

Amaal had mourned his brother for a time, mostly because that was the thing to do, and not because he thought the world had suffered any great loss because of his death. Blood ties were not enough to make him overlook Omar's numerous flaws. Indeed, he had thought to himself on more than one occasion that the world was probably a better place now that Omar was not in it. Still, it was in general a sad thing to lose a brother, even one as despicable as Omar.

And today—well, today had turned out fine and bright and blue, giving no hint that winter was on its way, save perhaps the patches of snow that gleamed in the sun on the highest peaks above him. Amaal had taken to walking in the woods, mostly because he did not have much else to do with his time. It was at least somewhat diverting to observe the birds and the various flora and fauna, although at this time of year there were no wildflowers to pick, and he did not know whether any of the berries he spied on the various bushes were edible or not. A djinn could manage poisons that would fell a human, but at the same time, he saw no reason to give himself a stomach cramp.

He'd ventured farther to the east than he had gone so far, not for any real reason, except that he had not yet explored this part of his territory and he thought he might as well get a better sense of all the lands that were his. The closest djinn was miles and miles away in a place called Claremont, so he knew he had no reason to worry about anyone trespassing on his property, knew he could roam freely through the woods.

After walking for a few miles, Amaal came upon a small clearing with a perfect oval of a pond in its center. The water looked very clear and clean, showing the pond's sandy bottom. In the summer, this might be a good spot to bathe; not quite the same as the sparkling swimming pool that had been installed in the rooftop deck outside his late, lamented penthouse, but better than nothing. He might have been a fire elemental, but that did not mean he didn't enjoy a good swim on a warm day.

As he stood there, looking down at the shimmering surface of the pond, a strange malaise suddenly swept over him. He put a hand to his stomach, wondering if perhaps he had eaten something that didn't agree with him, although any kind of sickness was exceedingly rare in a djinn.

His heart began to hammer in his chest, and almost before he realized what was happening, his legs had given way beneath him and he had fallen to the ground, face down in—luckily—the grass that surrounded the pond, rather than on its narrow, sandy shore. A strange shaking overtook his limbs, and the world seemed to spin around him.

Am I dying? he thought. The irony of expiring here, in the middle of nowhere with no one to know of his passing, was not lost on him. But no, a djinn could not simply drop dead for no reason. A mortal wound might lay him low, but he had suffered no such blow, had taken no injury on his walk. It was as if this dreadful weakness and sickness had descended out of the clear blue sky.

A rustling in the grass told him something was approaching him. With a great effort, he raised his head to see what it was.

He had expected to see a deer, or perhaps a coyote or even a bear. However, his eyes met those of a young woman who stood a few feet away. Her sun-streaked light brown hair blew around her face, which was surprisingly lovely, with regular, delicate features. In one hand she held a shotgun, but she clutched it by the barrel and didn't appear very comfortable with the idea of using it.

Even so, for one mad moment, he wondered whether she had shot him. No, that was impossible. He had heard no report from the gun, which should have boomed off the surrounding trees. Besides, while a shotgun blast might level a human, it certainly couldn't incapacitate a djinn to the point where he could barely lift his head from the ground.

She was human, so she had to be immune. How she had managed to survive out here in these mountains for so many weeks, Amaal didn't know, but he had more pressing issues on his mind. He hated to ask for assistance from a mortal, but he feared he had little choice.

"Help me," he whispered. The weakness of his voice shocked him, but at least he'd been able to form the words.

Her slender fingers tightened on the gun, pale against the blued steel. Otherwise, she didn't move. "Who are you?"

"My name is Amaal."

Her eyes narrowed. He noticed that they were a clear, piercing aquamarine blue, quite the most arresting eyes he had ever seen in all his long life. "What's the matter with you?"

"I—" Good question. The problem was, he had no idea what was wrong with him. Never before had he felt so ill, so helpless. Djinn were not supposed to feel this way. It was humans who suffered from illness and disease, who led short, brutish lives filled with all kinds of pain. "I don't know," he managed to whisper. "I was walking, and then I began to feel ill."

A strange sort of comprehension seemed to pass over the young woman's face. Some of the rosiness left her cheeks, even as her eyes widened and she gripped the shotgun, now raising it so it pointed directly at him. "Oh, my God," she murmured, although it was clear she had not intended those words for his ears.

"It works."

TWO

HER MIND WAS REELING. SHE'D CARRIED THE small black box in her backpack every time she ventured out from the small clapboard building that had once housed U.C. Riverside's wildlife research station, but she'd never really thought it would work. It was just a kind of lucky token, a bit bulkier than a rabbit's foot but serving basically the same purpose.

Really, it was all because of the voice on the radio.

The voice belonged to a man whose name was Miles Odekirk, and apparently he was based in Los Alamos, New Mexico. For more than two months, ever since the Heat swept over the world, he'd been broadcasting his message, telling of a group of survivors based in the small mountain town, warning anyone who might still be out there listening about the djinn, and how they were intent on killing any people who'd survived the deadly fever that had destroyed most of humankind.

Deirdre had seen firsthand what that dread disease could do. The wildlife station was usually staffed with a rotating complement of grad students and upper-division students, but no more than four or five at a time. She'd been there with three others—Leland, who was getting his master's in forestry and was studying the bark beetle infestation in the San Bernardino National Forest; Kate, getting the last bit of research done on her dissertation about deer populations in extra-urban areas; and Sean, who'd been a senior like Deirdre herself, and was there more as an assistant and general jack of all trades rather than to further any particular field of study.

Kate had left less than a day in, as soon as the first reports about the dread disease began to pop up on the internet. Leland and Sean and Deirdre had tried to convince her to stay, since they thought their isolation here at the station could only help them to avoid getting sick. That isolation hadn't mattered in the end, though—Deirdre never knew what happened to Kate, but both Sean and Leland were dead within twenty-four hours of her departure. Deirdre had done what she could, dispensing aspirin and trying to keep them hydrated. Not that it mattered. At the end of it all, they were gone, killed by a fever that burned so hot, it left only ashes behind.

She supposed she should be glad for that. Burying her compatriots would have been difficult, given how parched and hard the earth was at that time of year, in late September. And because conditions had been so dry, cremation would have been out of the question as well. One errant spark could have set the entire forest ablaze. It had been easier to focus on the practical aspects of disposing of their remains rather than the sorrow and horror she'd felt at their passing, the ever-present worry that she might be next.

Afterward—after she'd gathered their ashes and scattered them below the pine trees near the research station, and murmured the Lord's Prayer because it was the only thing she could remember from the Bible—Deirdre sat alone in the station's front office, wondering what in the world to do next. She didn't know why she wasn't dead, and kept waiting to come down with the deadly fever herself. Except she remained as healthy as the day she'd come up for her weekend at the station, her only real health issue the allergies that always seemed to get worse when she was deep in the pine forest. Still, the Flonase she always carried with her seemed to take care of the worst of her symptoms, and she knew she could get more at the convenience store down in Running Springs.

While she was taking care of her companions, she'd used the satellite phone at the station to try to call home, to check to see if her mother was all right. The first time the call went through, but no one picked up. After that, all she got was a fast busy signal, no matter how many times she hit redial. She knew what that meant. The lines were overloaded.

The day after that, there was nothing at all, not a fast busy signal, nothing coming through the satellite TV, either. Even so, she'd sat there with the shortwave weather radio, scrolling slowly through the bands, trying to find some evidence to tell her she wasn't the only person left in the world, too frightened to leave her current place of refuge. After five days, she determined that she had to leave, if only to go into Running Springs to scrounge some food. The station was supplied with enough rations to last about a week—and in her case they would last even longer, since she was the only one left and the pantry had been stocked to feed four people—but sooner or later, she was going to run out.

Besides, there might be survivors in Running Springs.

Just as she was about to head into town, however, she'd taken one last pass with the radio, one final search of the bands to see if anyone still was alive out there. And when she'd heard Miles Odekirk's voice come through the speakers, she'd cried, tears rolling down her cheeks as she realized she wasn't completely alone.

True, he was in New Mexico, which might as well have been on the dark side of the moon—especially after she heard what he had to say.

Strange creatures that looked human but weren't. Djinn. Elemental beings that even now were sweeping across the face of the earth, looking for all the immune survivors so they might finish the job they'd started. Deirdre hadn't wanted to believe any of it. She wanted to think that Miles Odekirk was a madman, someone immune who'd been driven crazy by his isolation and the losses she assumed he must have suffered.

However, there was something about the way he spoke—calm, dry, almost pedantic—that seemed to tell her he wasn't crazy. He didn't rant or rave. In fact, his no-nonsense delivery reminded Deirdre of her Botany 101 professor, although this Miles person sounded much younger than old Professor Barton, probably no more than forty at the most. He warned against venturing out alone, but said that at the very least anyone wishing to avoid the djinn had to stick to whatever cover they could find, whether that was an abandoned house or a thick stand of trees.

And he spoke of the devices he'd created, the ones that supposedly could repel the djinn and weaken them to the point where they were no stronger than an ordinary human.

Deirdre had taken his advice to heart. No, she couldn't stay in hiding forever, but she'd done her best to wear neutral colors when she ventured outside. Because of this, she'd been able to make several foraging trips to Running Springs, and had also ransacked the pantries of some of the houses in the area. She refused to allow herself to feel guilty about these petty thefts, since the small piles of gray dust she'd encountered in those empty homes and businesses told her that the people who'd owned them definitely didn't need those supplies any longer.

And once she knew she had enough supplies to survive on her own for a good while, she got to work.

The wildlife station had solar and its own well and a propane tank, so she was set in terms of power and water and gas for cooking as long as she was frugal about her usage. Heat hadn't been too much of an issue so far, although she worried about what she would do when the true snows of winter came. It wasn't a lack of firewood that had concerned her—the station also had a wood-burning stove, and a large stack of pine in the wood bins out back—but the very real fear that smoke coming from the chimney would certainly attract any djinn in the area. For the time being, she'd bundled up and piled extra blankets on the narrow bed in the room she would have shared with Kate.

Miles Odekirk kept repeating his instructions over and over, slowly and patiently. Deirdre had wondered whether it was frustrating for him to be sending his words out into the ether with no idea whether anyone could hear them. Possibly there were survivors somewhere who had access to a ham radio and could reply, but she wasn't so lucky; the broadband radio had been mostly for keeping up with weather reports, and anyone staying at the station had used the sat phone for actual communications. She hadn't found a ham radio during any of her foraging expeditions…not that she would have known how to operate it even if she had. It almost physically hurt to not be able to talk to Miles Odekirk, to cry out that she was here all alone and desperately needed someone to come help her. Then again, what could he have done? He was more than a thousand miles away, and there had to have been plenty of djinn haunting the miles in between the San Bernardino mountains and Los Alamos, just waiting to pounce on any hapless humans who dared to venture out into that desert wilderness.

But at least she would try to build one of his

devices. She knew her way around a soldering gun, thanks to having an older brother who'd always been into electronics and model rockets and other kinds of science geek stuff. Whether or not Douglas had survived was moot at this point; he'd known she was going to spend the weekend at the wildlife station, so surely if he'd lived through the Heat, he would have come in search of her. That he'd never appeared seemed to prove he was just as dead as everyone else.

She hadn't wanted to think about that. It had been better to sit in the small lab located at the back of the building, next to the area with the various cages that had once held injured wildlife, and use the pieces of Kate's laptop—she'd left everything behind when she fled the station, right down to her computer and her clothing—and Sean and Leland's iPads to put together the device that Dr. Odekirk had invented. Deirdre hadn't pretended to understand the mechanics of what she was doing; she just patiently followed the scientist's extremely precise instructions, using the touch screens from the pilfered iPads to construct several faces of the small, cube-shaped machine. Once she was done, it seemed to function—at least, lights went on and off when she moved her fingers over it in the places that were supposed to control its strength and intensity and range. However, without any djinn around, she couldn't really say whether it worked or not, and she wasn't about to go in search of them just to test whether the device was truly functional. She might have felt some days as though she was dying of loneliness, but it still wasn't worth risking her life to find out.

Still, Deirdre had found some reassurance in carrying the device in her backpack with her when she ventured out from the station to forage. Supplies weren't so low that she'd yet thought of hunting to supplement the items in the pantry. The forest might teem with life, but that didn't mean she was ready to kill and dress a deer, or even a rabbit or a squirrel. She'd found a shotgun and a .22 rifle in one of Running Springs' empty houses, and she'd brought the guns back to the station with her, although she doubted she'd be able to hit the broad side of a barn with either one of them.

This final trip to the lookout station had been her way of forcing herself to make a decision… any kind of decision. At this point, she really only had two options. She just needed to pick one and go with it.

Rationally speaking, there was really no reason to go down the mountain. She had her refuge at the research station. So far, she'd survived her various trips to gather supplies. No one had bothered her here yet, and she guessed no one would.

There was probably enough nonperishable food in Running Springs' pantries and stores to keep her alive through the winter. She could get over her squeamishness, teach herself how to hunt and fish and dress an animal. None of this sounded terribly appealing, but it was better than her other option, which was to gather her courage and leave the place that had sheltered her for the past few months, a plan of action that was terrifying on its surface, now that she knew what waited for her out there.

There was the device, true, but she had no way to test it. Otherwise, she would have packed what she could into Sean's Toyota truck—definitely the best vehicle at the station for that kind of journey —and headed out for New Mexico as soon as she was sure it worked. The djinn might have spotted her, but with their powers neutralized, they wouldn't have been able to do much about it, either. They couldn't have stopped her.

But she hadn't known whether it was really functioning the way it was supposed to. Lights that flashed on and off when she ran her hands over the surface of the little box were no guarantee of anything.

Except…she seemed to know now. This man —this person—lying on the ground in front of her, face pale and sweaty, had to be a djinn. No regular human being would be wearing clothes like that…and no human being would have been affected nearly to the point of fainting by the little black box that traveled with her in her backpack. Her gut clenched in dread, even though she could tell he was in no shape to offer any real threat.

"What works?" he asked, the strain clear in his words.

She didn't bother to reply to his question, instead gave him another. If he was a djinn, he certainly didn't deserve any courtesy from her. Voice rough, she made herself ask the question, even though she dreaded to hear the answer.

"You're a djinn…aren't you?"

As he stared up at the young woman, several possible lies flitted through Amaal's mind. However, he guessed she would accept none of them, this creature who appeared both fragile as glass and yet strong as steel, like a rapier from a bygone age. Besides, he feared the bright silk robes he favored had already given him away. No mortal would dress like this—or rather, no mortal who still walked in these woods would wear anything so clearly not designed for stealth. "Yes," he said simply.

Her fingers tightened even more, standing out white-knuckled as she gripped the gun. "Get up."

If only he could oblige her. He certainly didn't want her to shoot him, but on the other hand, his body was simply unwilling to obey her commands. "I don't think I can."

She made a sound of annoyance, then lowered the shotgun so she could hold it with one hand while she reached with the other to fish something out of the backpack she wore. After a moment's struggle, she produced a small, glassy-looking black box, about four inches on a side, just big enough to rest in the palm of her hand. She leaned the gun against her leg for a moment so she could run a finger over one surface of the box.

Immediately, Amaal felt the sickness and weakness that had threatened to consume him retreat a bit. Not all the way—no, he still was ill and weak and tired. He knew he could not move quickly enough to seize the gun from the young woman, even though the thought did cross his mind. However, he did believe he might be able to stand.

"Better?" she asked, and he nodded.

"I think so."

"Then get up."

Legs shaking, he pushed himself to his feet. He looked at the box she held and asked, "What is that thing?"

"There's no name for it," she said. "But it works. That's the important thing."

As he stared at the device, a sudden shiver of understanding passed through him. There had been rumors that a mortal scientist had devised an instrument which effectively neutralized the djinns' powers, rendering them weak, unable to use any of their inborn gifts, making them not much different from a human. Amaal had dismissed those rumors as fancy, especially since these fabled devices were supposedly being used a thousand miles away from where he now dwelled. He had not thought there was any need for concern, had not thought one of them would ever be used against him.

And yet here was a mortal holding one of those devices, a young woman who certainly should not have been able to get her hands on such a thing. If he had not been feeling so dreadful, he might have chuckled at the capricious nature of the universe, how it had brought him into her orbit. However, he saw no triumph in her delicate features for subduing him, only worry and fear.

"What are you doing here?" she asked.

"These are my lands."

She returned the device to her backpack. "What do you mean, your lands?"

Every syllable was an effort, but he forced himself to reply. "A-all of us djinn were given lands here on Earth for our own. Th-these are mine for many miles around, mine to do with as I please."

A short, humorless laugh emerged from her pretty lips. "You don't exactly seem like the master of your destiny…Amaal."

"I fear you are not seeing me at my best," he replied. It even hurt to raise an eyebrow at her, but somehow he managed it.

She nodded. "No, I guess not. Well, Amaal, you may think these are your lands, but they're mine, too." A pause, as if she was thinking something over, and then she commanded him, "Start walking."

"'Walking'?" he repeated.

"Yes," she replied. "You're standing, so I suppose you can walk." Once again she lifted the shotgun and pointed it at him. However, from the way her hands trembled slightly, he guessed she had no real notion of how to use it.

Her inexperience would have been amusing, except that he was worried she might do something to accidentally make the gun go off. Judging by how weak he felt at the moment, he feared any injury she caused him might not heal as quickly as it should have. If that proved to be the case, then a blast from that shotgun just might kill him. And even though he had lately found his life to be dull, he still had no wish to leave it.

"I can walk," he said. "Although not quickly."

"That's all right." Her chin jerked in a direction roughly northwest. "That way."

Since there was little else he could do, thanks to his current weakness, he began to walk. Each step was excruciating—not because it actually pained him, but because it required so much effort, as though he dragged his limbs through the world's thickest, stickiest mud. Even so, he found he had enough breath to ask, "Where are we going?"

"To the research station."

That reply sent a jolt of alarm through him. What, was she some kind of scientist? Did she plan to vivisect him, see how a djinn differed from a human?

No, she seemed too young to be a scientist. Perhaps in her early twenties, although he'd be the first to admit that he wasn't very good at guessing humans' ages. Their lives were so short, the decades passing over them so quickly, that it was hard for him to have a frame of reference.

"Is it far?"

"A couple of miles."

Miles. Well, Amaal supposed if he forced himself to concentrate on putting one foot in front of the other, and didn't think of either how far he had come or how far he had to go, he might be able to survive the experience. It would be too humiliating to give up in front of this beautiful young woman, even though he doubted that she had any designs on his person, except perhaps of the scientific sort.

They walked in silence for some time. Amaal could feel his legs growing heavier and heavier, as though every step drained a little more from him. At the same time, he could sense how that terrible little device she carried not only weakened him physically, but seemed to have separated him from the source of his power. He could not have called down the fire—his element—or used his inborn djinn gift of instantaneously sending himself from one place to another. No, all he could do was struggle along, wondering what this girl would do if he collapsed in front of her and refused to go one step further.

Some stubbornness within him would not allow him to do such a thing, however. Perhaps it was his fate to die at her hands, but he would not allow her to see how weak he truly was. His people might have believed in the next world, in an existence after this one, true, and yet he had no real desire to learn whether such a place actually existed.

After they had walked in silence for some time, he said, "I have given you my name. It is only polite that you should give me yours."

At first she didn't reply. In fact, the stony silence which greeted this request went on for so long, he thought she would not answer at all. At last, though, she said, "Deirdre. Deirdre Graves."

A mournful surname, although perhaps fitting for someone who had lived to see so many of her fellow humans dead. Not that any of them would require a grave—that was perhaps the cleverest part of the disease his kind had concocted, that it would not leave any messy corpses behind to pollute the world.

He doubted Deirdre would be cheered by this observation, however, and so he only said, "Thank you, Deirdre."

Another silence fell. No, it was not completely silent out here, for he could hear the wind singing in the tall pines, the crunch of the dry grass under their feet. Even so, it was quite uncomfortable to know that another person walked so close and yet seemed so disinclined toward conversation. Perhaps that was for the best. He had to use every ounce of energy he possessed simply to go on walking; talking to Deirdre at the same time would have required strength he needed to conserve so he didn't fall down where he stood.

At last, though, they came out into a small clearing. At the far end of the clearing was a low wooden structure painted white, with a modest little porch and several windows. To one side, a narrow dirt road snaked up to the building, and an extremely dusty pickup truck was parked there.

In fact, the truck's windows were so caked with filth that Amaal doubted Deirdre had driven it any time recently. Perhaps she was being prudent; it seemed that she had managed to escape detection up until now, but the sound of the truck's engine would surely have drawn the attention of any djinn in the area.

Including him, possibly, although prior to a few weeks ago, when he had been banished from his downtown penthouse, he had not spent much time here. Still, he couldn't help wondering what would have happened if he'd come across Deirdre before she had the terrible device operational. How she had managed such a feat, he wasn't sure. Someone must have given her instructions on how to build it, because he couldn't quite see how she could have come up with something so specific on her own.

"Inside," she said, the first word she had spoken for at least a half hour.

Walking up the three steps to the porch was more torment, but somehow Amaal managed it, although he was perspiring and panting as though he had run a race before he reached the top stair. She came up beside him and used her free hand to open the door to the station so he could enter.

This front room had clearly been a kind of office, for there were several desks, each with its own computer and phone. Although he didn't know much about human technology, he thought that the computers and the phones appeared to be older, certainly not anything that could be considered cutting edge or up to date. On one wall was a whiteboard with several names written on it, and tasks listed beneath them, such as taking out the trash, checking the animals' water, and so forth. One of the names written there was Deirdre's.

Clearly, this was the research station she'd spoken of. Had she been an employee here? Once again he thought her too young for such a post, but perhaps she had only been an assistant of some sort.

"Down the hall," she said.

He gave a resigned shrug and continued to walk, doing his best to ignore the way his breaths didn't quite seem to fill his lungs, or how it felt as though someone had tied heavy weights to his legs. It was still difficult for him to guess what Deirdre intended to do with him, but at least if his journey's end was now in sight, he should be able to sit down and get some rest. Indeed, he was not quite sure how he had managed to walk this far while the device continued to draw away every ounce of energy he possessed.

They passed several open doors. One room looked like a small but efficient laboratory. Two more were clearly bedrooms, with narrow beds placed up against the walls and some meager furniture to store personal items. Another door opened into the bathroom, which was just as utilitarian as the rest of the place.

And then they came to a larger space that took up the entire width of the station, which Amaal guessed had been a house at some point. This room was lined with cages, all of which were now empty. Despite the absence of any animals, he could catch just the faintest lingering trace of their presence, a certain muskiness in the air.

Pushed up against one wall was a large cage, much bigger than the others. What had it once held? Coyotes, or mountain lions? It did not seem sturdy enough to contain a bear, but perhaps if it had been tranquilized....

"In there," she said, inclining her head toward the cage.

He stared at her, aghast. Surely she didn't intend to confine him in that terrible wire box? Clearing his throat to get rid of the awful thickness that had settled there, he protested, "There is no need for that. Your device renders me completely harmless. All you need to do is lock me in one of the rooms we just passed."

The shotgun lifted again, pointed straight at his chest. "There aren't any bars on the windows in those rooms. And since your people are responsible for killing billions of my people, I hope you'll understand why I don't trust you. At all. Get in the cage."

He began to open his mouth to protest—then saw the way her finger tightened almost imperceptibly on the trigger of the shotgun. Just a bit more of a squeeze, and he knew that bits and pieces of himself would be splattered all over the walls of the room where he now stood.

Hands raised, he said, "I'm getting in the cage. There's no need for that."

His height forced him to crouch to climb in. Just bending in such a way made a rush of dizziness pass over him, and he collapsed onto the floor, feeling the wires that made up the cage press into the palms of his hands. Holding back a moan, he somehow managed to push himself into a corner, where he sat up and stared at Deirdre with weary resentment.

She closed the door of the cage and sealed it with a lock. Then she seemed to heave a breath as she backed away.

Despite his current misery, he saw how her hands shook. No doubt she had been petrified the whole time, worried that her device wouldn't be enough to keep her captive djinn at bay.

And strangely, what he experienced then was not a wish to hurt her, to punish her for putting him in such an ignominious position. No, he could clearly see the fear in her eyes, and what he wanted more than anything was to tell her that he meant her no harm, that just because the djinn had forever changed her world, it didn't mean he wished for her to follow all those who had already gone down into darkness and death.

He did not tell her these things, however, because he knew she would never believe him. Instead, he leaned his head against the wall of the cage and watched as she walked away.

THREE

A DJINN. A GODDAMN *DJINN*.

Deirdre's hands shook as she leaned the shotgun up against the wall in the lab. They didn't stop shaking even once she no longer held the weapon.

She had to be going crazy. Otherwise, she would never have attempted anything so nuts. And yet, when she'd come across Amaal, had realized the power she had over him, thanks to Miles Odekirk's crazy little black box, a strange fury had possessed her. She wanted this djinn to pay. For one terrible second, she'd almost lost control, had almost blown him away then and there.

What had stopped her? She really didn't know. But as she'd stared down at him, she realized she wanted something more than revenge. She wanted to know *why*.

Whether he'd actually tell her anything of what she wanted to know, she wasn't sure. He'd actually been courteous and polite during the trek over here, even though she guessed he had to be in pain from the device's effects. His handsome features had been taut, drawn, as though he'd had to force himself to take every step, make every movement, when all he'd probably wanted to do was lie down where he stood.

Handsome. That was one word she hadn't thought she'd ever use to describe a djinn. Miles Odekirk hadn't said much about their looks in his radio broadcasts. He'd been much more concerned with letting any surviving humans know of one way to fight them. And because the djinn had done such a monstrous thing, Deirdre had assumed they must look like monsters.

But they didn't. Or at least, the one she'd captured definitely did not.

How close to human were they? She had the means to find out. The lab here wasn't so well equipped that she'd be able to sequence Amaal's DNA or anything, but she'd still be able to analyze his blood, do a smear so she could get a look at his chromosomes. Of course, that meant she'd have to get close enough to him to get a sample. He didn't seem as though he was in much shape to fight her, however. No, he looked about as weak as a kitten.

Despite her anger toward the djinn in general,

she couldn't help experiencing a pang of guilt right then. She'd left him in that cage with no water, nothing to cushion the hard steel of the wire against his flesh. That wasn't like her—she'd always been picking up strays when she was younger, forcing her mother to find no-kill shelters for them, since the owner of their rented house wouldn't allow them to have any pets.

Did going through the apocalypse change you that much?

Deirdre wasn't sure she wanted to know.

Instead, she went into the station's small, utilitarian kitchen and got the pitcher of water out of the refrigerator. Luckily, it was a compact, efficient appliance, and so she'd been able to justify keeping it plugged in and using the electricity the solar panels on the roof generated to keep things cool. She poured some water into a mug, then headed back to the wildlife holding room. Amaal was still where she had left him, leaning into a corner of the cage. His bright blue eyes watched her as she entered and put the key in the lock, then opened the cage door and extended the mug of water to him.

"I thought you might be thirsty."

"Thank you," he said, gravely courteous, and took the mug from her.

His fingers brushed against hers for a second, and she had to keep herself from jumping back.

Was it because he'd touched her, or was it because his skin felt so cold, so clammy? Somehow she knew his flesh shouldn't feel that way, and guessed it must be another side effect of the djinn-repelling device.

"You're cold," she said as she shut the door to the cage and locked it again. "I'll go get you some blankets."

Before he could reply, she'd fled the room, going to the bedroom that Sean and Leland had shared. Mouth set, she stripped the blankets from both of the beds, and took a pillow as well.

Then her gaze moved to the small closet. Inside it was a chest of drawers. Deirdre set down the blankets and pillow she held, then opened one of the drawers. Leland had been tall and thin, and the muscular Amaal would never be able to fit into his clothes. Sean, on the other hand, had been very athletic—in fact, he'd started to drive her crazy with his constant talk about his damn cross-fit workouts—and she thought his stuff might work for her captive djinn. Amaal could stay in those gaudy silk robes of his if he wanted, but the chill of his touch told her he must be cold. Jeans and a sweatshirt and some socks would probably work far better at keeping him warm.

Why don't you get him a binkie while you're at it? she thought sourly as she added Sean's abandoned clothing to the pile. *You're not exactly treating him like a prisoner.*

Well, even prisons were supposed to provide their inmates with decent food and clothing. Deirdre supposed at some point she'd have to feed Amaal, but first she might as well do what she could to make him a bit more comfortable.

Clearly, he hadn't been expecting this sort of consideration, since his eyes widened slightly when she reentered the room with her bundle of clothing and blankets. Once again undoing the lock, she said, "Here. I thought this might help."

In silence, the djinn took the blankets from her, then ran a hand over the sweatshirt on top of the pile. He inspected each of the items she'd brought him, then looked up at her, eyebrows lifted slightly. "Why?"

She made her voice deliberately hard. "I can't trust you, because you're a djinn. But that doesn't mean I want you to be cold."

"These garments do look warmer than the ones I currently have." His eyes met hers, and she had to force herself not to look away. For some reason, she'd never thought that a djinn would have eyes so blue, like snippets from the summer sky. "Why is it so cold in here? I'm surprised you have not taken ill."

In her own flannel shirt and bulky sweater— pilfered from one of the shops in Running Springs

—she hadn't noticed the chill all that much. She shrugged, saying, "I have a wood-burning stove, but I couldn't use it. The smoke would have attracted you djinn."

His mouth tightened slightly at the phrase "you djinn," but his voice was calm enough as he replied, "You needn't worry about that. This is my territory. If any other djinn noticed the smoke, they would think it was because I had made a fire. So please, if you do have wood for the stove, I would appreciate it if you could use it for its intended purpose."

For a second, Deirdre was inclined to retort that she wasn't going to do him any favors, but she stopped herself. It was chilly in here, and even though the weather had been mild enough lately during the daytime, temperatures overnight always dipped into the twenties. She herself had been suffering the last few nights, even with the blankets from hers and Kate's beds piled on top of her—and she wouldn't be able to add any more to that pile, because she'd just given the spare blankets from Leland's and Sean's beds to Amaal.

"Okay," she said. "I'll go get a fire started. If you're sure it's safe."

"You are safe from any other djinn here, yes."

As she walked away, she realized that Amaal hadn't said she was safe from him. Then again, he wasn't in much of a position to be making threats.

It was pretty obvious that, with his powers stripped from him, he had no chance of getting out of the cage where he was currently confined. From what Miles Odekirk had said, it sounded as if the device would continue to blank a djinn's powers as long as the machine was operating, so Deirdre figured she should be safe for now. The device would have to be recharged after a while—although a single charge seemed to last for days—but she could plug it into one of the outlets in the lab if necessary and have it keep working.

So she went out to the back porch, to the one of the wood bins there, and got out an armful of logs. Good thing that Leland had coached her on how to use the stove, because otherwise she would have been at a loss—wood-burning stoves weren't exactly standard issue in suburban San Bernardino. Luckily, she still had plenty of matches, since she hadn't used the stove at all for the past few months.

The logs were dry and well-seasoned, and caught quickly. Whoever had done the retrofit of this house into the research station had done a good job, because the stove was positioned so much of its warmth would flow out of the kitchen and down the hall, helping to spread the heated air throughout the building. In fact, after a minute or two of standing near the stove, Deirdre began to rethink the bulky wool sweater she wore over her flannel shirt. She went into her own room and traded both garments for a T-shirt and a hoodie with "Running Springs" silk-screened on the back—another acquisition from one of her foraging trips into the little resort town.

Once she had changed, she didn't immediately go to where Amaal waited for her in his cage. Instead, she headed into the lab, where she got a blood-testing kit down from the cupboard. Maybe she should have waited, but she figured that the djinn seemed extra tired from his walk here, and she might as well try to get a sample when he wasn't at all capable of fighting back.

When she went into the room with the cages, she saw that Amaal was leaning against the wall of his pen, eyes shut. In fact, he was so still and pale that for one terrible second she was afraid he had died. But then his eyes opened, and he even offered her a faint smile.

"That does feel better," he said. "The warm air, that is." His gaze moved to the kit she held in one hand. "What is that?"

She moved closer to the cage. "It's a blood-testing kit. I'm going to take a sample of your blood."

Strangely, he didn't seem too discomfited by that revelation. "Why?"

"Because I want to study it."

"You're a scientist?"

She had to fight back a bitter laugh. *Not even close....* "No," she said. "I was a student...before. In my senior year."

"Ah. I thought you looked too young to be a scientist."

From his weary tone, it was hard to tell whether he was being sarcastic or not. Deirdre knew that, at twenty-four, she'd been older than many of her fellow classmates. Unfortunately, she'd been on the six-year plan at the university, having to go to school only part-time for nearly half her tenure there, simply because she needed to work enough hours to be able to afford the tuition. She'd lived at home and had done her best to control costs, but even then, blasting through in the traditional four years just hadn't been an option.

"No, you need a Ph.D. to be a scientist," she said. "I was a long way from that." She got the syringe and the vial out of the kit, set the labels aside for now. "Are you going to give me any trouble over this, Amaal? Because I've also got a handgun I can bring in here to make sure you cooperate."

He shook his head. "No trouble," he said.

The weariness in his voice sounded convincing. Only one way to find out, she supposed.

Doing her best to ignore the uneasy feeling in

the pit of her stomach, Deirdre went to the cage and unlocked it. "Come out."

He crawled over to the door and squeezed out. Although she guessed he hadn't changed yet because there hadn't been enough time, she wished he'd swapped out those djinn robes for the sweatshirt and jeans she'd brought him. As he painfully stood up and the robes flapped open, she realized just how much bare chest and equally bare stomach they exposed. She'd really never seen a man built like that who wasn't a model or an actor, and his physique was a little overwhelming when he was standing that close to her.

"You can sit down over here," she said, eyes carefully averted, and pointed to the folding chair and small table that had been set up against the wall.

Even the few steps he took over to the chair were stumbling, hesitant. He didn't so much sit as fall into that chair, then looked up at her expectantly. "I am ready."

Without replying, she pushed up the sleeve of his robe and then tapped her finger against the crook of his arm, doing her best to ignore the bulge of the bicep just above the spot where she was working. Luckily, he had a vein that seemed fairly close to the surface, so she chose that one and inserted the needle, then watched as the syringe filled with his blood.

She wasn't sure why she'd expected it to be green.

But it was a rich dark red, human-looking enough. Just as Amaal himself was, although she had to admit that she hadn't met too many people who were quite as perfect in appearance as the djinn.

"What are you going to do with it?" he asked. He sounded genuinely curious.

"I'm going to check your blood type," she replied. "And I want to look at your chromosomes. There isn't the right equipment here to sequence your DNA, and I wouldn't know how to do it even if there was, but I can still look for some basic stuff."

"Ah." Those bright blue eyes glinted up at her. "Do you want me to get back in my cage now?"

"Yes, that's all I needed."

He pushed himself out of the chair and made his laborious way across the room to the waiting cage. She could tell that the act of lowering himself to the ground so he could crawl back into the cage was painful for him, but she made herself stand quietly and watch until he was all the way inside. Then it was the work of a few seconds to slip the lock back in place and click it closed.

Even as she did so, she couldn't help experiencing a brief stab of regret. He certainly seemed docile enough. Maybe she should just let him stay in Leland and Sean's old room—

No, she told herself. *He's a djinn. He's dangerous. For all you know, he's exaggerating how much the device really drains him and is just trying to trick you into letting him out of that cage.*

"I usually eat around six," she said, her voice deliberately hard. "Can you wait that long?"

"That is only a few hours from now, correct?"

Deirdre nodded.

"Then I will be fine. I think I will try to sleep."

Not sure how she should reply, she only nodded again, then gathered up the little vial of his blood and left the room.

Time to see…whatever she could see.

He waited until he knew she was gone to reach for the little pile of clothing she'd left for him. There hadn't been enough time to change earlier, but now the cold was bothering him more than ever, despite the faint heat of the wood stove drifting down the corridor to the room where he was confined. And, plain and unattractive as they were, the garments Deidre had given him would be much warmer than his open silk robe and billowy trousers.

First was the sweatshirt, heavy and thick, and softer on the inside than he'd expected. Then the trousers of that heavy blue fabric that mortals seemed so drawn to. They were somewhat snug, but again, warmer than his silk pants. And the socks were thick and warm and soft all at once, comforting on his bare feet.

Thus attired, he rolled his djinn garments into a small ball, then took the pillow and blankets and burrowed into them as best he could. Yes, that was better. He was hardly cold at all now, although he wondered how warm he would be once night fell and the temperatures outside dropped. The mountains and their weather were something he was still learning to live with, but even in the luxurious home that had been provided for him, he'd experienced these sharp extremes, although they hadn't affected him directly. The sun might ride high during the day, but its warmth was as fleeting as the light it provided.

From down the hall he heard a faint metallic clink. Deirdre, he supposed, working in the laboratory. Human science had interested him very little—djinn had no need of it, after all—and so he wasn't quite sure what she was doing. Looking at his blood under a microscope, he supposed. Wasn't that what mortals did, put specimens in slides and then squinted at them to see what might be in those specimens?

He didn't quite know why Deirdre was so motivated to study his blood, but perhaps she wanted to know what it was that separated djinn from humans. On the surface, after all, they did resemble one another very closely. Indeed, that was why there were djinn who had taken humans for their partners. Some of humanity's more perfect specimens could possibly pass for djinn in dim light…if you squinted.

This young woman who now held him captive —she really was quite lovely, even as tired and as strained as she appeared to be. It had most likely been difficult for her to be alone for all these weeks, forgotten by the world.

A strange rush of sympathy passed over him, and Amaal wanted to shake his head at himself. Here he was, lying in a cage, and he was feeling sorry for his captor? But then, he guessed this sort of behavior was not exactly usual for her. When confronted by one of those she knew to be her enemy, she had done the only thing she probably thought she could. It certainly wouldn't have made much sense for her to leave him there in that glade, not once she knew what he was. She most certainly must have feared that he would have come after her.

Not that he would have ever done such a

thing. He was not one of those djinn who were intent on cleansing the world of every mortal who wasn't Chosen, those few immune humans who had been lucky enough to be selected as partners for eternity by their djinn. The aftermath of the Heat was a horribly messy business, when you got right down to it. The fever the djinn had sent... that was one thing. It killed cleanly and quickly. But to then hunt down those who were lucky—or unlucky, depending on how you looked at it—enough to be immune? No, he certainly did not have the stomach for that kind of sport. In the early days, after the Heat but before the reavers had killed off most of the survivors, Amaal had come across the scene of one of those "cleansings." It had taken the better part of a *very* good bottle of burgundy to rid his mind of those terrible images.

He supposed Deirdre had every right to fear him. And he also supposed she wouldn't believe him if he told her she had nothing to fear.

Well, he would just have to prove his trustworthiness, one way or another. For one thing, he had no desire to stay in this damned cage any longer than was necessary. If she wished to keep him here so she could analyze his blood or perform other tests—although he drew the line at anything that involved cutting him open—he was fine with that. But he would much rather stay in one of the bedrooms he'd noticed as he walked down the hallway. There was no reason to keep him confined like this. He was not an animal, after all.

Although he feared she might think he was. Had she seen anything of what his fellow djinn had done to humanity's survivors, or had her isolation shielded her from the Heat's terrible aftermath? He couldn't be sure; she clearly feared him, but not so much that she hadn't somehow found the courage to face him down.

And there was the device. Where in the world could she have gotten that thing? There was no way she could have traveled the thousand miles that separated her from the place where the infernal machines had first appeared. Could she have somehow managed to figure it out on her own? That didn't seem very likely. By her own admission, she was only a college student, not a scientist or an engineer.

He wondered whether she would tell him the truth if he asked her outright. It was hard to say. So far she had seemed forthright enough with him, although wary and not inclined to reveal much of herself. Again, he supposed that was to be expected.

Even so, he wished she would come back in here. It had been pleasant to have someone to talk to, even if his conversational partner had also locked him up in a cage.

He scrunched the pillow into a small ball and rested his head against it, and hoped his tenure in this cage wouldn't be too prolonged.

FOUR

DEIRDRE PEERED INTO THE MICROSCOPE. She'd already mixed the djinn's blood with the reagents the lab had on hand and had discovered that he was Type O, RH negative. That had surprised her somewhat—for some reason, she'd halfway expected that the reagents wouldn't react to his blood at all, that the djinn must possess a blood type which didn't even exist in humans. However, while his blood was a fairly rare type, it was still completely normal.

Now she was performing karyotype analysis, matching his pairs of chromosomes and looking for abnormalities. Of course, the main one leapt out at her immediately, was so obvious that at first she thought she must have performed the chromosome separation incorrectly, even though she'd performed the procedure many times in her genetics class.

All humans had forty-six chromosomes, grouped into twenty-three pairs. Abnormalities in those groupings could cause Down syndrome, or rarer genetic problems like Klinefelter syndrome or Turner syndrome.

Amaal didn't have forty-six chromosomes. He had forty-eight.

Deirdre rubbed her eyes and stared down at the slide again, but what she was looking at didn't change. It wasn't that her vision was blurred or she was overly tired. All right, she knew she was tired, but her eyesight had always been perfect. Good thing, too, considering she couldn't just pop in to see the optometrist the next time her prescription changed.

As far as she could tell, Amaal was a perfect physical specimen. He certainly didn't appear to be suffering from any kind of genetic disorders. Her best guess was that all djinn must have forty-eight chromosomes. Maybe it was on that last pair where all their differences from humans resided— their ability to control various elements, their longevity and strength. At least, those were particular traits that Dr. Odekirk had called out, more as a warning than anything else.

Deirdre straightened and rubbed the kink at the back of her neck. Probably she'd spent too long bent over that microscope. And she knew she could sit here and stare at that slide for hours and hours, and it wouldn't change the very obvious fact that Amaal was different from her—or any other human—at the genetic level.

If she'd had a full-on lab—and if she actually knew what she was doing—maybe she would have been able to delve into his DNA, find out exactly where those differences lay. But she didn't have any of the correct equipment for that kind of analysis. She was only a student with some biology courses under her belt, not a geneticist or a doctor.

She took Amaal's blood sample and slides over to the lab's mini-fridge, and carefully set them inside. When she'd taken inventory of the research station's supplies as soon as she realized she was going to be alone here for a very long while, she'd found some beer hidden in the back of the mini-fridge. Sean's, probably; Leland certainly wasn't the type to hide a six-pack of Harp ale in behind a bunch of biological samples.

Since Sean wasn't going to need that beer— and because there was no need to hide it any longer—Deirdre had relocated the six-pack to the refrigerator in the station's kitchen. She'd allowed herself one bottle each Sunday, but now they were all gone.

Too bad, because she thought she could have used a beer right about now.

Failing that, she poured herself some water and drank it down, wetting her dry throat. That was better. Now, though, she thought she'd better go check on her captive.

When she entered the room where he was being held, she found him leaning against a corner of the cage, the pillow she'd given him wadded up behind him, his eyes closed and his head tilted to one side. She noticed that he'd changed out of his djinn clothes and into the garments she'd left for him; looking at him now, it was hard to believe that he wasn't human, that he wasn't someone she knew from college, maybe a grad student, since his appearance suggested that he was in his late twenties. However, she knew he wasn't human, and probably much, much older than he looked.

"Amaal," she said softly.

His eyes opened at once. So very blue, with dark lashes that made them seem even brighter and bluer in contrast. "Deirdre," he said. "What did you find?"

"You have a human blood type," she told him. "Does that surprise you?"

"I'm not sure." He stared up at her, expression frank. "That is, we djinn and you humans certainly look enough alike that it shouldn't seem that odd that our blood might be similar. I suppose I'm more surprised that no one has discovered such a fact before now."

"Well, I doubt you djinn gave our scientists much of a chance to study you."

"That is probably true." Shifting a little, he put up one hand to the back of his neck in an unconscious imitation of the same gesture she'd made only a short time earlier. Watching him, though, Deirdre experienced another pang of guilt. She doubted he would have a crick in his neck if she hadn't forced him to stay in that cage.

On the other hand, letting him roam free seemed pretty much out of the question.

"Are you hungry?" she asked. "I don't have a lot, but I have some pasta, and there's spaghetti sauce from a jar. It's better than nothing, I guess."

"That would be fine."

Watching him, she wondered how he could be so unruffled, so apparently calm. If someone had stuck her in a cage, she would be doing her best to figure out how to get herself free. Then again, the device had probably weakened him enough that he didn't have much fight left. He might have decided it was better to conserve his strength rather than waste it in futile displays of defiance.

It was hard for her to say one way or another, because he might look human, but he wasn't, which meant his thought processes could be completely alien to her.

In the meantime, she might as well make that pot of spaghetti. She'd been putting off boiling the pasta because she didn't want to waste the propane, but now she could heat the water on top of the wood stove and not have to worry so much about being wasteful.

"I'll have it ready in a little bit," she told him, then hurried away before he could reply. There was something disconcerting about those direct blue eyes of his, as if he was able to watch her and somehow know what she was thinking.

No, that wasn't possible. At least, Miles Odekirk had never mentioned anything about djinn being psychic. Even if they were, Deirdre doubted Amaal would be able to read her mind now that all his powers were being blocked.

She went in the kitchen and filled the pot with water, then set it on top of the wood stove, which appeared to be chugging along just fine and didn't require any more firewood—for the moment, anyway. The pasta sauce and the spaghetti she'd "liberated" from the general store in Running Springs during one of her foraging trips, but it had been sitting on the shelf for some time, waiting until she was ready to make it up.

Had Amaal ever had spaghetti before? She had no idea. It wasn't as if she could jump on Google and learn everything she needed to know about djinn folklore while she was waiting for the water to boil, so she was pretty clueless when it came to these strange elementals and their history with humans.

She supposed she could ask.

No, it was probably better not to speak to him very much. Then she could do a better job of thinking of him as a research subject and not anything more. Not a living, breathing, intelligent being…who just happened to look like he should have been on the cover of *Men's Fitness* magazine or something.

Damn.

Steam began to curl up from the pot of water, so Deirdre dumped the entire packet of spaghetti noodles into the pot and got out a wooden spoon to stir them. Good thing this kitchen was equipped with most of the essentials; people would often come and stay for a weekend, or even a whole week or more, depending on what they were researching. True, everything was a hodgepodge, with dishes and cutlery that didn't match because most of the items were donated, but aesthetics weren't exactly of prime importance in this kind of setting.

It was too bad she wasn't putting together a more labor-intensive meal, because that way she could have distracted herself from thinking about Amaal. The more she tried to ponder the oddities of his chromosomes, the more she saw those piercing blue eyes fixed on her.

Which doesn't matter, she told herself as she fished a strand of spaghetti out of the pot to check it for doneness. *He's a djinn. A* djinn.

The djinn had destroyed everything. Everyone she'd ever known was dead because of them. The enormity of the loss still hadn't quite sunk in, partly because she'd been so isolated here, hadn't seen for herself what her world's ending truly meant. But if that djinn-created apocalypse wasn't a good enough reason to push aside any concerns for Amaal's comfort, to remind herself that there was no need for her to treat him with any kindness, she didn't know what was.

And yet....

She'd never been very good at hardening her heart. God knows she'd had plenty of reasons, starting with a father who'd walked out when she was eleven and her brother Douglas was thirteen, leaving their mother to struggle to keep the household going on only her nurse's salary. But Deirdre still hadn't hated him, had only morosely wondered what was wrong with her. Surely if her father had really loved her, loved his family, then he would have stayed. And because her mother had always seemed pretty much perfect in her eyes, and her brother had certainly been a son to be proud of, geeky, yes, but also excelling in track and field, Deirdre figured the fault must have lain with her.

Maybe a therapist could have helped her with that issue, but there sure as hell hadn't been enough money for that kind of luxury, especially considering how haphazard her father had been with his child support payments.

The spaghetti was done. She drained it in the sink, then put some sauce in a bowl and nuked it in the microwave before pouring it over the pasta, which she'd dished onto a couple of mismatched Corelle plates.

Should she take both plates with her, or leave her own food here in the kitchen to be consumed later? There wasn't any reason why she needed to eat with Amaal. It wasn't as if he was her guest or something. Somehow, though, the image that flashed into her mind of him eating alone in his cage made pity stir within her again. She did her best to remind herself that he was a djinn, someone who could kill her without a second thought, and yet....

Shaking her head, she took both plates—and a couple of forks, although she certainly wouldn't give a djinn even the dullest butter knife—with her back to the room where Amaal waited for her in his cage. He looked up as she entered, and even smiled at her as she came toward him with a plate in her hand.

That smile...how could he smile? Especially at her, his captor. But he did, and Deirdre wasn't sure how she should react. Since she'd already set her own plate down on the table across the room, she had one hand free to undo the lock, then open the door to his cage.

"Here you are," she said, handing the plate to him. "Sorry there isn't any garlic bread."

"Or chianti," he added, those sky-colored eyes glinting at her.

She'd never been big on wine, but a glass of chianti sounded good right then. Why hadn't she pilfered some booze when she was looting the grocery store in Running Springs? Probably because the bottles would have been heavy and bulky to carry, and she'd been so nervous and stressed out that losing even a tiny bit of her faculties to alcohol hadn't seemed like a very smart idea.

"Maybe next time," she said lightly, then backed away so she could close the cage door behind her.

"I'll take that as a promise."

To her shame, a flood of color rushed to her cheeks. She'd been turning away as it happened, though, so maybe Amaal hadn't seen. She went and sat down at the table, then picked up her own fork and helped herself to a mouthful of spaghetti.

The djinn ate as well, slowly and methodically.

He didn't offer any praise for the meal, but then, she hadn't really expected any. It was just spaghetti sauce from a jar dumped on some bargain pasta, after all, not something a Cordon Bleu chef had whipped up.

The silence between them was so profound that she almost jumped when Amaal finally spoke. "If you weren't a scientist, then what were you doing here?"

She knew she didn't have to answer him. Giving a djinn personal information about herself might give him some kind of opening he could exploit. On the other hand, it seemed rude not to reply, and she didn't think providing a few minor facts would change all that much. "Helping out, mostly," she said. "I could get an extra two college credits for putting in fifty hours during the quarter up here. I fetched and carried for the grad students, looked after the animals."

"Ah, yes…the animals who once inhabited these cages." He looked at the wire structure that trapped him before continuing. "What happened to them?"

"I let them go," Deirdre replied. "They were all wild animals that had been injured in some way. Hikers would find them and bring them here. I guess in the past people conducting research would have lab animals, but the university stopped that a while back, and it was mostly a small-scale wildlife rescue by the time I got involved. Anyway, the animals were pretty much healed up, and I knew I'd soon run out of things to feed them, so I set them free."

"Was this what you wanted to do?" Amaal asked. "Help animals?"

That question touched on a raw nerve, one she'd managed to ignore for a while, since her thwarted ambitions weren't of much import now that the world had ended. "I thought about it," she said, her tone brittle. "But vet school wasn't going to happen for me. It was just too expensive. I would have been paying off the student loans for years and years."

"Your family did not have money?"

A derisive laugh escaped her lips before she could think to hold it back. "That's an understatement. We were doing okay when I was little, but then my father decided to trade my mother in for a newer model, and things were always tight after that."

Amaal's forehead puckered into a frown as he appeared to process her remark. "Trade in—oh, you mean he wanted to be with a younger woman?"

The truth put so baldly only made Deirdre scowl as well. "Yes. He was in sales. His territory was California and Nevada. After one trip when I was around eleven, he came home, packed his things, and left. And he never came back. He lives in Las Vegas with his new wife...or at least," Deirdre amended, realizing the chances of her father and Trudi surviving the Heat were also literally one in a million, "they did live there. I guess they're dead along with everyone else."

"I am sorry."

Deirdre set down her fork, then got up and walked across the room to stand next to the cage. "Are you sorry, Amaal? Why would you be, when you're one of the beings who helped kill them?"

Not even a blink. "I am not."

"What do you mean, you're not?"

"I mean that it was not all djinn who created the Heat and decided it should be let loose on the world." He couldn't stand, of course, not in that cramped pen where she was holding him, but he set his plate of half-eaten spaghetti aside and straightened as best he could, his gaze meeting hers. "I was not one of those djinn."

How could she possibly believe that? It sounded to her as though Amaal was only handing her whatever story he thought she wanted to hear. "So, what—you just stood off to one side and let your friends destroy the world?"

His perfect features went very still, and he glanced away from her and down at himself, at the U.C. Riverside sweatshirt he wore. "I fear that is very much what I did. I am sorry for that as well, although I doubt I could have done much to stop them."

Deirdre remained standing where she was, knowing she should walk away, go someplace where she could gather her thoughts. It didn't seem possible that the djinn weren't some huge monolithic block, all of them dedicated to the destruction of mankind. Then again, she was all too ready to believe that Amaal lied to her now, was doing his best to paint himself in a better light so she would be lenient with him, maybe even set him free.

Like that was going to happen.

He moved as close to the spot where she stood as the cage would allow. "I know you have no reason to believe me, and I have every reason to lie to you. But I swear that I am telling you the truth."

Her throat felt tight, and she doubted it was because she hadn't done a good job of swallowing her last mouthful of spaghetti. "If you're really telling me the truth—"

"I am."

"Then why? What did we ever do to you?"

He let out a sigh. "That, I fear, is a very old story. And because I am weary, thanks to your device, I do not have the energy to tell you the whole thing. My people have resented yours for a very long time, and they coveted this world. At last the opportunity came to take it for their own, and that is precisely what they did."

"Just like that," Deirdre said, her voice hard.

"Just like that," he repeated. "I did not agree with the wholesale death they caused, but I also could not argue with their assertion that humans had been very poor stewards of this world and therefore had lost any right to it."

Poor stewards. As much as she wanted to argue with that statement, she knew she couldn't. Not really. Humanity had done a pretty good job of screwing up old Mother Earth, after all.

Still....

"That's why you were given these lands?" she asked then. "Because you djinn are taking over, carving it up for yourselves?"

"'Carving' is a bit harsh, but yes. We will try to restore this world to what it once was. It will be the work of many years, but then, we djinn have many years to work with."

Despite the tiredness in his voice, she could hear the calm conviction behind it. The djinn would take over now, and humanity would soon be only a memory. And she honestly couldn't say whether that was even a bad thing. Her own losses weighed heavily and always would, but the planet didn't care whether she survived, or whether her mother and brother and everyone else she'd ever known were dead.

Tears stung her eyes, and she turned away. The last thing she wanted was for this djinn to see her crying. It just hurt too much.

Everything hurt.

"I—I need to clean up the kitchen," she said, her back still to him.

"Deirdre—"

"I'll see you in the morning."

And she grabbed her plate and fork and fled the room.

FIVE

AMAAL LEANED HIS HEAD AGAINST THE CAGE wall, hating the encircling wire frame more than ever. He had never been the type to offer comfort, but as he watched Deirdre all but run from him, he'd wanted nothing more than to reach out and take her in his arms, hold her so she would not weep anymore.

For she had been crying. He'd caught the glint of tears in her beautiful aquamarine eyes before she turned her back on him. And he knew she'd fled so he wouldn't be able to hear her sobs.

Well, she had plenty of reasons to mourn, no doubt. Several months had passed, and it seemed that she'd achieved a measure of calm during the time she'd spent alone here, but he guessed that their conversation had reopened those old wounds, had allowed her to see that the hurt would not heal for a long, long time.

If ever.

Amaal had recently suffered a loss of his own, but he knew it was not quite the same thing. He had lost one brother, not his entire family, his entire world. And, to be perfectly truthful, he had never been very fond of Omar. He had suffered his brother's whims because that was what family was supposed to do, but being Omar's brother had been quite exhausting. It was better when he went about his business and didn't contact Amaal for months or even years, because it seemed whenever Amaal was dragged back into Omar's orbit, something dreadful usually occurred.

This last time was no different, except that Omar had finally over-reached himself, and paid the ultimate price. And all Amaal could feel about the whole sordid matter was a certain weary relief that he would never have to deal with Omar's indiscretions again.

Was his captivity now a punishment of some sort for the assistance he had offered his brother? Amaal knew he had lied and covered up for Omar on too many occasions. At the time, he had thought he'd only done so out of a vague sense of family loyalty—and a much stronger desire to appease his brother so he might be left alone—but Amaal knew that his own punishment could one day be at hand. Now it seemed it might have finally come.

His arm ached. He pushed up the sleeve of his borrowed sweatshirt and then carefully lifted the adhesive tape that held the gauze in place where Deirdre had drawn blood. The flesh there now looked bruised, purplish-red. Had some sort of infection already begun? No, she had been very careful, had wiped down the area with alcohol, had used a fresh needle extracted from a paper wrapping. More likely, his body simply wasn't healing the way it should. A minor pinprick like that would have disappeared almost as soon as she had made it, if his djinn powers of regeneration had been working correctly. It seemed that terrible device was interfering with anything that made him different from a mortal.

Frowning, he pushed the tape back down and ran his finger over it, hoping there was enough adhesive left for it to properly stick to his skin. He had to hope that the wound would be marginally better in the morning. If not, he would ask Deirdre to take a look at it. Surely she couldn't refuse, not when she had been the one to cause that pinprick in his skin in the first place.

For some reason, the thought of her slender fingers touching him, of the wild waves of her hair falling around her face as she bent toward him, made a shudder go through his body. Weak he might be, but he still recognized that shudder for what it was.

Desire. Need.

She was so very beautiful. And it had been too long since he had been with a woman.

And it will be longer still, he told himself as he reached for the pillow and blankets, knowing there was little he could do now except try to sleep. *For it is clear enough that Deirdre Graves has no desire to be with you in that way, and even if you could somehow convince her, there is little chance of you being able to rise to the occasion as long as that device of hers is still operating.*

Impotence was not a failing he had any experience with. Now, though, he was no more capable of being physically intimate with his human captor than he was of escaping from this damn cage.

He pulled the blankets around him, thinking it was a good thing that Omar was dead. If he had survived to see his brother in such an ignominious position, he would never have allowed Amaal to live it down.

Deirdre had just finished scraping off her plate when she realized she'd left Amaal's plate in the cage. Well, there was no way in hell that she was going back in there to retrieve it. He'd just have to push it off to one side while he slept, and she could get it in the morning.

The tears had stopped, thank God. She knew she shouldn't have allowed him to get to her like that, but when he'd confessed that the djinn had done all this so they could take the Earth for their own, it was as though she'd suffered the shock of loss all over again. They would do whatever it took to secure their prize, which meant she knew there was no chance of survival for anyone.

Including her.

Oh, Amaal might say pretty words in that formal way of speaking he had, with that faint, faint accent which made him sound like some rich Middle Eastern guy who'd spent his teen years getting educated at British prep schools, but Deirdre knew she didn't have a chance of surviving in the long run. He'd said these lands were his and that no other djinn would come here to bother her, and yet she doubted that was the whole truth. If she kept him here long enough, surely someone would have to notice he was missing. They'd notice, and they'd come to investigate, and then eventually they'd find her. And kill her.

Life hadn't been all that great lately, but that didn't mean she was ready to let it go.

She pulled in a breath and made herself finish washing her plate, mostly because it would only be that much more difficult to clean if she allowed the sauce remaining on it to harden overnight. *All right, think,* she told herself. *He hasn't been missing for very long. If we go back to wherever he's been living—*

No, that was crazy. Here at least she was on her home turf, where things were familiar. If they went to Amaal's house, he'd have the advantage.

Or would he? As long as she kept the device operating, he'd be weak. He couldn't fight her.

But he wouldn't be in the cage, either. Somehow she doubted he'd forgive her anytime soon for penning him up like an animal. He might talk sweet, but she was crazy if she didn't think he'd do whatever he could to get his revenge. She couldn't hold out against him forever; if nothing else, she'd have to sleep eventually.

What difference did it really make, though? She might live for a few more days, or even a year or two if she was lucky, but in the end, she was an anomaly, a relic, something that should have gone extinct with the rest of the humans. Whatever trick of biology had caused her to be immune when hardly anyone else was, it had been a cruel one. Why continue to live when you knew you'd eventually be hunted down and killed?

Taking Amaal back to his house might buy her a little time, though. She'd read between the lines of a few of the things he'd said, and guessed that the djinn weren't all that social, didn't tend to mingle very much. If he was even a little bit grateful to her for releasing him, he might put in a good word for her.

Or maybe he'll turn you into his pet, she thought as she put her dish away. *Put you in a cage, just like you did to him.*

No, Amaal wouldn't do that. She couldn't say she knew him at all, but there was something charming and also somehow slightly world-weary about him. He didn't seem like the vengeful type, despite her fears of a few moments earlier. Now that she'd had a bit of time to calm down, to catch her breath, she realized she hadn't been reading him very well. After all, hadn't he just confessed that he'd stood aside while the other djinn destroyed mankind? That wasn't the action of someone who'd put a woman in a cage.

Or at least, she hoped not.

She turned off the light in the kitchen and moved quietly into the hallway. After she'd heard Miles Odekirk's broadcasts about the djinn, she'd stopped turning on the lights at night, had instead forced herself to blunder around in the dark rather than risk attracting any attention. This evening, though, she'd figured it was safe, just as Amaal had said using the wood stove would be safe, since any djinn in the area would only think it was him.

The room down the hall was quiet. Had Amaal already fallen asleep? For that matter, did djinn sleep? In a way, she hoped they did; it was sort of awful to think of them living so long and never getting the respite of slumber.

Deirdre thought of her captive lying in that cage, huddled in the blankets she'd given him. He was so tall that he couldn't stretch out all the way, even lying diagonally. Such a position had to be almost as uncomfortable as being forced to sleep on the floor. Did she really want to do that to him?

He's a djinn. He doesn't deserve your pity or compassion.

Her inner voice was growing weaker, however. Did she want to be the kind of person who had no regard for another, even if he happened to be a djinn? How did that make her any better than those of his kind who were even now hunting down humanity's survivors?

It didn't, she realized. If she went down that path, she'd be just as bad as they were.

She drew in a breath, then went to her room, to the backpack that still held the device. Its range could be adjusted, according to what Miles Odekirk had said on the radio, but even at its tightest focus, the device's effects covered the entire building. That was why she hadn't worried about keeping it on her person at all times. Now she pulled out the little black box and shoved it under her pillow. If the djinn tried to poke around the station and look for it, he wouldn't have much luck.

Well, not without going through her first, anyway.

That matter taken care of, Deirdre went back out to the hallway and headed down to the room where Amaal was confined. She'd left one of the overhead lights on, so she could see him clearly enough, curled up in a corner of the cage, pillow smashed beneath one cheek. He appeared to be asleep.

As soon as she entered, however, his eyes flickered open, and he pushed himself up to a sitting position. "What is it?"

Without immediately answering, Deirdre went over to the cage and undid the lock, then opened the door. Standing back a foot or two, she said, "You can get out."

That blue gaze met hers. "Excuse me?"

"I can't—" She stopped there, frustrated, not sure what she'd meant to say. "I realized how uncomfortable this has to be. Wouldn't you rather sleep in a bed?"

"I would." His head tilted slightly as he appeared to consider her. "Is that what you're offering?"

"Yes. You can have one of the beds in the

room Sean and Leland were using. It's not as if they need it anymore."

With more alacrity than she would have expected, given the sapping effects of the energy-draining device, Amaal squeezed out of the cage and stood.

"Bring the blankets and pillow," Deirdre said. "I stole them off the beds there, so you'll need to put them back."

"Of course." The tall djinn bent and retrieved the items in question, then stood up again.

"This way."

You're crazy, she told herself as she went back down the hallway toward what had once been Leland and Sean's room. *Certifiable.*

Maybe so, but she couldn't deny the relief in her at knowing she wasn't going to continue to torture Amaal by keeping him in a cage.

When they got to the doorway, she flicked the switch, turning on the small round light in the middle of the ceiling. "It's not much," she said, and it wasn't. The sleeping quarters here had been purely utilitarian—two twin beds in each room, two nightstands, a low dresser in the closet. Not even a desk, because there was ample workspace up in the front office.

"It is much better than a cage," Amaal replied. His tone was so neutral, she wasn't sure how to take the remark. Probably better to accept it at face value and move on.

"True." Deirdre hesitated, then went on, "There's a bathroom down the hall. That is, if you need it."

This time his mouth quirked slightly. "The bodily functions of djinn are not terribly different from those of humans."

Interesting. It seemed as though there wasn't that much to separate humans from these elementals—well, except that odd pair of chromosomes. She wished she had the kind of expertise that would allow her to determine exactly which traits those chromosomes controlled. That might help her to understand more about the djinn, figure out why so many of them had no problem at all killing humans, despite all their similarities.

As it was, better not to say too much. "Um... okay. I'm across the hall—but I'm going to have that pistol under my pillow, and I'm a *very* light sleeper, so don't even think about trying something."

"I will not try to escape, if that is what you are worried about." He paused for a few seconds, watching her. "Not when you have done me the courtesy of letting me out of that cage."

Courtesy? He had a strange way of looking at things. After all, he was still her prisoner, just one with slightly more freedom of movement. "Well, thanks for the reassurance." She moved toward the door, then added, "Good night, then, Amaal."

"Good night, Deirdre." His lips curved slightly, but he didn't smile. Not quite, anyway.

She nodded at him and left, trying to rid herself of the nagging sensation that he'd somehow come out ahead in that conversation.

Yes, this was much better. The bed upon which he lay was narrow and hard, but still a spectacular improvement over the floor of the cage. Amaal still didn't quite know what had moved Deirdre to free him from the cage, but he wasn't about to argue with her apparent change of heart.

He stared up at the ceiling, at the faint shadows of the trees outside the window, rendered ghostly by the light of a gibbous moon. All his limbs felt weighted with weariness, which meant the device was still operating. He had no idea of its range, but he'd noticed that Deirdre didn't have it with her when she'd brought him his supper, which meant she'd probably secreted it somewhere in the research station.

Not that he had any intention of going to look for it—not yet, anyway. If too many days passed and he had not yet been able to gain enough of her trust to convince her to shut it off, well, then perhaps he would have to find the damnable thing. Living like this was not terribly comfortable, but he could endure it for a time if he must.

You should take it at some point, though, he thought. *Not for yourself, but to give to the elders. They will probably wish to study it.*

True. What they would do with it, when they had no more of a scientific bent than any other djinn, Amaal was not sure. Still, giving them such a valuable piece of human technology would surely earn him their favor, and after that debacle with Omar, he thought it certainly could not hurt to have a few good marks in his particular column. Perhaps he could even convince them to give him back his penthouse.

But he was getting ahead of himself. For now, he thought it best to prove to Deirdre that he was no threat to her. This most likely would not be terribly difficult—after all, she'd already unbent enough to let him out of the cage, to give him a real bed to sleep in. She could begin to relax around him. He thought he would like that very much. It would be good to see her smile, for she seemed wrapped in sorrow.

Not that he could really blame her for her sadness. He could not fully comprehend the sort of losses she'd suffered, since of course he had no basis of comparison. Omar was gone, true, but the rest of the djinn were still here. Indeed, they had far more to look forward to than they had in a very long time. This earth and all its beauties was theirs, and now all they had to do was determine the best way to become its stewards. In a generation or so, humanity would be all but forgotten.

Well, except those who had survived to become Chosen. Why no one had selected Deirdre as his partner, Amaal wasn't quite sure. Certainly she was lovely enough, and of the correct age. But then, this place called Southern California had possessed almost a surfeit of physically magnificent human specimens, and he supposed that the djinn who had decided to take a Chosen had wanted someone a bit showier. Deirdre's was a subtle sort of beauty, the delicacy of a wildflower rather than the full-throated bloom of a rose.

But she was still very lovely. Amaal could not deny that fact, just as he couldn't deny the desire he'd experienced for her a while earlier. That fit had passed, luckily, but he feared he would have to address it sooner or later…or rather, he would have to see whether Deirdre would be amenable, once she had gotten used to him. It would not have to mean much, only a joining of bodies searching for the sort of release they both probably needed.

At least, Amaal knew he did. Some time had

passed since his last liaison, partly because every-thing in the djinn world had been in turmoil, and he had decided it would be better to wait to seek out another woman until after he was settled in his new home. Unfortunately, that new home wasn't quite what he had been expecting—he still thought that most djinn women would be more impressed by the penthouse he'd been forced to abandon rather than the chalet-style home he now occupied outside Running Springs—but surely someone would have been amenable to a few cozy winter months here in the mountains.

Now, of course, all those plans would have to be set aside. Then again, wooing Deirdre would have its own challenges, challenges he thought he might enjoy confronting, and defeating. Her mouth looked so very soft and full. He would enjoy kissing her…and he had to hope the feeling would be mutual.

Well, as with most matters, time would tell.

SIX

Lying in her bed, eyes now opening to the pale light of a winter morning, Deirdre heard the door to the bathroom shut, and the shower start a moment later. For a few wild seconds, she thought that must have been Leland or Sean, getting up to begin their day, and that everything she'd suffered over the past few months had only been a terrible nightmare.

But then she remembered that Sean and Leland were dead, and so was everyone else. Those reassuring, normal morning sounds had come from Amaal, her captured djinn.

Panic hit next, and she scrabbled under her pillow, looking for the device she'd hidden there. Her fingers closed around the hard little box, and she blew a breath of relief out from between her lips. Thank God. She didn't see how Amaal could have possibly taken it, since her warning to him that she was a light sleeper was true enough, but when you were dealing with a djinn, anything seemed possible.

After pushing back the covers, she climbed out of bed, the device still clutched in one hand. A cautious peek out into the hall confirmed that the bathroom door was indeed shut, the water loud even through that closed door. Deirdre supposed she should have told him to be careful with the water. Too late for that now. The solar water heater generally was good for about two showers before you had to give it a rest, but so much depended on how long those showers actually were.

Since she slept in a sweatshirt and sweatpants to keep warm, all she had to do was slip her feet into a pair of Uggs she kept handy before padding over to the closet. Inside it was the backpack she'd worn the day before, but that seemed too obvious a hiding place, especially because Amaal had seen her carrying the device around in that same backpack the day before. No, tucked back into a corner of the closet was her laptop case, black and inconspicuous. She opened it quickly and slid the device into a side pocket, then zipped the case shut again.

That task done, she found her brush and ran it through her hair, and gathered all of it into a scrunchie. At least that way she wouldn't look quite so much like she'd just rolled out of bed, although she'd need to get in the shower herself at some point.

For now, she padded down the hall to the kitchen to get a pot of coffee started. She made more than she usually would for herself, figuring that Amaal would probably want some.

Or at least, she guessed he might. He seemed familiar enough with human food and drink, or he wouldn't have suggested chianti the night before.

Other than that, she didn't have a lot to offer him. She'd accumulated a decent hoard of protein bars and breakfast bars, the kind of stuff that wouldn't go bad for another six months or so. With no milk and no eggs, she couldn't bake muffins or make bread. She supposed she could have used powdered milk, but that didn't take care of the egg problem. It hadn't been worth the effort to find a reasonable substitute. The protein bars provided decent nutrition, and she'd made sure to supplement with multivitamins and fresh field greens when they were in season. Lately, though, she'd had to rely on canned goods when it came to fruit and vegetables.

She'd just poured herself a cup of coffee when Amaal appeared at the door to the kitchen. Although he still looked tired—Deirdre doubted those dark circles under his eyes were normal for him, and guessed they were another side effect of the device—he seemed cheerful enough, his dark hair still damp from the shower, the stubble gone from his cheeks and chin. He must have found Leland's razor. He'd been meticulous about shaving, while Sean usually let himself get scruffy on the weekends he'd spent here at the research station.

"Is that coffee?" Amaal inquired, appearing to sniff the air.

"It is," Deirdre replied. "I made extra—I thought you might want some."

"I do. Perhaps it won't be enough to counter the effects of your device, but I am sure it will help."

She sent him a sideways glance, wondering if the comment was meant as a subtle dig, but his expression was guileless enough. It would be hard to know whether he was being sincere, since she really didn't know him at all. But at least he hadn't attempted to find the device, or disturb her sleep in any way, and so she supposed she should take his remark at face value.

"Maybe," she allowed, and went to get another mug from the cupboard. This one was emblazoned with the slogan, "Be greater than average," followed by the actual equation for finding an average. Leland's, she recalled; Sean wasn't the sort to have anything quite that scientific on his coffee mug. "I don't have any milk —" she began, but Amaal shook his head.

"Black is fine."

Well, that made things easier. She poured coffee into the mug and then handed to him, reflecting that this had to be one of the stranger episodes in her life. When she'd gotten out of bed the day before, the last thing she would ever have expected was to have a djinn living under her roof, sharing morning coffee with her.

Amaal sniffed the coffee appreciatively, then took a sip and nodded in approval. Deirdre knew it was good because she'd been making coffee since she was twelve years old, trying to be helpful by getting a pot going in the morning for her mother. This particular batch was mocha java, something she'd pilfered from the coffeehouse down in Running Springs.

"Thank you for this," Amaal said after sipping again at the coffee. "I hadn't really expected coffee...or a hot shower."

For the briefest instant, Deirdre had a flash of his muscular body standing under the shower head while water ran down his smooth skin. Heat flared in her cheeks, and she picked up her own cup of coffee and took a hasty swallow. Where the hell had *that* come from? Yes, those stupid djinn robes he'd been wearing the day before had shown off enough of his form that the image would be indelibly stamped on her brain, but still....

Thank God that today he was in more of Sean's borrowed clothes, some faded jeans and a long-sleeved T-shirt with the Heineken logo printed on the back. No shoes; socks peeked out from underneath the slightly ragged hem of the Levi's he had on. Of course, in those clothes he looked disturbingly human. If Deirdre hadn't known better, she would have thought Amaal was just a regular guy...or at least, an insanely good-looking regular guy.

"Solar water heater," she said, the first thing that popped into her mind. "They tried to make the station as self-sufficient as possible."

"Which was why you were able to survive out here on your own for so long."

Those blue eyes seemed far too keen as he looked down at her. Was he imagining her in the shower as well? No, that was crazy. She had no idea whether djinn would even think of having humans as sexual partners. The prospect didn't seem very likely, considering the way the elemental race appeared dedicated to ensuring that no humans remained.

Despite that very obvious fact, something about Amaal's regard made Deirdre uncomfortable. He wasn't looking at her like something he wanted to destroy. No, she'd seen that expression on too many guys' faces at bars and parties not to know he was checking her out. Subtly, not in a blatant way, but definitely assessing.

Which only made her remember that she didn't have on a speck of makeup, and that she was wearing some extremely unflattering sweats.

So what? she asked herself. *You're not trying to impress anyone.*

Even so, she had to refrain from reaching up to smooth her hair, or to bite her lower lip in the hope that might make it look a little more rosy. These weren't actions she would have even considered around Sean or Leland, so it seemed that Amaal was having some kind of an effect on her, whether she liked it or not. Of course, Leland had been so engrossed in his work that he probably hadn't even noticed she was female, and Sean already had at least two on-again, off-again girlfriends. One of them had come with him to the station once, and she'd been an almost stereotypical California girl—bright blonde hair, big blue eyes, tanned and fit, large bust straining against her too-small T-shirt. It had been pretty obvious what Sean's type was...and Deirdre knew she wasn't it.

Not that she'd really wanted to be, either. The only time they'd been able to have any kind of decent conversations had been when they were talking about taking care of the animals at the station, or when discussing the prospects for skiing this next winter. Sean had been an avid skier; Deirdre wasn't, mostly because it was too expensive to begin with, and she also couldn't afford to get laid up with a broken arm or leg or something. But at least long-range forecasts had been a neutral topic for discussion, and better than working together in complete silence.

The early snow that had fallen a few weeks earlier seemed to be a promising indicator for the rest of the season...not that anyone would be skiing up in Big Bear or Wrightwood any time soon.

"There's not a lot to eat," she said, changing the subject. The last thing she'd wanted to do was go into any detail regarding the things she'd had to do to survive over the past few months. "But I have breakfast bars, protein bars, that kind of thing. They're not bad."

Amaal seemed to accept this bit of information without too much dismay, because he nodded, his expression noncommittal as he took another sip of coffee. Then a wicked glint entered his blue eyes, and he said, "It's unfortunate that you've blocked my djinn powers, because I could have summoned us any kind of breakfast you would like."

Deirdre knew she probably shouldn't fall for

such an obvious ploy. However, she couldn't help asking, "What do you mean, 'summon'?"

Amaal didn't blink. "I mean that all I would have to is snap my fingers, and we could have a buffet laid out here to tempt any appetite. Omelettes,   pancakes,   muffins,   fresh fruit…bacon."

The word actually made her mouth water. She thought of those rare occasions during her childhood when her mother had actually had the time to cook bacon for Deirdre and her brother, the times when the savory smell of bacon on the griddle seemed to fill the entire house. Never mind that she'd all but given up red meat lately, both for the health benefits and because the entire meat industry was sort of appalling from a sustainability standpoint. She'd allowed herself to feel virtuous about her food choices, even though right now the thought of having a few pieces of bacon—or a cheeseburger—was enough to make her want to throw all her scruples right out the window.

However, she wasn't so hungry that she would be stupid enough to turn the device off. If Amaal got his powers back, she highly doubted that his first action would be to summon her a breakfast worthy of the most ostentatious Sunday buffet. No, he'd probably either simply disappear, if he was feeling generous, or maybe enact some kind of revenge on her for locking him up in a cage, if he was feeling hostile.

Either way, she'd still be hungry…and kicking herself for allowing a djinn to trick her with false promises.

"That's all right," she said, her tone deliberately careless. "The breakfast bars are pretty good. I especially like the peanut butter ones. Should I get you one?"

For a few seconds, he didn't answer. If he was annoyed with her for turning down his offer, it didn't show. Actually, he looked more amused than anything else, one corner of his mouth lifting in a half smile.

"Certainly," he replied. "I will admit a certain fondness for peanut butter."

Since he'd called her bluff, there wasn't anything she could do except go to the pantry and retrieve one of the breakfast bars in question. Amaal set down his mug of coffee and took the bar from her, pausing for a moment to read the ingredients. As if that should matter. Either he was going to eat it or he wasn't.

Apparently, he didn't find anything that troubled him, because after he was done inspecting the wrapper, he carefully tore it open. Watching him, Deirdre could see how his fingers shook slightly. He was doing a pretty good job of pretending that the device wasn't affecting him too badly, but little telltales like the tremor in his hands showed that he wasn't holding up quite as well as he'd like her to think.

He took a bite, then nodded. "That is not bad," he allowed before adding, "but not as good as bacon."

"What is?" Deirdre responded, then went over to top off her mug of coffee. She knew she needed to let the caffeine settle a bit more before she ate anything.

Another bite, and he chewed meditatively before responding with a question of his own. "You don't trust me, do you?"

A short bark of a laugh escaped Deirdre's lips before she could stop it. "No," she said frankly. "Why in the world would you think that I would trust you?"

"You let me out of the cage," he said, his gaze earnest now, lacking any of the irony she'd noted in most of his previous interactions with her. "Why would you do such a thing if you didn't trust me on some level?"

"Because...." The word trailed off as she tried to think of the best way to respond. The truth was, she still didn't know for sure why she'd done something so reckless. Any rational observer would have thought that letting a djinn roam free in the research station was pretty spectacularly stupid. There was no reason for her to believe he

wouldn't try to suffocate her in her sleep—
although she had to admit that Amaal was so
weak, thanks to the device, he probably couldn't
even smother a kitten. Shrugging, she said, "It
would have been cruel to keep you in that cage. I
guess I didn't want to think of myself as being
capable of such a thing. After all, cruelty is more
up you djinns' alley, right?"

Again he was quiet for a moment. He set
down the breakfast bar he'd been eating on the
counter, then lifted his mug of coffee so he could
drink from it once more. "Some of us, yes," he
said, and suddenly Deirdre was able to see real
sorrow in his face. The glint was gone from his
eyes now, and his mouth drooped slightly. "To the
detriment of all around them."

It was crazy, but looking at him right then, she
had the wildest impulse to go over and give him a
hug. She had no idea what kind of losses he'd
suffered, or who he was thinking of to appear so
sorrowful, but something about her words had
triggered a deep sadness in him.

Of course she wouldn't give in to that
impulse. He was weak, but allowing herself to get
close enough where he might try to grab her, or
strangle her, or....

No, he wouldn't do any of those things.
Hadn't he already said that he wasn't one of the
djinn who'd been instrumental in destroying

humanity? Deirdre would be the first to admit that she didn't always have the best instincts about men—after all, she'd idolized her father and thought he could do no wrong, right up to the point where he walked out the door and never came back—but she somehow knew that Amaal wasn't a murderer. He didn't have that edge about him.

Or maybe he was just a really, really good actor.

"Well, detrimental to humans, anyway," she remarked, and took another swallow of coffee. "I guess you djinn can manage well enough."

"Not as well as you might think." Amaal picked up his neglected breakfast bar and bit into it. He chewed contemplatively for a moment, then said, "Really, you'd only have to allow me my powers for a minute for me to fetch us a real breakfast."

"No."

That flat response only made him shrug, as if he'd been expecting the denial but had hoped he might be able to get her to budge on this particular point. He was quiet as he ate the rest of the breakfast bar. Once he was done, he folded the wrapper in half, and then in half again, flattening it against the countertop. Deirdre watched him, surprised, because she often indulged in the same sort of compulsively neat behavior and certainly hadn't expected to see it in a djinn, of all people.

It was almost as if he wasn't so very different from her.

She really didn't want to entertain that kind of thought. Better to remind herself of those extra chromosomes, of lord knows what other kinds of alien biology lurked behind that all-too-human face. She needed to remember that he was very, very different from her, no matter how he might appear on the outside.

To cover her confusion, she went back over to the pantry and got herself a breakfast bar as well. Oatmeal raisin, which she didn't like as well as the peanut butter, but which needed to get eaten, too. Amaal noticed, since his eyebrows lifted slightly at her choice, although he didn't comment.

But then he asked, "What do you do all day here?"

She hadn't been expecting that question. The answer that immediately leapt to her mind was, *Keep an eye out for you djinn.* Fat lot of good that had done her. All that watching with binoculars, going to the lookout, scanning the sky for any hostile intruders, and when she finally did run into a djinn, it was because she'd nearly tripped over him in a mountain meadow.

"I clean, some days. Others, I go into

Running Springs or the houses around it to see what kind of food I can scrounge."

Amaal's head tilted slightly to one side. "Then why were you so far from home yesterday when you came across me?"

"What does it matter?"

"I'm curious." He paused, then added, "You see, I must confess that I was finding it rather difficult to fill the hours at my home. That is why I asked you what you do with your days."

Again she experienced a rush of sympathy for him. Solitude wasn't always the easiest thing in the world to manage, especially if you weren't used to it.

"There's a fire lookout station about a mile or so from where I found you," she said. "I'd go up there every once in a while to get a different vantage point on things. I suppose I kept hoping something would change, that I would see some sign of life. But I never did."

His gaze wouldn't quite meet hers. Deirdre supposed she couldn't really blame him for that. After all, he'd already apologized to her, made it clear that the world's current emptiness had nothing to do with him. What else could he do except offer more apologies, empty words that didn't mean very much in the end?

"Anyway," she went on, hoping she sounded unconcerned by the whole situation, and knowing she probably didn't, "that's what I do. I used to put feed out for the birds, but I ran out of what we had here on hand, and I couldn't quite see lugging twenty-pound sacks of it up from Running Springs when I had to get my own supplies. The birds just had to fend for themselves."

"They'll all be taken care of," Amaal said softly. "The animals, I mean."

She sent him a puzzled glance. "'Taken care of'?"

"So many animals left behind when their owners died. We djinn had no wish to see them suffer. That is why we made sure that they would always have enough to eat, would not suffer from hunger or disease. It seemed the least we could do."

Deirdre stared at him, at the vaguely sad expression he wore. It had puzzled her, immediately after the Heat took out everyone in the vicinity, why she didn't see any stray cats or dogs in Running Springs or its environs. She'd thought she could rescue at least a few of them, bring them back with her to live at the research station. But the little resort town had been suspiciously empty when it came to abandoned domestic animals. The only explanation seemed to be that the fever had taken them as well.

They hadn't died of the Heat, though.

Through some mysterious mechanism, the djinn had looked after them, made sure they stayed healthy and whole.

That news should have cheered her. Instead, Deirdre only felt the aching knot of sorrow and worry that she'd carried with her ever since the world ended grow a little bit tighter, a little bit harder.

In a whisper, she said, "So you showed more mercy to the animals than you did to human beings."

And before Amaal had a chance to reply, she turned away from him and fled the room.

SEVEN

THAT COULD HAVE GONE BETTER. AMAAL RAN a hand through his shaggy shoulder-length hair and wondered whether he should go after Deirdre. It was so hard to know whether she would be at all receptive to his offers of comfort.

No, probably better to stay here in the kitchen. The fury and the hurt in her voice as she'd flung that last condemnation at him seemed to indicate she needed some time to sort through everything he'd said to her. He'd thought letting her know how the djinn had cared for the animals would make her feel better, since she'd previously indicated that she'd wanted to be a veterinarian and would have pursued that field if it weren't for her family's money constraints. Apparently, that had been the wrong tack to take.

He let out a sigh and then went to pour the last of the coffee from the carafe into his mug. Perhaps that was poor etiquette, but it didn't seem as if Deirdre had any desire to drink more.

No, it appeared that all she wanted at the moment was to put as much space as possible between the two of them.

Up until that point, however, things had seemed as though they were going well. She'd talked to him almost normally, even if he couldn't yet convince her to turn off the device.

That would have been a welcome relief. He'd done his best to act as though it wasn't constantly draining him, sapping his energy so that every step, every breath required extra effort, because he didn't want Deirdre to know how weak he truly was. He did not enjoy the sensation at all, to put it mildly. Never in his life had he felt ill, or even tired, and so the constant drain on him was taking its toll. Still, the situation could have been much worse. She could have left him in the cage, but her better nature had prevailed.

He drank the rest of his coffee, then put the empty mug on the countertop. As he came out into the hallway, he heard the sound of water behind the bathroom's closed door, and realized Deirdre must be in the shower. Yes, that would be a good place to isolate herself and seek the privacy she obviously needed. At the same time, he couldn't quite keep his thoughts from straying to an image of her standing under the shower head, water flowing over her naked body, wet hair a curtain of silk down her back.

Device or no, that imagined sight made a thrill of desire rush over him. She was so lovely, even this morning in those baggy clothes and with her hair pulled away from her face in a messy ponytail. He wondered if she knew how truly beautiful she was. His experience with human women was not large—unlike some of his kind, he'd never had any desire to go slumming in such a way—and yet it seemed that most women, human or djinn, who possessed that kind of beauty had some awareness of it, and of its effects on others. Deirdre, on the other hand, appeared oblivious to her own looks. Perhaps she'd stopped caring because she thought no one else would ever see her, that she was utterly alone.

Ah, but he was seeing her, and she wasn't alone. And as much as he would have liked to linger here and perhaps catch a glimpse of Deirdre as she emerged from the bathroom—with any luck, wrapped in a towel—he knew that to do so would probably only anger her that much more. No, it was better to stay away until she was dressed again and ready to see him...whenever that might be. He didn't know her well enough yet to guess whether she was the sort of woman whose anger flared up quickly and was gone, or whether she was one of those who would brood over any slight or setback.

The room where he'd slept did not offer any amusements. He supposed he could have taken advantage of Deirdre's occupation in the shower to slip away from the research station; surely the range of effect from the device couldn't be infinite, which meant as soon as he reached a certain distance from that black little box, he would be himself again, and in possession of all his powers.

However, he was reluctant to escape. For one thing, Deirdre was already angry enough with him, and he had no real wish to upset her further. Also, the thought of not seeing her anymore was far from appealing. He supposed at some point he might find a djinn woman who would erase any memories of Deirdre Graves, but for now he would much rather stay here and confront the challenge she presented.

And of course there was the very real worry that another djinn might find her, a djinn who would care nothing for those crystalline blue eyes or that perfect rose-petal skin, a djinn who would kill her simply because she was human, and prey. Amaal could try to convince himself that the device would protect her, but did he know that for sure?

He passed the bathroom door and the door to the room where he'd slept, and entered a chamber he guessed must be the laboratory. Although unfamiliar with a great deal of human technology, he recognized the microscope on the nearest worktable easily enough. Moving closer, he saw a piece of paper covered in choppy, nearly illegible handwriting—Deirdre's, he assumed. He couldn't really decipher most of what she'd written, but at the bottom of the sheet of paper she'd printed in large block letters, *48 chromosomes!!! What does it mean??*

Below that were more scribblings he couldn't quite make out, obviously written in some haste, as though she was working through something and wanted to get it out and onto paper before she lost the thread of her thoughts. Underlined several times was something he thought said, *Djinn powers = extra chromosomes???*

Amaal knew nothing about genetics except what Deirdre had attempted to explain to him the evening before, but it seemed to him that she might be have discovered a truth there. How else could one explain the similarities between humans and djinn, and yet their enormous differences?

"What are you doing?" Deirdre's voice, tight and angry.

He looked up, guilt coursing through him—a somewhat unprecedented sensation. "I am sorry. What you told me yesterday about the differences in my blood from yours—I was curious. But I should not have been looking at your notes. Then again," he added, essaying what he hoped was a charming smile, "I fear I cannot make much of them."

She crossed her arms. Now she was fully dressed, in jeans and a sweater that fit her somewhat better than the baggy garment she'd worn earlier. Her hair was damp, falling in waves past her shoulders. Clearly, she'd only blotted it and left it to dry on its own. "That doesn't matter. You still shouldn't be snooping around my stuff."

"No, I suppose not." A table up against the far wall caught his eye. Unlike the one where the microscope was located and where he'd found Deirdre's notes, this other worktable was a mess of wires and circuits and other bits and pieces he couldn't begin to identify. Off to one side were what appeared to be a disassembled laptop computer and a couple of tablet devices, while on the shelf above was a radio of some sort. "What is all that?"

"None of your business."

He raised an eyebrow at her. "There's no need to be rude."

Some of the angry tension seemed to go out of

her neck and jaw, and she appeared almost contrite. "Sorry. I—well, sorry." She moved past him, going to the worktable with its assemblage of junk. "This is where I built the device."

Even though he'd guessed she must have assembled it herself, he still couldn't prevent himself from staring at her in surprise. "You *built* it?"

A wry smile. "Well, I couldn't exactly go down the hill and get one at Best Buy, could I?"

Amaal didn't know what this "Best Buy" was, but he assumed it must be some kind of retail establishment. "This is the sort of thing you learned at the university?"

This time she actually chuckled, then shook her head. "No. It was—" She seemed to stop herself there, then said, "I got the instructions from someone else who built one."

Obviously, she was reluctant to divulge any more information than that, but he'd heard enough now to put the pieces together. "Someone in New Mexico?"

Shock flared in her aquamarine eyes. "How did you know that?"

He stepped closer, came over to stand next to her. To his relief, she didn't attempt to move away. Staring down at the bits and pieces on the table, rather than at her, he said, "I thought it did not concern me, for all this was happening in a territory far from my own, but I had heard rumors of some sort of devilish device being used to thwart the djinns' power. That is why I had some knowledge of it, even though I never expected to see such a thing so close to my home."

"Oh." Deirdre fiddled with a bit of loose circuit board, then set it back down on the table-top. Also looking down, she said, "The man who invented it was sending out the instructions. I just followed them. I'm not an engineer or anything. But it worked."

"Yes, it did," Amaal said. She was so close that he could smell the sweet scent of the shampoo she used rising from her damp hair. A warm scent… coconut and vanilla. Again he had to fight the urge to take her into his arms. This was certainly not the time, and even though his spirit was certainly willing enough, he feared that his flesh, weakened by the device as it was, might be far too weak.

This time she did glance up from the work-table. Her expression was almost puzzled, as though she was having a difficult time trying to determine his true feelings on the topic. "You don't sound very angry about it."

"Well," he said calmly, "while I would be the first to admit that the sensation is extremely unpleasant, I also must admit that I understand why you built the thing, and why you used it.

Indeed, I am rather impressed that you were able to succeed so well at something that was far outside your area of expertise."

A little flush of color tinged her cheeks. "I kind of surprised myself, too. I guess having my brother show me how to solder circuit boards paid off."

"Your brother?"

Once again she looked away from Amaal and began fiddling with a bit of wire. "Douglas was my older brother. He was always sort of a science geek. Anyway, he liked to build things—he put together his own computer when he was only fifteen years old. I was always sort of fascinated by his projects, so he taught me how to do some of this stuff, even though I didn't always understand the principles behind it." The faintest gust of a breath, as though she wanted to sigh but couldn't quite allow herself to do so in front of him. "He's gone now, I suppose. I mean, I know if he'd lived, he would have come to look for me."

"I'm sorry," Amaal said. It seemed he had repeated that short, useless phrase far too many times already, but he didn't know for sure how else he should respond. He certainly couldn't bring back those she'd lost, and he'd already done his best to explain that he had no part in those deaths. Some impulse compelled him to add, "I recently lost my brother as well."

She set down the bit of wire and looked up at him, surprise clear in her lovely features. "You did? I didn't know—" And she seemed to stop herself there, even though what she'd intended to say seemed obvious enough to him.

"You didn't know that djinn could die?" She shook her head, and he continued, "We have very long lives and are difficult to kill, but we are not immortal, not in the way your people might have thought. Omar was…a difficult person. He ran afoul of the wrong man and paid the price for his wrongdoing."

Deirdre seemed to digest that information for a moment, quiet as she absorbed what he had told her. Then she said, "You don't seem very upset about it."

He lifted his shoulders. "I have come to terms with what happened to him. He broke the laws of our people, and so I cannot condemn the man who took his life, not when he only did so to protect his woman."

From the way Deirdre frowned, Amaal guessed that his answer had only provoked more questions. However, she didn't say anything at first, instead seemed to once more ponder his words. When she spoke, her comment surprised him. "Maybe that's even harder, in a way. I mean, my brother lived a blameless life. I mourn him, just as I mourn everyone else I've lost. But it must be rough to lose someone who wasn't a very good person. You don't quite know how you're supposed to feel about them, and then you feel guilty for being relieved that they're not around anymore."

Staring down at her, Amaal could only think of how perceptive she was, this young woman who hadn't lived even a tenth of the years he had spent in this existence. And yet she seemed to have gone to the very heart of the matter. He had wondered at himself, wondered if there was something wrong with him because he had shed no tears for his brother's loss, but now he knew that was not his own failing. Why affect false grief for a deeply flawed person, simply because they had shared the same blood?

"That is precisely it," he said. "I hope that Omar finds some peace in the next world, for he certainly found none here. At the same time, I must admit that it is rather a relief he is gone."

She didn't reply, only nodded. Her weight shifted almost imperceptibly, and Amaal thought that perhaps she had intended to move toward him but then thought better of it. Rather than offer a comforting gesture, it appeared she thought the best thing to do was change the subject, for she said next, "What about your parents?"

"They are still alive, if that is what you are asking," he replied.

"What did they do when Omar died?"

"Nothing," Amaal said, and went on to clarify, "That is, I am sure the elders informed them of his death, but I have heard nothing from them on the subject."

This reply seemed to shock her, for her eyes widened, and she turned toward him, asking, "And that's not considered strange?"

"Not really." How best to explain all the many differences between djinn culture and the world she'd grown up in? That would be a subject for many conversations. However, since she clearly expected him to say more on the topic, he continued, "Once a djinn reaches his or her majority at the age of two decades, their parents are not terribly involved with their lives. It is enough to raise them and send them on to do as they will."

"That sounds...cold."

"To a human, perhaps." All he could do was offer her another shrug, for there had been times in his life when he couldn't help comparing the somewhat cold and distant manner in which djinn families generally conducted themselves to the intricate connections humans seemed to culti-vate. "We live a very long time, you see. Would you really have wanted your mother and father to continue to meddle in your affairs for millennia?"

That question elicited a wry grin. Amaal was glad that he could make Deirdre smile, even if the topic they discussed was not all that amusing. "I guess not," she said. "Although, like I told you, my father was kind of out of the picture after I turned eleven. Still, I get your point." She turned even more toward him, leaning into the worktable. "So in all those millennia, your parents only had two children?"

"Yes. Djinn do not have large families, as a rule. My parents joined for the purpose of having children, but once the two of us were born and had both grown to our majority, they dissolved the relationship and went on their way. That is how it is always done."

From the way Deirdre frowned, he could tell she did not much like the sound of that kind of arrangement, and her next words only confirmed his suspicions. "No 'til death do you part,' I guess."

Not except for Chosen and the djinn who have selected them, Amaal thought, but he did not say it aloud. The last thing he wanted was to explain the odd setup that had allowed some of humanity to survive, for then he would have to explain why he'd had no real desire to claim a human woman as his own. And, looking at Deirdre, he was beginning to wonder why he had made such a decision in the first place. He had never even studied the list of names the elders had provided, those who would be immune and who were of the correct age to be made Chosen. He had not thought he could bear to be saddled with a human for all eternity.

And yet now he wasn't quite sure whether he'd made the right decision.

"No, nothing like that," he said. "Only those we wish to be with for a time, and then go on our way."

Her mouth pursed, and she pushed herself away from the worktable and went over to where her microscope sat, began tinkering with the controls. Amaal guessed she was not doing anything particularly useful, had only wanted a reason to walk away from where he stood.

"I knew some guys who would've liked that arrangement," she said, still peering into the microscope. "No strings, no commitment."

"I am not sure it is quite like you think," Amaal protested. As much as he wanted to go over to her, he sensed that she needed this space between them. "Many of those liaisons last forty, fifty, even a hundred years or more. It is not quite like what your people used to refer to as 'one night stands.'"

"Still...." A shake of her head, and she went back to peering in the microscope.

Had she been wounded by a former lover,

someone who had only wanted a short-term relationship, who had no thought for their future together? Amaal could see why she might take such a negative view of the way the djinn managed such things, if that were the case. Then again, she had been in college when the Heat struck. He could not confess to knowing much about that lifestyle, but he knew enough to understand that it was a time when young mortals were planning their futures, were not, in general, ready to settle down.

He wished he could ask her. However, despite everything they had been discussing, he knew that making such an inquiry would be too intrusive. They might have slept under the same roof the night before, but they were still strangers to one another, for the most part. And he could tell from the way she was pretending to work with the microscope that she had no desire to continue the conversation.

Making his tone as mild as he could manage, he said, "I can see that you wish to work. It is a sunny day—I think I will go and sit on that bench I saw out front on the porch."

"That's probably a good idea." Then she added, sounding a bit softer, "Make sure you don't take a chill, though. The sun's out, but the wind can be pretty harsh if you're in the shade."

"I'll be careful," he replied. As he went out, he

couldn't help but feel slightly cheered, despite the way they'd left the conversation.

After all, if she cared nothing for him or his welfare, why would she be worried about him taking a chill?

EIGHT

DON'T CATCH A CHILL. DEIRDRE WANTED TO shake her head at herself, but instead she bent back over the microscope. *What are you, your mother?*

Not even remotely close. Alison Graves had been an R.N., someone who always seemed in control, even when in reality her world was falling apart. Not once had Deirdre ever heard her mother utter a bad word about her father, even in the face of his obvious betrayal. Maybe she complained to her friends, but Alison was old-fashioned about certain things, and one of them was bad-mouthing her children's father anywhere they might hear.

Deirdre was pretty sure she wouldn't have been able to display that kind of forbearance. No, she would have told everyone what a cheating asshole Stephen Graves was, and would have made sure he paid as much alimony as the law dictated. As far as she could tell, her father hadn't paid any kind of spousal support, and although he did send child support payments, sometimes they were late, and sometimes he skipped a month, saying that his commissions were below what he expected and that he really couldn't afford it. He never let the payments lapse for so long that even Alison might have lost her patience and hauled him back into court. No, it was always just enough that he could pad his bank accounts a little, maybe pay for a vacation for him and his new wife.

Anyway, Deirdre was pretty sure her mother would never have put Amaal in a cage, djinn or no. She didn't have that kind of temperament.

Yeah, you put him in a cage, Deirdre thought. *And then you let him back out again, and now you're fussing about him catching cold, so it's not like you grew up to be some kind of hard-ass.*

That was for sure.

And actually, could a djinn even catch a cold? Amaal had said djinn could die, so Deirdre supposed they could get sick as well. Or maybe they didn't get sick in general, but all bets were off when the device was affecting them.

She didn't have a frame of reference, so it was hard to say.

Neither did she really know what she was

looking for in this slide of his blood. He had red blood cells and white blood cells, just like a normal person. From what she'd been able to tell, the differences between humans and djinn weren't visible on the cellular level, but buried far deeper in their DNA. Maybe if she'd been able to talk to Miles Odekirk, he might have had some insights. No, he'd said he was a physicist. Did someone with a Ph.D. in physics need to know that much about genetics?

Probably not.

She got up from the stool where she'd been sitting and went over to the window. Not to check on Amaal, because the bench where he was supposedly trying to relax wasn't even visible from this side of the building, but to take a look at the day. As he'd said, it was sunny and clear, a fresh breeze ruffling the dry grass. Even so, the temperature couldn't be much warmer than the low fifties at best, not at this time of year, not at this altitude.

Had he taken a jacket? Sean's old puffer jacket hung at one end of the closet in the room he'd once shared with Leland, but Deirdre didn't know whether Amaal had realized it was there.

Are you going to take it to him? she jeered at herself. *Maybe bring him some milk and cookies, too?*

He'd been standing way too close to her over

at her workbench. Had he even realized that he was inside what she thought of as her private bubble, or did djinn not have the same notions of personal space?

It was hard to say. He hadn't made a move, tried to touch her or anything like that. Actually, she was the one who'd almost reached out to lay a comforting hand on his arm as he talked about his brother. Deirdre hadn't expected the rush of compassion that had moved through her when Amaal spoke of losing his brother, of wrestling with his feelings about that loss. But she could relate all too well, because she'd grappled with many of the same emotions while coming to terms with her father's death. At least, she assumed Stephen Graves must be dead, just because everyone else was. And she hadn't known how to weep for him because she was still so very angry with him, for what he'd done to their family. It was easier to mourn her mother and Douglas, because she loved them both unre-servedly.

Damn it.

She left the window and went in to the bedroom she'd given Amaal for his use. Sure enough, there was the jacket, still hanging at one end of the closet. Deirdre pulled it off the hanger and bundled it under one arm, then went down the hall and out the front door. Amaal wasn't sitting on the bench, but instead stood out in the open area just beyond the porch, face lifted toward the blue sky, eyes shut as though he was completely focused on absorbing as much of the sun's energy as possible. The breeze caught at his shoulder-length hair, blowing it away from his face so that every perfect plane and angle was clearly illuminated.

God, he really was good-looking. Deirdre realized she was staring, so she cleared her throat and said, "I brought you a jacket."

His eyes opened, reflecting the deep cerulean blue of the skies above him. "It is warm enough here in the sun."

"Maybe, but that wind is pretty brisk." She stepped off the porch and went over to him, then extended the jacket in one hand.

Amaal took it from her and slipped it on. At once he smiled. "Thank you. That does feel better."

Why did that smile make her knees feel a little wobbly? He was a djinn, a completely different species. She shouldn't be reacting to him like this. Voice sharper than she'd intended it to be, she said, "I told you that wind could be brutal. You probably shouldn't stay outside too long in it."

The smile didn't fade. "I won't. I just wanted to feel the sun for a bit longer."

"Okay. When you come inside, there are some

books in the break room if you need something to occupy yourself."

"I will look for them."

Deirdre offered him an uncertain smile and went inside. It was only after she'd closed the door behind her that she realized he probably could have escaped if he'd really wanted to. She'd been in the lab for a good fifteen or twenty minutes after he went outside, and she guessed that he could have easily walked past the device's field of effect in that space of time.

But he hadn't. He'd stayed.

She wasn't sure she wanted to know why.

Amaal came back inside, shut the door, and then shrugged out of his borrowed jacket. It had been good of Deirdre to bring it to him, because that way he'd been able to remain outdoors in the sunlight much longer than he could have if he'd only been wearing a sweatshirt on its own. An elemental of fire, he welcomed the fires of the sun, for they gave some of his own energy back to him, allowed him to fight the effects of the device Deirdre had built, if only for a little while.

It had occurred to him, as he stood out there in the sunshine, that he could have turned and begun to walk west, toward his home. He had no idea precisely how far he would have to go before the device stopped draining his djinn powers, but it could not have been more than a quarter-mile or so. Even as weak as he currently felt, he knew he could have covered that distance during the span of time when Deirdre was still inside in the laboratory. It wasn't as though she had come out immediately to check on him.

As to why he hadn't left...well, the answer was not so far away, only down the hallway in the lab, most likely hunched over her microscope once again. He still didn't know for sure whether she was conducting further tests, or whether she was only using the lab and its equipment as a pretext for staying away from him. Perhaps it would have been easier for her if she had left him in the cage. Guilt over such a course of action set aside, she wouldn't have to worry about interacting with him as an equal, or wondering what mischief he might get into as he roamed about the wildlife station.

At any rate, he knew that Deirdre was what had kept him here. He had never spent any appreciable amount of time around a human before, because although of course he had left the otherworld from time to time to see Earth's beauties or to sample its cuisine or visit its museums, he had never had a liaison with a human woman. Some djinn said the novelty was worth the complications, but Amaal had never thought such diversions were worth the inevitable trouble they caused.

Now, though...he thought of how Deirdre had looked when she came out to bring the jacket to him, of how the fresh breeze had caught her loose hair and brought pink to her cheeks. Or perhaps that flush did not have terribly much to do with the wind. He did not wish to flatter himself, but he couldn't help but notice the way she sometimes blushed around him, the way her eyes did not quite want to meet his. As far as he could tell, some kind of attraction already existed between them, even if she did not wish to acknowledge it.

Would a human woman's lips be as soft and full as those of a djinn? Would her body feel the same when he held her in his arms?

There was only one way to find out for sure, but Amaal realized Deirdre was not ready to take such a step. He thought he could indulge her for a while; the effects of the device were certainly not pleasant, but as long as he could go outside from time to time and "recharge," so to speak, he thought he could endure them for at least a few more days.

After that...well, he supposed he would see.

Amaal seemed happy enough to be outside, although he came in after a while and went into the break room, which was supplied with an odd assortment of paperbacks that had been left there by various students and teacher's assistants over the years. Deirdre hadn't stopped to think that maybe her djinn captive couldn't even read English, despite being so fluent in it when speaking, but when she peeked in the break room on her way to the kitchen to get herself a glass of water, he seemed to be engrossed in a tattered, dog-eared copy of *Twilight*.

She had to hope that particular selection wouldn't give him any ideas.

Lord knows she'd been having ideas of her own, ideas she tried to shove out of her head as soon as they appeared. Her thoughts kept circling back to the way he had looked standing out there in front of the research station, bright sunlight picking out flecks of gold and russet in his dark brown hair. Again she'd had to remind herself that he wasn't human at all, was some kind of strange other that might look like a mortal man but was anything but. It only helped her so much, probably because in that sweatshirt and puffer jacket and those faded jeans, Amaal might have been just another student working at the station with her.

The difference, however, was that she'd never

had a burning desire to kiss any of her fellow students. This djinn, on the other hand….

God. Deirdre tucked a stray strand of hair back behind one ear and set to work creating a fresh slide with Amaal's blood. She really didn't expect to find anything new in this one, but at least it gave her something to do. And if she did another chromosome stain, she could remind herself once again that he wasn't like her, that his DNA was as alien as that of a tardigrade.

Well, not exactly. But it was the only way to keep pounding it into her head that he wasn't like her.

Why hadn't he left? Surely whatever house he'd been given had to be more luxurious than this renovated '30s-era cottage. And she knew the device was, if not actively causing him pain, at least making him feel like someone suffering a very bad hangover. That couldn't be pleasant.

And it couldn't be her scintillating personality, either. She'd been doing her best to avoid him, except for those few moments when they'd shared revelations Deirdre now wished she'd kept to herself. Amaal didn't need to know her life story. And yet she'd already told him about how her father had walked out, about the way her brother had showed her how to solder and work with circuit boards.

Then again, Amaal had also shared his own

confidences. His brother definitely hadn't sounded like a very nice person. Deirdre wondered who the woman was that Amaal's brother Omar had tried to kidnap. A djinn, she assumed, beautiful and exotic. Would a djinn woman even put up with that sort of behavior, though? Surely djinn women had their own powers and could probably take care of themselves. Then again, maybe not. Amaal hadn't said much about his female counterparts, so maybe they differed from the male djinn in terms of the powers they commanded.

It was hard to say for sure, because Amaal was the only djinn she'd ever seen. She knew nothing about the women of his race, except the bits and pieces that had come out when they were discussing the djinns' concept of families and relationships. And that had all sounded very unappealing. Despite her parents' nasty split, Deirdre had always hoped she might one day find a real soul mate, someone she could spend the rest of her life with. She didn't like the djinn model of hooking up with someone for a few years or decades or whatever, then dissolving the relationship and moving on when both of the parties involved eventually got tired of one another.

True, she hadn't exactly had the best luck so far, but she also wasn't naïve enough to think that the guys she'd dated in college were prospects for long-term marital bliss. Or rather, she'd tried to tell herself that, but had fallen hard for Tristan Summers, a guy she met in her Biology 102 class the last quarter of her junior year. He'd sworn she was the most beautiful woman he'd ever met, the smartest and most creative, and had built grand castles in the sky in terms of discussing their future. Deirdre had been positive he was going to ask her to marry him, although Tristan was also taking his time to get his bachelor's degree, and those sorts of plans would have to wait until after they both graduated. They'd spent a mostly blissful summer together, but only a few weeks after classes had started up again in late August, he'd bluntly informed her that he didn't think it was going to work out and that he'd started to see other people.

"See other people." There was a joke. Deirdre was just glad that she'd always made sure he used a condom.

Anyway, she definitely hadn't circled back to a place where she could trust anyone, and when it came to trustable individuals, she was pretty sure that a djinn was at the bottom of the list. If she couldn't figure out a way to stop dwelling on that wicked twist to Amaal's mouth, or the way his clear blue eyes danced in the sunlight, then she'd give herself permission to admire his obvious physical attributes without allowing herself to go any further than that.

Maybe she should let him go. After all, he hadn't done or said anything that would make her believe he would tell the other djinn where she was holed up. It probably would be safe enough.

No, she couldn't quite bring herself to do that. An acquaintance of twenty-four hours wasn't enough to inspire the sort of trust such an arrangement would require, although Deirdre also knew that if she really didn't trust Amaal, she probably should have left him locked up in the cage, no matter what her conscience told her about treating another intelligent being in such a way.

Well, she would just have to see how things went. If she couldn't stop herself from brooding over him no matter what she did, then maybe it would be time to send him on his way.

That evening they had boxed macaroni and cheese, made with water since they didn't have any milk. Amaal didn't care for it much, but he didn't comment, for he knew that Deirdre's resources were limited. And he said nothing the next morning when their meal was yet another round of breakfast bars.

Matters went on like this for several days. He stayed out of her way because he had guessed that his presence troubled her, and he would rather have her come to her own understanding of her attraction to him instead of having him attempt to force the situation. For himself, he became increasingly more aware of how deeply he wanted her, no matter how much the device drained every spare ounce of energy he possessed.

After his third night there, however, Deirdre stood at the pantry the next morning and shook her head. "We're going to run out of food soon at the rate we've been going through it."

"Then go into town and get some more," he suggested. "You know you have nothing to fear from other djinn, for they know this is my territory and will stay away."

She turned back toward him, a frown etching the clear, delicate skin of her brow. "And leave you here alone? I don't think so."

"What other choice do you have? I am certainly not up to the task of walking into town, not with that device beating on me. I doubt I could go much farther than the turn-off from the forest service road."

Her eyes narrowed as she appeared to mull her predicament. "I'm not sure…."

"Or," he went on, not bothering to hide the amusement in his voice, "you could turn off the device for a moment or two, and I could summon any kind of food you might require."

She let out an exasperated huff of a breath. "You know I can't do that."

He shrugged and leaned up against the scratched tile of the kitchen counter. "Well, it seems you have a conundrum to deal with. You either leave me, and risk me wandering off, or you take me with you, and risk my collapsing from pain and exhaustion because of the device you use to keep me in check."

"Or I could lock you back up in the cage while I'm gone."

No, he didn't like that alternative at all. However, one of the times she'd been in the shower, he'd pilfered several paper clips and a stray bobby pin from one of the desk drawers in the front office of the research station, and he thought he wouldn't have too much trouble picking the rather crude lock to the cage, in the unfortunate event that she decided to do such a thing.

"If you must," he said. "As long as you aren't gone for too long."

She seemed to consider him for a moment, and then her gaze strayed to the window. "I really don't have to worry about any djinn attacking me?"

"No. At least, I am fairly certain that would not happen. We do tend to respect one another's boundaries." Amaal felt safe enough in giving her this reassurance, for certainly in the time he had spent at his new mountain home, he had never seen another djinn, nor sensed their presence.

"Then I could drive into town," Deirdre said, her tone musing. "That would be a lot faster than walking."

He knew there were several vehicles on the property, for he'd seen them parked around the rear of the research station—an older Subaru of some sort, an even older compact car he didn't recognize. Then there was the big shiny red truck he'd noticed on his first approach to the station. Or rather, it had probably started out new and shiny, but now had more than two months' worth of dust and dirt caked on it. "I suppose you could."

That seemed to decide matters for her, because she said, "All right. You'll have to go in the cage. I'll try to be as fast as I can."

Amaal didn't even attempt to argue. "Of course."

At least she gave him some blankets and a pillow, and he took a book in with him. With his back propped against the cage, the pillow working well enough to protect him from the hard wire, he reflected that this wasn't so bad.

Besides, he didn't intend to spend any more time in here than he had to.

Once he'd heard the roar of the big truck's engine recede into the distance, Amaal fished one of the paper clips out of the pocket of his borrowed jeans, then unbent it and crawled over to the cage door. It was held in place with a simple padlock, not even one that had a combination. He reflected that if he'd had his djinn powers, he could have snapped the damn thing with one twist of his fingers, but that solution was denied him…for now.

The angle was awkward, but he could lean back against the cage wall and just barely get his thumb and index finger out through the wide mesh. He poked the same fingers of his left hand through the mesh as well in order to hold the lock steady while he worked.

His first attempt only succeeded in bending the paper clip at an awkward angle. He pulled it back in through the cage's mesh wall and straightened it out again, then poked it into the keyhole of the lock with less force this time. Ah, yes, that time it stayed in place. Trying not to shift the lock too much, he transferred it and the paper clip to his left hand so he might use the second paper clip to reach inside the lock and manipulate the tumblers. This seemed to be going well—until the second paper clip slipped out of his fingers and fell to the floor with a faint metallic tinkle.

Damn it.

The room wasn't overly warm, but sweat began to form on his forehead nonetheless. He didn't quite know why it was so important to him to succeed at this task—after all, it wasn't as though Deirdre wouldn't let him back out again once she returned from her foraging expedition—but right then he wanted some measure of control. He wanted to figure out where she'd hidden that damnable device.

All he had left was the bobby pin. He extracted it from his jeans pocket and managed to bend it partway open, then slipped it into the lock. Its end was slightly thicker than the paper clip, and therefore a bit easier to use to manipulate the lock's tumblers. Even so, they didn't seem very cooperative, sliding back into place the very second he thought he had them beaten.

Finally, though, he heard the lock click, and it slipped open. Murmuring a quick prayer under his breath, he removed the lock from the cage's latch and opened the door. By then he'd given himself a serious kink in his neck from having to lie in such an awkward position for such an extended period of time, but it was worth it to pull himself out of the cage and rest there on the floor for a moment, reveling in his freedom.

Eventually, however, he pushed himself to his feet and retrieved the two bent paper clips from the floor so he wouldn't be leaving behind any evidence of his escape. At once he went to the window and looked out, but there was no sign of

Deirdre or the truck. Even going at a good clip, he guessed it would take her at least an hour to get into Running Springs, collect the items she'd been looking for, and return to the research station.

Good.

He peeked in the lab but then discarded that notion. His instincts told him she would want to keep the device close, especially during the night-time hours when she was asleep and vulnerable, and so he went on to her bedroom.

There was little here to suggest that she'd spent the better part of two and a half months in this chamber. No personal items other than a scarf draped over the back of a chair, nothing to show that anyone had been staying here at all. Her belongings were stowed neatly in the closet and the dresser, and he went through them all, calmly and methodically. Perhaps it was a particular point of interest to learn that her few underthings were silkier and lacier than he had expected, but he filed that bit of information away for now, making sure to replace everything exactly where he had found it.

And yet…no device. It wasn't in any of her dresser drawers, nor was it hidden beneath her pillow, or even under her mattress, although it cost him some effort to lift the thing, only to realize there was nothing to be found underneath it.

Very well. He turned toward the closet. The upper shelf was bare, and only a few items of clothing hung from the hangers, although Amaal guessed she must have pilfered some of those sweaters and shirts from the shops down in Running Springs. Meager as her wardrobe was, it still appeared to be far more extensive than someone coming to the research station for only a weekend might have needed.

She'd had a purse with her when she left, not the backpack she'd been wearing when she first encountered him in that mountain meadow. And there was the backpack, leaning into a far corner of the closet. But wait...there appeared to be something *behind* the backpack.

Amaal crouched down to look more closely, although even that simple movement felt nearly as taxing as running a mile. He pulled in a breath and moved the backpack aside, revealing a slim black case, most likely for a laptop computer. It was empty—he'd seen the laptop sitting on one of the tables in the laboratory—and yet one corner of it bulged strangely.

His heart began to beat a little faster, although he tried to tell himself that the bulge could be anything, including a spare charging unit for the laptop. With hands that shook slightly, he pulled the case toward him and reached inside. His fingers closed around a small cube-shaped object.

God is good, he thought.

The device sat squarely in the middle of his palm, dark and innocuous in appearance. Two of its sides were covered in a glassy substance; recalling how Deirdre had somehow managed to manipulate the gadget by running her fingers over those surfaces, Amaal attempted to do the same thing.

It was as though a giant had plowed a fist into the center of his chest. He let out a gasp and fell over in a heap, the device slipping from his fingers.

Wrong…way….

Somehow he retained enough strength to reach for the thing again. This time he moved his fingers in the opposite direction, and the pressure and the pain immediately receded. In fact, the sensation was rather like drinking a gallon of coffee all at once—every nerve ending flared to life. The fuzziness that had invaded his mind during the past few days was gone. He was strong, strong and completely himself again.

He let out a laugh and sprang to his feet. As far as he could tell, his powers had returned, but there was only one way to find out for sure.

A snap of his fingers, and a meat pie appeared in one hand. He bit into it, savored the seasoned beef and the vegetables and the spices. It was so good, he summoned another one, and then a goblet of wine to wash them down.

Ah, now he felt like himself again, the rich food and the wine mingling in his belly, giving him a sense of well-being he had not experienced for some time. It was probably a good thing that Deirdre was not there, because he would have pulled her into his arms and kissed her heartily, whether she desired such a thing or not.

However, he knew he could not allow himself to become drunk on this freedom, this sense of exhilaration. She would be back soon enough, and she must never know he'd learned where she had hidden the device that gave her control over him.

For a moment he considered summoning a third meat pie, or perhaps another goblet of wine, but then decided it would not be a good idea. He was not sure how he would react to having that much alcohol in his system once the device was turned back on, and so he only blinked away the empty goblet, then bent to replace the device in Deirdre's laptop bag. Again, he paused to wonder whether he should turn it back on at all, but he feared he would not be able to conceal how good he actually felt. Better to turn it on, but at an even lower level than where it had been set previously.

Yes, that would work. At once he felt weariness wash over him, but it was more manageable. As long as Deirdre did not look at the device too closely, couldn't tell that its settings had been slightly altered from where they had been before, all should be well.

In the meantime, he needed to return to his cage and wait for her to return.

NINE

THE SENSATION OF JOUNCING ALONG THE forest road in Sean's big Toyota Tundra truck was so exhilarating, Deirdre almost wanted to laugh out loud. As she drove, she recognized far too many landmarks that she'd already gone by multiple times on foot, but now they passed quickly enough, eating up ground in minutes that had taken her more than an hour to cover. Despite Amaal's reassurances, she couldn't help continuing to glance in the rearview mirror or out through the side window to see if any djinn followed her, alerted by the dust trail she was leaving behind, but the skies remained clear, as did the road in front of and behind her.

Sooner than she'd expected, she pulled into the outskirts of Running Springs. She'd already gone through the one grocery/general store here, but she'd always been forced to leave a lot behind, since she could only carry what would fit in her backpack. Now she was able to load up on more breakfast bars, oatmeal and cream of wheat, powdered milk, soup, beef jerky, canned chicken and tuna, and so much more—Kleenex and toilet paper, dish soap and deodorant. Whatever would help make life at the research station a little more comfortable.

In addition to the groceries, she went into an outdoor outfitters store and found more sweaters and shirts and pants for both her and Amaal, and boots and parkas and anything else that looked remotely useful. A little voice told her she probably didn't need half this stuff, but it felt so good to be able to take what she wanted, to not be constrained by the space restrictions of her backpack.

By the time she was done—or rather, by the time she'd determined that she couldn't really squeeze anything else into the bed of the truck— at least an hour had passed. The truck only had a half tank of gas, but Deirdre wasn't sure how to fill up with all the electricity out. She thought she'd read somewhere how to switch a gas pump over to manual, but she certainly couldn't recall the procedure now. Besides, that half tank would last for a good long time if all she was doing was going back and forth between the station and Running

Springs. Actually, the gas would probably start to go stale before she used it all up, and that didn't even count what was in the tank of her old Nissan Sentra or Leland's ancient Subaru Outback, or in the gas tanks of the abandoned cars in town.

She really didn't want to think about the gas going stale. Again, there was probably a way to convert one of the vehicles to ethanol, but she didn't know how to do that, either, or make ethanol. In fact, if she had to sit down and make a list of all the things she didn't know how to do, it would have been depressingly long. Usually, she liked tinkering with problems, figuring out how to make things work, but right now she was just tired.

Surviving the end of the world could be damn exhausting.

And beneath it all, she also didn't want to think about why she was stocking up so much, or getting so many things for Amaal. Just how long did she think this little domestic arrangement was going to last? Sooner or later, she'd have to let him go and hope that he really wasn't the vengeful type. Never mind that the thought of having him gone, of having to live in the research station all by herself again, made her stomach start to clench.

She didn't want to be alone. No, it was more specific than that, if she really wanted to be honest with herself. She wanted to keep Amaal around.

All right, she'd stuck him back in the cage before she headed out on this particular expedition, but he hadn't seemed too upset about the situation, had even smiled ruefully as he climbed inside.

And, to be honest, he could have left multiple times before this. It wasn't as if she could stay awake and watchful around the clock. If he'd wanted to leave one night while she was asleep, all he would have had to do was slip out the front door, close it quietly, and be gone. She did tend to sleep lightly, but if he was stealthy enough about it, he could have managed his escape. Plus, there were all the times she'd been in the shower. He could have left then as well, if that had been his intention

But he was still at the station, four days after she'd found him. What did that tell her?

He wanted to stay, too.

Despite herself, she smiled at the thought. This whole thing was crazy. She knew that. If Amaal had been a regular man, a fellow survivor like those who supposedly had gathered in Los Alamos, that would have been one thing. But he wasn't. His people had destroyed the world—or at least, they'd destroyed humankind. Planet Earth itself seemed to be chugging along just fine. Which left her and Amaal where, exactly? He hadn't made a single advance toward her, nor she toward him. Truth be told, she'd spent most of the past few days hiding out from him in the lab, frightened of what any further shared confidences might do to their relationship.

And yet…he was still there.

Deirdre was so preoccupied, she only caught the dark blur out of the corner of her eye at the last minute. Some instinct made her slam on the brakes, the truck skidding on the washboard surface of the dirt road before the traction control caught. Dust swirled up around the windows, and she sat there for a moment, fingers clenched on the steering wheel. Had she hit something? She hadn't felt a bump, but….

Hands shaking, she undid the seatbelt and climbed out, then moved cautiously toward the front of the truck. Hunched there by the roadside was a dog—a gorgeous German shepherd/husky mix, if the animal's thick fur and distinct saddle-shaped markings on its back were any indication.

Oh, God, she'd hit the poor thing. Even from where she stood, she could see the way the dog was favoring one of its hind legs. If it would let her get close, she could take it back to the station, use the first aid supplies there to patch it up as best she could, but….

"Hey, sweetie," she said in a low, coaxing voice, since she really didn't know the dog's sex. "Can I take a look?"

It just lay there, panting, golden eyes staring

up at her beseechingly. Encouraged by the dog's lack of reaction, she came closer, then knelt next to it. The animal whined when she touched its leg, but it didn't snap at her. Even after living on its own for the past few months, the dog looked healthy and well-fed. Was that what Amaal had meant when he said the djinn would take care of the animals?

And now she'd gone and run one of them over.

"Hey, sweetheart," she murmured. "I'm going to lift you now. Want to go for a ride in the truck?"

Despite everything, the dog's tail beat against the gravel, little puffs of dust rising into the air. Deirdre's spirits lifted slightly. No, she'd never had a dog of her own, but she knew they loved to go on car rides.

When she bent to lift the dog, she could tell that it was a female. She was heavy, too, probably between fifty and sixty pounds. Luckily, she seemed to recognize a savior in Deirdre, because she didn't struggle, allowed herself to be carried over to the passenger side of the truck, where Deirdre somehow managed to get her into the seat.

That task accomplished, Deirdre went back over to the driver-side door and climbed in, then resumed her journey at a much slower pace. The last thing she wanted was to hit any other stray animals, and neither did she want to jounce the poor dog around and cause her any more pain.

Even though it probably took only ten or fifteen minutes, that final part of the journey was excruciating. At last, however, the research station came into view. When she saw the empty front porch, Deirdre experienced a stab of disappointment, thinking Amaal should have been there to greet her. Then sanity reasserted itself, and she realized that of course he couldn't be waiting for her on the porch, not when she'd locked him up in the cage before setting out on her foraging expedition.

Nothing for it. Telling herself he probably wouldn't have been of much help in his current weakened state anyway, Deirdre parked the truck as close to the rear entrance of the station as she could, since it was a shorter trip to the animal holding area there than it would have been if she'd come in through the front. Then she got out and lifted the dog from the passenger seat, and staggered up the back steps, only to realize that of course the back door was locked. There was no way she could continue to hold the dog while she dug around in her purse for the keys, and so she gently set the animal down on the stoop, retrieved the keys, and opened the door.

"Almost there, sweetheart," she said, and once

more picked up the dog. Through all this, the animal had only whimpered once or twice, seemed ready to wait and have a human take care of her.

As she came into the room, Amaal stirred in his cage. "Who's that?"

"I don't know," Deirdre replied. She set the dog down on the high metal table that had once been used for this very purpose. "She ran across the road as I was coming back, and I hit her. Thank God I wasn't going fast, but one of her hind legs was injured."

"That is unfortunate."

Deirdre reflected that was one word for the situation. After murmuring a reassurance to the dog, she went over and unlocked the cage, then stepped back so Amaal could climb out. He did so slowly, one hand going to the small of his back as he straightened, as though the cramped conditions had given him a crick somewhere.

Well, there wasn't much she could do about that. She assumed he'd eventually unstiffen now that he wasn't cramped in that cage any longer. After turning away from him, she went over to the cupboard where they'd kept all the veterinary supplies, glad that she'd left it all in place, even after the last of the animal patients here had been set free.

"Do you know anything about healing

animals?" she asked as she got out the antiseptic and the bandages. It seemed that the dog's leg had been bruised and abraded, but as far as Deirdre could tell, it wasn't broken. At least she wouldn't have to worry about putting a splint on the poor thing.

Amaal came over to the table where the dog lay and placed a hand on her head. At once she let out a happy little whine and seemed to smile up at the djinn, her tongue hanging halfway out. Deirdre watched, somewhat surprised by the animal's positive reaction to Amaal's touch. For some reason, she hadn't thought that djinn and dogs would get along.

"Unfortunately, no," he said in answer to her question, his long, strong fingers scratching behind the dog's ears. "We djinn have no healers at all, because we have no need of them, thanks to the way we heal from wounds so quickly, and never suffer from disease. About all we do have is *doulas,* or midwives, since even for djinn women, the task of bringing a new life into the world can be something of an ordeal. However, a djinn woman never has to worry about complications from childbirth. Our women recover from the experience very quickly, and are often back on their feet in less than a day."

Must be nice, Deirdre thought, although something about hearing Amaal talk about childbirth and pregnancy in such a matter-of-fact tone made her a little uncomfortable. A stupid reaction, she told herself, since they certainly weren't intimate, and would never engage in the kind of activity that might lead to having children. Not that she'd be able to bounce back so quickly even if they did. She was human, after all, and would never be anything different.

"Well, then," she said briskly, "I guess it's a good thing that I have some experience. You can keep petting her, and that should keep her mind off what I'm doing."

"I am happy to," Amaal responded, continuing to stroke the dog's ears. "She is quite a beautiful creature. What do you think you will call her?"

A name for the dog hadn't even crossed Deirdre's mind. After all, giving a name to an animal meant you viewed them as a pet, which also meant you planned to keep them around for a while. Then again, why shouldn't she keep the dog here? It would be lonely once Amaal left, and the thought of having to slide back into that kind of solitude wasn't appealing at all. A dog would help to make the loneliness a bit more bearable.

"I'm not sure," Deirdre said. She poured some of the antiseptic onto a cotton pad and carefully wiped down the abraded area on the dog's leg. The animal jerked in reaction, but she didn't try to jump down from the table. "Why don't you help me name her?"

Amaal seemed pleased by this request—his eyes lit up, and he nodded. "What about 'Sasha'?" he asked, after pausing for a moment to consider. "After all, she appears to be part Siberian husky."

That sounded like a good name. Whether she'd respond to it, when obviously she must have had a different name given her by her owners, Deirdre didn't know. The dog wasn't wearing a collar, so she didn't have any tags to show what her real name once had been. "I like it," she said, placing a soft cloth against the animal's leg and taping it in place as carefully as she could.

"You're a good girl, Sasha," Amaal said, his tone gentle as he continued to rub the dog's head. She whined and pushed against his hand, obviously more than happy about all the attention she was getting.

"Yes, she is." Deirdre hoped her makeshift first aid would do some good; thank God she hadn't found any evidence of a break. As far as she could tell, Sasha had only bruised the bone, and as long as she took it easy and stayed off the leg as much as possible, she should heal and be none the worse for wear. "I need to get her down now."

"Do you need any help?"

"No, I'm fine." It probably would have been less awkward to have Amaal assist her, but Deirdre didn't want him to strain himself. He was being smiling and helpful, but the shadows under his eyes remained—although she thought he looked a bit better than he had when she'd left, with more color in his face and more light in his eyes. That didn't make much sense, since one would think that being confined to the cage would have had a negative effect.

Oh, well. She wasn't going to waste time trying to figure it out. Instead, she slid her arms under Sasha's belly and then carefully lifted her from the examination table and set her on the floor. The dog took a few hesitant steps, clearly trying to figure out how best to walk with her leg sore and bandaged up, but then her tail began to wag and she went over to the cage, sniffing around for a moment, before she continued with her inspection of the animal holding room.

"Can you keep an eye on her?" Deirdre asked. "I need to bring in all the stuff from the truck."

This time, Amaal didn't offer to help, possibly because he knew his offer would only get shot down again. "Of course. I'll take her around the station so she can get familiar with everything."

No point in protesting. Hopefully, once Sasha had gone everywhere and smelled everything, she'd feel like lying down and resting. For now, at least Amaal would be watching her to make sure she didn't get into too much mischief.

Deirdre went back out to the truck and grabbed as much as she could carry. At least she'd put everything in reusable shopping bags with sturdy handles, and so she could move more at a time than she would if she'd just thrown everything haphazardly into the back of the truck. Still, it took a good ten minutes to get all of the items she'd procured into the station and put more or less in their respective positions, although she went ahead and dumped all the clothing items on her bed, telling herself that she'd get them sorted out later.

When she was done, she found Amaal and Sasha in the kitchen, the dog slurping water noisily out of a bowl Amaal had set on the ground for her. "I could tell she was thirsty," he said with a smile.

"That's fine," Deirdre replied. Then she realized that she'd gone and gotten all these supplies, but of course she hadn't thought she'd need to get anything for a dog. "We don't really have anything to feed her. I guess I'll have to go back into Running Springs and see what I can scrounge up."

Amaal nodded, although a flicker of concern came and went in his blue, blue eyes. "Will we both have to go in the cage?"

At once remorse reappeared and smacked Deirdre in the head. What the hell had she been thinking, anyway? After four days together, and with ample opportunity to leave when she was otherwise occupied, he'd proven that he wasn't going anywhere. "No," she said firmly. "I suppose the two of you can stay out of trouble for a half hour or so."

Even as Amaal smiled in response, however, Deirdre couldn't help wondering whether she was making a very big mistake in allowing herself to trust him.

Amaal watched the big red truck disappear around a bend in the road. Standing next to him on the front porch, Sasha let out a little whine and looked up at him as though asking why Deirdre was leaving.

He smiled down at the dog, at her big amber eyes. A wolf's eyes, he thought, and the rest of her was also rather wolf-like, although Sasha had the saddle pattern that denoted some German shepherd blood, and she was stockier, not as rangy as a true wolf.

It was tempting to consider going back into the closet where Deirdre had secreted the device so he could turn it off again, but Amaal decided it was better not to indulge himself in such a way. For one thing, he had already had his "fix" that afternoon, and also, he feared that if he kept going back to the device and shutting it off, he would give himself away. Besides, he wasn't entirely sure how long Deirdre would be gone this time. She'd already gathered the majority of the items they needed and was only going back to get food for the dog. This trip would be much shorter.

Pushing thoughts of the device out of his head, he took Sasha outside so she might sniff around and do her business if necessary. Clearly, the matter had been more urgent than he'd thought, because she squatted and urinated almost immediately—or perhaps she was only marking her territory.

Clouds had begun to move in from the west, obscuring the clear blue of the sky from earlier in the day. Amaal stared up at the clouds, wondering whether they held rain or snow, and if they did, how long it would be before the storm gathered its full strength. A fire elemental, he couldn't sense weather patterns the way his djinn brethren who controlled the air were able to, but it didn't require too much of a sensibility about such things to realize that the fine, mild weather they'd been enjoying was about to break.

He hoped it would hold off until Deirdre returned. Once he was far enough away from the device, he could blink himself into Running Springs to fetch her, but then he would have to explain that he had only left the station out of worry for her safety. Besides, Deirdre had made it sound as though she'd been coming up here off and on for at least the last year. Surely she must have dealt with a storm or two. And that truck she was driving was big and sturdy, certainly capable of handling muddy roads.

Sasha, once she had finished smelling her way around the bare dirt and weedy flowerbeds in front of the research station, limped her way up the three stairs to the front porch and stood by the door, looking at Amaal expectantly. It seemed obvious enough to him that she had had enough outdoor fun and was more than ready to go back inside where it was warm and cozy, thanks to the kitchen's wood-burning stove.

"All right, all right," Amaal told her, chuckling a little. His kind rarely kept pets, because their short lives were barely a flicker compared to the span of time that djinn spent in this existence, but he had to admit that dogs could be amusing. He went up the stairs to meet her, then let her inside. She hurried to the kitchen and began nosing around, then stopped when she realized all that waited for her there was the bowl of water he'd set out earlier. "I'm sorry," he said. "Deirdre is going to get you some food. You'll have to wait."

Apparently, Sasha wasn't happy to hear the "w" word, because after that last gentle admonition, she sank down onto the vinyl floor, chin on her paws, snout pointing toward the door.

"I miss her, too," Amaal said, and was vaguely surprised to realize how true those words were. Earlier, he had been occupied with escaping from the cage and locating the device, but now that he had nothing better to do than sit and wait, he realized that the research station felt empty without Deirdre in it. True, she wouldn't be gone long this time, but....

Despite the ever-present weariness that was the device's continuous gift, he made himself go back to the front of the building and look out the window there. Of course, it was far too soon for Deirdre to return, since the round-trip journey would take her at least half an hour even if all she did was run into a store once she was in Running Springs and grab several bags of dog food. Still, he felt he should keep watch.

The sky darkened, lowering. Amaal resisted the urge to turn on one of the lamps, for he knew they had to ration their power. The solar panels that provided their energy were more robust than he had imagined, but even so, the power they provided was far from limitless. The gas for cooking came from a propane tank located a few yards away from the building. Sooner or later, it would run out, however, no matter how sparing they were with their resources. What then?

The sensible thing to do would be to turn off the device and go to his home, which offered far more comforts and which he could keep warm and lighted through the entire winter season, no matter how long and how cold that might be. Unfortunately, convincing Deirdre that this was the most logical course of action would be difficult. They had nothing to tie the two of them together, really, except this strange not quite captor-and-captive situation.

If only there were some way to persuade her there should be much more connecting them than the chance encounter that had led to his captivity here.

He smiled and nodded to himself, even as a plan began to form in his mind. They had spent enough time together, despite her doing her best to avoid him while working in the lab. He'd caught the way she watched him out of the corner of her eye, then abruptly turned away as soon as she realized he was looking back at her. Deirdre might not wish to acknowledge the heat building between them, but he figured he might as well use it to his advantage.

And then he would see what happened.

TEN

THE FIRST SNOWFLAKE FELL AND HIT HER ON the nose as Deirdre emerged from the feed store, where she'd located a nice big stack of Science Diet dog food. She didn't stop, but continued to the truck and dropped the two twenty-pound bags of dry food into the bed. Once she was done, however, she squinted up at the sky and muttered a curse. She'd been so preoccupied with focusing on the road so she wouldn't hit another dog—or coyote, or stray cow, or whatever else decided to wander into her path—that she hadn't paid much attention to the weather. It had been cold enough that she'd put on a jacket, and that one precaution had been the extent of her preparations.

Well, one snowflake wasn't exactly a blizzard. Jaw set, she climbed into the cab of the truck and turned it around, heading for the forest service road that would lead her back to the research station. It wasn't very far, after all, just a little over three miles.

More flakes settled on the truck's windshield, but they melted almost as soon as they touched the glass. The same for the snowflakes falling on the hood of the vehicle. That was all fine and good, except Deirdre couldn't help noticing the way those flakes kept falling faster and faster. She'd been up here in the winter before, of course, but never when it was actively snowing, only after enough sturdier vehicles and come and gone from the station that the way was pretty much cleared.

Then again, her little Sentra hadn't been this big four-wheel-drive truck. She was pretty sure the Tundra could get through almost anything. Of course, its ability to plow through snow and mud was hampered by her driving skills. She'd always thought of herself as a pretty good driver, but she'd never been behind the wheel of an off-road vehicle like this before. With any luck, she'd make it back to the station before she had to figure out the four-wheel-drive controls.

The snow fell faster. Deirdre could see it sticking to the ground, only a faint white film now, but one that was destined to grow thicker as the storm really bore down on the mountain. She wished she could turn on the radio and get a weather report. Unfortunately, weather reports and forecasts and reassurances that a storm wouldn't be too bad were now a thing of the past. It was early in the year, but they could still get a heavy snowfall, one that might be two or even three feet of snow. She just didn't know. The thought of all that snow frightened her. It was one thing to see it all pretty and gleaming white on the mountaintops, and quite another thing to think about how so much of it might fall, it could pile up all the way to the windowsills. And to be stuck up here all alone....

But she wasn't alone. Her fingers tightened on the steering wheel, and she made herself slow down even further, although every instinct was telling her to drive faster, to get back before the weather got even worse.

No, you're not alone, she thought as she turned on the windshield wipers and cranked the defroster. *Amaal is waiting for you, and Sasha. No matter how bad this storm might be, you won't have to go through it by yourself.*

That thought reassured her. She made herself imagine the djinn and the dog, both of them waiting for her in a place that was warm and illuminated. The three of them could hunker down and wait it out. She'd already stocked up with enough supplies to last them at least a week, maybe two. No snowstorm lasted that long in this part of the world; it wasn't as if they were in

Alaska or Siberia or someplace like that. Southern California's taller mountains got more snow than most people might think, but not *that* much.

She felt the truck's tires slip on the icy, rutted road, and she slowed down even more. It was excruciating to inch along at around fifteen miles an hour, but she didn't dare go faster than that. Someone who was experienced with driving in these sorts of conditions could probably have managed it. Unfortunately, she didn't have that kind of experience. Usually the worst thing she'd had to deal with when driving in bad weather were all the people who suddenly seemed to lose what little driving skill they had as soon as rain started to fall.

At last, though, she saw warm light up ahead through the snow, and let out a little sigh of relief as she recognized the research station's square windows, now set off by the lamps Amaal must have turned on. Another time, she might have given him some grief for wasting the electricity, but in that moment she could only give thanks that he'd offered this beacon to her, this way of guiding her home.

She pulled up to the front porch, then hurried out of the truck, trying not to slip on the snow. Her hiking boots had decent treads, thank God, but they were also suede, and already starting to get soaked through. As she wrestled one of the bags of dog food out of the bed of the truck, the door to the research station opened and Amaal hurried out. She almost told him to get back inside, but she had a feeling he would have ignored her. Without speaking, he grabbed the second bag of dog food, and then they both went indoors.

It wasn't so bad, after all—he'd only turned on two lamps, but they still gave a warm and welcoming light. And it was warm in here, the air scented with wood smoke from the stove.

"I was starting to worry," he said with a glance toward the windows. The snow was falling more thickly than ever, cutting visibility down to a few yards.

"So was I," she responded. "Luckily, the truck could handle it. Thank you for getting that other bag of dog food."

"It is nothing. But come along to the kitchen," he went on. "Your shoes are soaked."

She couldn't argue with that, since she could feel the icy chill from the sodden suede already working its way through the thick socks she wore. Without speaking, she followed him into the kitchen, where Sasha sat by the stove, tail wagging frantically, although Deirdre guessed the dog's enthusiasm at seeing her was more due to the large bag of dog food she was carrying. She set it down next to the pantry, while Amaal placed his beside it. When he straightened, he was breathing heavily. That twenty-pound sack of Science Diet must have felt like a hundred pounds, thanks to the device working away on him.

Once more she experienced a pang of guilt. Would it be so awful to turn the damn thing off? Whatever the other djinn might have done, Amaal certainly showed no sign of being anything like them. He was courteous and calm, quietly funny when she least expected it, but was that all an act? Maybe he was showing her the face she wanted to see, not the one he truly possessed. It was so hard to know for sure when she had no frame of reference. She'd never met another djinn. She'd never even given djinn a second thought...until Miles Odekirk's voice on the radio informed her that the otherworldly race was responsible for humankind's destruction.

Well, she could think about that later. For now, she quickly unlaced her hiking boots, then set them next to the stove. Sasha eyed them with some interest, and Deirdre gave her a stern look.

"Don't you even think about chewing on those," she said. She had a backup pair, but the soles were worn down, not in good shape like the boots she'd taken from the outdoor shop in Running Springs. The thought of trying to go outside in those worn boots to get more firewood was definitely not appealing.

"She won't," Amaal said. He had fetched a pair of scissors from one of the kitchen drawers, and now went over to one of the bags of dog food so he could open it. "She'll have better things to occupy her mind."

Right—the dog would much rather have a nice bowl of Science Diet to munch on than a pair of boots. Deirdre went and got a bowl out from the cupboard, then set it down on the floor next to the one they were using for Sasha's water. She also fetched a measuring cup from the same drawer where Amaal had found the scissors, and handed it to him.

"Here you go. This is a lot easier than trying to tip the right amount out of that heavy bag."

He took the cup from her, flashing her a grateful smile at the same time. Once again, she experienced that slightly weak-kneed sensation that seemed to take over anytime he smiled at her. Damn. She really needed to do something about that.

Problem was, she didn't have any idea what. Her brain should have been telling her he was alien, and therefore shouldn't be able to affect her like this, but her body appeared to have different ideas.

As soon as the food hit the bowl, Sasha was there, head down so she could start munching away. Amaal put the bag of dog food back over by the pantry, and Deirdre went to get it and set it inside the pantry itself so she could close the door and ensure that Sasha wouldn't try to get into the open bag. She seemed like a very well-behaved dog, but she would have had to exercise a lot of self-control not to help herself to a midnight snack when she thought no one was looking.

"Well, the dog's taken care of," Deirdre remarked. "I suppose I'd better figure out what we can have for our own dinner." Her gaze moved to the clock that hung on one wall; it wasn't quite six o'clock, but by the time she'd put something together, they'd be sitting down to eat at what she thought of as a more reasonable hour.

"Yes, that's probably a good idea."

Amaal's tone was so neutral, she wasn't quite sure what to make of it. He'd probably begun to tire of the bland meals she'd been preparing for the two of them, but there was a limit to what you could do with canned goods and dry pasta. The refrigerator here worked, of course, thanks to the station's solar panels, and yet that only helped so far, since the power had been out in Running Springs for months, and so anything frozen or refrigerated there had long since spoiled.

Holding back a sigh, she went into the pantry and looked at some of the new items she'd brought back—more jars of spaghetti sauce, canned vegetables, a variety of pasta, some dry salami and pepperoni that didn't need to be refrigerated. She'd even gone ahead and gotten some evaporated milk as well, thinking that maybe she could put together some kind of white sauce with it and grated parmesan cheese, but none of that sounded terribly appealing.

The djinn's voice came to her from just over her shoulder. "I fear that none of this will change into what you would really like, no matter how long you stare at it."

Deirdre almost made a sharp response, but she realized there was no point in snapping at Amaal when she'd been thinking pretty much the same thing. "I know. And I also know I should be grateful for what we do have here."

"There is an alternative, you know."

She turned away from the pantry's shelves and gave Amaal a skeptical look. He stood only a foot or so away, arms crossed, a slightly amused expression on his handsome features. "And what might that be?"

"Turn off the device, and I can summon any meal you would like."

Once again a retort sprang to her lips...and once again she kept herself from giving voice to it. After all, hadn't she just been thinking about powering down the device? Clearly, if Amaal had wanted to leave before now, he would have. And yet...could she allow herself to trust him? Maybe he'd only been waiting for his chance, waiting when she'd be vulnerable and he was in possession of his full strength again.

It was so hard to know for sure, and yet Deirdre realized that she'd have to make a decision one way or another. Amaal had borne up remarkably well, but having that device grind on him day and night had to be wearing him down. And he hadn't done or said anything threatening, had generally tried to be helpful. Still, could she trust him? Should she?

She couldn't know for sure. What she did know was that right then she felt as though she'd kill for something that wasn't canned or dried in some way, some *real* food. The stuff she'd been subsisting on had kept her alive, but that was about all she could say for it.

"All right," she said at last. "But you have to wait here while I turn it off."

"Of course," he said politely. "I wouldn't think of following you to the place where you have it hidden."

He leaned against the counter, as if to indicate that he planned to stay in this spot, and Deirdre took that as a sign to leave. She gave him a half-hearted nod, then went down the hallway to her bedroom, where she pushed aside her backpack and got the device out of her laptop case. As she slid her finger over the touchscreen to power down the little gadget, she hoped she wasn't making the worst mistake of her life.

Amaal felt it the second she turned off the device, strength and energy flowing into all his limbs, his entire body suffused with a sense of well-being. Up until that very moment, he wasn't quite sure whether she would go through with it, whether she would decide at the last moment that she couldn't take such a risk with him.

But apparently once she decided on a course of action, she stuck with it, and so she had turned off the pernicious little machine. He heard her footsteps coming down the hallway, and a moment later she appeared at the entry to the kitchen, her expression all diffidence, as if she had expected him to turn into some kind of monstrous creature and immediately pounce on her.

Well, to be fair, he would like to pounce, although not in the way she probably feared. Now that his strength and energy were restored, he wanted her more than ever. Her hair was untidy from being blown in the wind, but her cheeks were pink and her lips rosy, inviting. She truly was the most exquisite creature he'd ever seen.

First things first, though. She had taken an

enormous leap of faith by shutting down the device, and he would have to prove to her that her trust in him was not misplaced.

"Better?" she asked. Her tone was casual, but he could see the tension in her slender body. She still wasn't quite sure of him.

He would have to fix that.

"Much better," he replied. "Now that I am able to give you anything you like, what do you want for dinner?"

She pressed her lips together for a moment, moistening them. "Anything?"

"Anything."

A breath, and then she responded, "Chicken cacciatore. Fresh garlic bread. A salad with oil and vinegar dressing and tomatoes and olives and grated mozzarella cheese."

"That's very specific," he said, doing his best to hold back a chuckle.

She smiled then, light filling those shimmering blue green eyes. "It is. It's a salad I used to get at my favorite Italian restaurant. I swear, I've had dreams about it. And their chicken cacciatore was my favorite, too. So I guess I just want some Italian comfort food."

"That is fine. I can do that without a problem." Actually, it all sounded very good to him; it had been a while since he'd sampled chicken cacciatore. "And a nice Montepulciano to go with it."

Her nose didn't precisely wrinkle, but Amaal could tell Deirdre wasn't precisely enraptured by this suggestion. "I'm not much into wine," she said.

"Perhaps because you never had a chance to savor it," he said. "The right food with the right wine is perfection. I would very much appreciate it if you would indulge me in this."

"Well...." The syllable trailed off, and she glanced toward the window. By that point, a bluish-purple dusk had fallen, although Amaal could still see the snowflakes swirling around the building. "It's not like I have to drive anywhere, I suppose."

"True." He didn't bother to add that, now he had full possession of his powers again, there was no need for them to drive anywhere. Deirdre was still nervous, worried that she had made the wrong decision in turning off the device. He needed to prove to her that her trust in him hadn't been misplaced.

"Is there anything I need to do to help?" she asked, and he shook his head.

"Nothing at all. Perhaps if you have something a bit nicer to wear for dinner?"

She looked down at herself, at her faded jeans and baggy sweater. "Well, I'm pretty sure I didn't pack any evening gowns, but I'll see what I can do."

"Excellent."

Wearing a slightly puzzled expression, she left and went back down the hallway, presumably to go to her bedroom. He could have conjured an evening gown for her, of course, but he doubted she would have worn it. For a moment he considered switching out the borrowed human clothing he wore for his infinitely more comfortable djinn robes, then dismissed the idea. Again, he didn't wish to make it seem as though this meal was anything particularly special. Besides, he'd noted on their first meeting—despite his discomfort— that Deirdre was a bit put off by the traditional attire of the djinn male. He supposed it revealed too much of his body, and while he thought little of being exposed in such a way, he knew it made her uncomfortable.

However, he did swap the faded sweatshirt he wore for a fine sweater of black merino wool, and the jeans with their ragged hems for a pair that was newer and more presentable. Once he was satisfied with his own appearance, it was time to turn his attention to their dining accommodations. Before this evening, they'd taken their meals at the hand-me-down table and mismatched chairs in the research station's small dining area off the kitchen, but Amaal did not think that space at all adequate for tonight's dinner.

Frowning slightly, he went out to the building's front room, which had once served as a combination office and reception area. He'd barely seen Deirdre use it—why should she, when she spent the majority of her time in the laboratory? —and so he hoped she wouldn't mind if he refashioned it to suit their current needs. Of course, the most practical thing to do would have been to whisk the two of them away to his own house, but he doubted she would be agreeable to such an arrangement. Better to do a bit of redecorating here and see what happened. After all, he could always change it back if it turned out his companion was less than pleased with the alterations he'd made.

A wave of one hand, and the dingy metal desks and chairs disappeared, along with the worn plastic blinds at the windows. Now the room, which spanned the width of the building, was divided into two distinct sections, with a round table and a pair of chairs off to one side, and several low divans off to the other. A wintry evening such as this called for a fireplace, and so he brought one into existence on the wall nearest the set of divans, a fire already crackling away in the marble hearth. Draperies of embossed velvet framed the windows, and candles flickered from nearly every surface.

Yes, that was much better.

Another wave of his hand, and an embroidered silk cloth covered the table. Dishes patterned in warm shades of brick and burgundy sat on top of that cloth, and iridescent wine glasses, fragile as soap bubbles, joined them. All that was left was the food, but Amaal thought he had better wait to conjure it until Deirdre reappeared. He could keep their meal warm for a time, but he wanted her to see him bring it into existence before her eyes.

"Oh, my God."

Amaal turned to see her standing at the doorway that opened on the former office space. No evening gown, of course, but she'd changed into a nicer sweater, one in a deep blue-green shade that brought out the watercolor tints of her eyes, and her hair was brushed. Those delectable lips gleamed with a soft gloss. Sasha was at her side, panting slightly. No doubt the dog was enjoying the additional warmth provided by the fire in the hearth.

"Do you like it?" he asked.

She came into the room and looked around, eyes wide with wonder. "You did all this?"

"Yes. I like to enjoy my surroundings along with my meal, and the chamber where we have been dining seemed somewhat inadequate. I hope you don't mind that I took a few liberties."

"'Liberties'?" she repeated, and shook her head. "This is...I can't even say." A shift, and she faced the fireplace, still with that incredulous expression on her delicate features. "And you made a fireplace go there, just like that?"

"Just like that, yes." He extended a hand toward the table on the opposite side of the room. "But if you would sit now?"

An absent nod, and she moved toward the table, then stood hesitantly as he pulled out a chair for her. This was a human custom, not a djinn one, but even if Deirdre hadn't been expecting it, he thought it a good idea to show her that small courtesy.

She took the cloth napkin from where it rested under the forks at her place setting and put it in her lap. Amaal sat down and did the same thing, then asked, "Some wine?"

Her puzzled glance moved across the tabletop, which was empty except for their plates and cutlery and glasses. "Um...sure."

He thought the wine into being, a nice ten-year-old Montepulciano from Tuscany. It appeared in his hand, cork already removed, and he poured a good measure into both their glasses.

From the diffident expression she wore, he could tell she was still hesitant about the wine.

Was that simply because she hadn't been a wine drinker back in the time before, or did she fear how she might react around him once the alcohol began to take effect?

Perhaps a little of both. Amaal knew he would never force her, would never make her do something she didn't wish to, but if the wine loosened a few of her inhibitions, all the better.

He raised his glass. "To riding out the storm."

The toast seemed neutral enough that it didn't cause her any more concern. She lifted her glass as well and clinked it against his. "To riding out the storm."

They both sipped. Her expression became almost fiercely bland, as though she didn't want him to guess what she thought of the wine. Well, there certainly wasn't much she could find fault with, for it was full and rich without being tannic at all, and reminded him of the times he had visited Tuscany, had walked along those roads in the sunlight, with the vineyards stretching everywhere on the hillsides around him, rich and golden and full of life. It was a good memory to have on an evening like this, with the snow falling outside and the wind keening around the corners of the building.

"You seem very far away," Deirdre remarked.

Amaal came back to himself...and to the woman who sat opposite him. Why on earth would he lose himself in reveries of Tuscan holidays when he had such beauty here with him now? Perhaps it was only that he knew he most likely would never be able to return to the places he had visited when it was only permitted for djinn to come to this world for a short time. Now that they had settled here, they were supposed to stay on the lands they had been given, except on those occasions when business might call them elsewhere.

"I was thinking of Tuscany," he said, and sudden interest lit up her face.

"You've been there?"

"Oh, yes. We djinn were great world travelers, once upon a time. I suppose I was only remembering the sort of land where this wine was grown."

She looked wistful. "I never went to Europe… or anywhere, really, except a couple of day trips to Baja California. We didn't have the money for that sort of thing."

Amaal wished he could take her to Tuscany and kiss her beneath a grape arbor. Since that pleasant image would most likely never become a reality, he could only lift his shoulders and say, "That is unfortunate. There are many beautiful places in this world. But then," he hastened to add, "many of them are here in California, so it is not as though you were deprived of all the world's beauties."

"I suppose so." She lifted her glass of wine and took another sip, then looked down at the tabletop and raised an eyebrow at him. "Are you only going to ply me with wine, or is dinner going to be forthcoming at some point?"

Of course. He'd been so distracted by her, he'd almost forgotten. "Dinner is served, milady," he said, and waved a hand. At once the dinner she'd requested was there before them, a perfectly sized portion of chicken cacciatore on each of their plates, a basket full of garlic bread off to one side, and a bowl of salad as well. Sasha's ears perked up immediately, and she came to plunk herself down by the table, well within arm's reach if any table scraps should appear.

Deirdre stared down at the food, her eyes even wider than they had been when she'd first viewed his alterations to the room. "This smells heavenly."

"I am sure it tastes heavenly as well. Go ahead —with all the work you did today, you deserve a good meal."

Deirdre picked up her fork and took a few rapturous bites, then paused. "There wasn't much point to it, though, was there?"

Amaal paused with a chunk of chicken speared on his fork. "To what?"

"To all that work I did, when you can just

wave a hand and make anything you want appear."

"Ah, well." He set down his fork and went on, "At the time, you had no plans to free me. You were doing what you thought needed to be done."

"Maybe." Her shoulders lifted, and she took a bite of cacciatore, then another. "And maybe I was crazy to turn off the device."

"No, you most assuredly were not." He reached for the basket of garlic bread and set a piece on his plate before offering it to her. She selected a piece as well, and he put the basket back in its original place. "If I were someone else—my late brother, for example—then perhaps such an action would have been ill-advised. But I assure you that I am completely harmless."

"I don't know about the 'completely' part," Deirdre returned, her tone clearly skeptical. "After all, you're a djinn."

"All djinn are not created equal," he replied imperturbably.

"They're not?"

"Of course not." Amaal poured some more wine into her glass, then topped his off as well. "We are all individuals, just as you mortals are."

"Were," she said, her tone flat.

He kept himself from frowning. The last thing he wanted was for the conversation to veer into a discussion of the Heat and what the djinn had done to humanity's few remaining survivors. "There are still some of you," he said, then went on before she had a chance to respond. "We were not as numerous, but we all had our differences. And while many might have done things I don't approve of, there are other djinn like me who would have preferred a different outcome. I mean you no harm, Deirdre. Surely you should understand that by now."

A nod, but her eyes wouldn't meet his. She broke off a piece of garlic bread and ate it slowly, her thoughts obviously in turmoil. "I wouldn't blame you if you did. After all, I put you in a cage."

At once he reached out and laid a hand on her arm. She startled, but he noticed that she didn't attempt to pull away, either. "And I cannot blame you for that. You didn't know who—or what—you were dealing with. It was an obvious precaution, one I am sure I would have taken if I had been in your position. So please, don't think I hold that against you."

Once again she was quiet for a moment. Then she said, a rueful smile touching her lips, "You're being awfully nice to me, Amaal."

"Am I?" He smiled at her as well. "Well, I suppose it is because you are easy to be nice to. I enjoy your company."

"Even though I haven't given you much of it."

"You were working."

Another silence. She dished some salad and put it on her plate. "Pretending to work, more like it." She looked up, and this time her eyes did meet his. Amaal thought he saw a small shudder work its way through her slender frame, although he couldn't say precisely what had caused that reaction. "I suppose it was because I didn't know what to do around you. How to behave. You're…you're a djinn. I don't think I even really knew what a djinn was until a few months ago."

He gave her a sympathetic nod. "I understand. Or at least, I can understand why you would need time to work through what you were thinking or feeling. My people have existed since before mankind, and so you have always been a part of our existence, but for most of humanity, we were only a myth or legend, if even that much. I suppose I would have felt much the same if I'd suddenly had a dragon living under my roof."

Her mouth curved into a small smile. "Are you saying dragons don't exist? After djinn, I thought anything was possible."

"No, I fear not. And neither are fairies nor mermaids nor any of the other fancies men's minds have conjured over the centuries. There is man, and there are djinn, and that is all."

Deirdre ate a few bites of salad. When she was done, she said, "I guess in a way that's a relief. I don't think I could handle too many more mythical creatures turning out to be real."

"I have no doubt that you would handle them with as much grace as you've shown in all other situations," Amaal said, his tone gentle.

"You don't have to flatter me," Deirdre responded, a slight frown touching her delicately arched brows. "I've already turned off the device, remember."

Did she think he paid her compliments only because he wanted something from her? Well, perhaps that belief wasn't completely incorrect. He did want something.

He wanted her.

"Is it flattery to tell the truth?" he asked. "For that is all I am doing."

She didn't appear entirely convinced, but at least she didn't seem inclined to offer any further arguments. Instead, she shrugged, picked up her glass of wine and drank from it, and then returned to her neglected chicken cacciatore. Seeing that she wished to be quiet for a moment, Amaal also turned his attention to the food on his plate.

After a few moments had passed—during which Amaal noted the way their new canine companion watched every bite that went from their plates to their mouths—Deirdre set down her fork and reached for her glass of wine. Once she'd had a few sips, she said, "I guess I'm just trying to figure you out."

"What is there to figure out?"

She sent him a sideways glance, complete with lifted brows. "Oh, come on, Amaal. I brought you here and put you in a cage, I kept a device running that sapped your energy and blocked your powers. And now you're sitting here and having dinner with me like none of that mattered."

"It didn't," he said. That response only earned him another dubious look, and so he continued, "What I mean to say is, everything you did, you did to protect yourself. You feared me. That is entirely understandable. Besides, it is not as if you have caused me any lasting damage, no hurt except some temporary discomfort. Unlike my brother, I am not one to hold a grudge. I am sitting here and having dinner with you because I like you, Deidre, and I enjoy your company."

She stared at him, apparently at a loss for words. Her fingers played with the stem of her wine goblet, and she lifted the glass to her mouth so she could drink from it again. At length she said, "I'm...not sure how to respond to that."

"Well, I would hope you would respond by saying you enjoyed my company as well," he told her. "Or is that not the case?"

Obviously flustered, she replied. "No. I mean,

yes, I suppose I've gotten used to having you around."

Her color had risen, and he noted how her breathing had sped up as well. As far as he was able to tell, he was having more of an effect on her than someone she was simply "used to."

Good.

But her next actions surprised him. Rather than remain seated, she rose from her chair, plucking the napkin from her lap as she did so. "I —I think I'm getting full. It's been a long day, and the wine is making me sleepy."

Very well. If that was how she wanted to play it—

He stood as well, and came around the table so they were only a foot apart. Her eyes flared in alarm, but he noticed how she didn't try to back away.

"It is a little early to be going to bed," he said, putting a slight emphasis on the word "bed."

"I know, but—"

Her mouth looked far too full, far too enticing. He bent and pressed his lips against hers, reveling in their softness, tasting the richness of wine on her skin. For a second her mouth opened to him, and her slight body was pressed against his...

...and then she pulled away, visibly shaking.

"I can't do this," she whispered. "I *can't.*"

And she was gone, fleeing from him down the hallway to the safety of her room. Amaal watched her go and let out a small sigh, even as Sasha looked up at him and whined softly, her tail thumping gently against the floor.

"I know," he said. "I must give her some time."

But not too long, I hope.

ELEVEN

Deirdre leaned against the door of her bedroom, her body trembling with reaction. If she closed her eyes, she could still feel Amaal's lips touching hers, the warmth of his breath against her mouth...the way her body had flooded with sudden heat. For one insane second, she had wanted him, wanted him so badly that she'd thought about dragging him over to one of the couches he'd conjured on the other side of the room so they could continue what he'd started.

Which was just crazy. He was a djinn. A *djinn.*

Oh, God.

She stood there, weight against the door, and wondered what she would do if she heard his footsteps coming down the hall, heard him rattle the doorknob. If he tried to force his way in, she knew there was no way she could stop him. She'd turned off the device, which meant he had all his powers at his disposal.

He could do anything he wanted, and there wasn't a damn thing she could do about it. Even if she even tried to go for the device and turn it back on, she guessed he would stop her before she could lay hands on it.

But as she waited at her door, hardly daring to breathe, she realized she couldn't hear anything at all, except the soft sigh of the wind around the eaves of the building. No footsteps. No sound of him coming after her at all.

Which meant…what? That he'd understood she couldn't quite process their kiss yet, that she needed some time to figure out what to do next?

Or was he simply sitting down and finishing the rest of his meal, since he figured he could pop into her room anytime he liked?

Deirdre hadn't thought about that. A closed door meant nothing to him, or a locked one, although the only doors in the station that had actual locks were the ones in the front and back, and the entrance to the animal holding room. No point in shoving the chair under the doorknob, either; a djinn could break the piece of flimsy furniture like a toothpick.

All right.

Since there didn't seem to be much else she

could do, she went and sat down on her bed. It felt reassuringly solid beneath her. She needed that right then, since the rest of her world seemed as if it had been tilted on its side.

How could she have let him kiss her?

No, scratch that. There hadn't been a whole hell of a lot of permission involved. He'd seized the moment, that was all. True, she'd enjoyed the kiss during those first few seconds, before her cortex kicked in and reminded her of something that her lizard-brain appeared to have forgotten, that the person kissing her wasn't a man at all, but a djinn, someone from an entirely different species. He might not look it, but he was just as alien as though he'd come from another planet.

At last there was a gentle knock at her door. "Deirdre? Are you all right?"

It crossed her mind not to answer at all, but she decided that wasn't a very good idea. "I'm fine," she said.

"If I offended you, I apologize. It is possible I misread you. When you looked up at me, I thought…." The words trailed off, and were followed by a long pause. Then he said, "But it appears I was wrong."

Oh, yes, he was so very wrong. Or rather, she didn't want to acknowledge that he might have been right, that he might have seen something in her expression that told him she wanted him.

Because she'd be lying to herself if she tried to say she didn't find him attractive, that there wasn't something about his company she found appealing, even when doing her best to stay out of his orbit.

Before she realized what she was doing, she was already off the bed and at the door. However, she didn't intend to open it. That would definitely give the wrong impression.

"It's okay," she said, then stopped. Was it okay? Probably not, but that was the sort of useless phrase she tended to employ in awkward situations when she didn't know what else to say. "I mean, I'm sorry if I was giving you mixed signals. It wasn't my intention. But...."

"But...?" he prompted.

Not sure how to respond, she did her best, tripping and stumbling over the words. "But I guess I don't understand. You're djinn. I'm human. That's not normal. Or is it? You never said anything about djinn and humans...." Again her words trailed off, and she wished she hadn't sounded quite so incoherent.

However, Amaal seemed to understand what she was trying to say. "It is a...delicate topic, one I would prefer not to discuss through a closed door."

His point was clear enough. He would tell her what she wanted to know, but only if she allowed him to do so face to face. Deirdre swallowed, then reminded herself that, for better or worse, she and Amaal were stuck here until the storm dissipated. Or maybe not—she supposed he could make himself vanish to wherever he wanted, no matter what the weather was like. However, it didn't seem as though he had any intention of leaving anytime soon.

She put her hand on the doorknob, then turned it before she could lose her nerve. Amaal stood there, but not so close that she was in any danger of tripping over him. "All right," she said. "Because I want to hear what you have to say."

A nod, and he extended his hand down the hallway, clearly indicating that he wanted her to go back to the living area he'd magicked into being. Well, she wouldn't argue with him about that, because at least it was warm and cozy in there.

Without speaking, she walked in the direction he'd indicated, then sat down on the small sofa closest to the fireplace. She noticed the dining table had been cleared and that all the leftovers from their meal were gone. Had he blinked them out of existence the same way he'd brought them into being, or had he done something infinitely more prosaic like put them away in the refrigerator?

To her relief, Amaal sat on the other sofa, a

respectable distance away. Deirdre wasn't sure what she would have done if he'd tried to sit next to her.

"Again, I am sorry if I misinterpreted your feelings," he said. "That was not my intention. As for the rest—" He stopped there, expression worried and yet intent, as if he was watching her and sorting through what he wanted to say. "Throughout history, there have been accounts of djinn being with humans. Most of the time, the humans did not know who they were being intimate with, only thought the person who shared their bed was another mortal like themselves."

"The djinn lied?" Deirdre asked, her tone sharper than she'd intended. Not that Amaal had misrepresented himself in such a way to her, since she'd known what he was almost from the first moment they met, but....

"Sins of omission, mainly," he replied. "Not intended to hurt their mortal lovers, but rather to protect them from the repercussions of being with someone who was not of their kind. But my kissing you—that is certainly not unprecedented. Our two peoples are not so very different, after all."

"To look at," Deirdre said, knowing how shaky she sounded. Amaal's explanation hadn't been all that reassuring, except to let her know it wasn't so very strange for him to have kissed her.

She wasn't so sure about that. It felt plenty strange to her. She added, "Inside, in our DNA…we're different."

"Not different enough for it to change things," Amaal said. "What if I told you that humans and djinn had interbred, that there were people in your world who had mingled blood? Not so very many, for we djinn generally tried to avoid having such offspring, but they exist. Or at least, they did at one time. I have no idea whether any of those with mixed blood survived the Heat."

This was something she'd never expected to hear. All right, humans and djinn appeared almost identical, morphologically speaking, but it was hard to believe that the djinns' otherworldly DNA would be compatible with that of human beings. And yet here was Amaal calmly telling her that such children were a fact of life.

Is that would happen if she let him kiss her again, take her to bed? Would she have one of those mixed-blood offspring, or were the odds stacked against such a pregnancy occurring, even though such a thing had happened before?

Not that this was a world to bring children into. For all she knew, the djinn who had busily gone after any immune survivors would look on such a mixed child as an abomination, and would hunt it down as well.

"I'm not sure what you want me to do with that information."

Amaal's head tilted slightly to one side as he appeared to consider her words. "'Want'?" he repeated. "I am not sure it is a matter of me 'wanting' you to do anything. You said you wished to hear the truth, and so I am doing my best to give you the information you requested." A pause, and then he added, "I suppose some part of me hopes that you will understand a little bit better now, that you will see there is nothing so terribly strange about my attraction to you. Because I am attracted. When I first saw you, even as drained by the device as I was, I thought you were one of the most beautiful women I had ever seen."

Color flooded her cheeks, but Deirdre made herself say lightly, "I told you earlier that you didn't need to flatter me."

"I am not flattering you. I am telling you the truth."

There he went again. And he looked so earnest, sitting there in his dark, close-fitting sweater and jeans. In the warm, flickering light from the flames, his startlingly blue eyes appeared almost green. She hated to admit it, but she liked looking at him.

And she liked the way he told her she was beautiful, even if she didn't completely believe those words. Pretty enough to attract male attention, sure. She wasn't blind or stubborn enough to argue that she hadn't noticed the way men's gazes tended to slide toward her when she walked by. But that wasn't quite the same thing as being told you were the most beautiful woman a man had ever seen, especially when the man in question was a djinn and had seen djinn women, who Deirdre assumed must be as physically perfect as their men.

Apparently he took her silence for tacit acceptance of his words, because he got up from where he sat and came over to her, sinking down onto the couch at her side. His hand sought hers, and she didn't try to take it away. His fingers were warm, unlike the previous times she'd touched him, when the effects of the device had made his skin cold and somewhat clammy.

"You can tell me to stop," he murmured, and bent and kissed her again.

Oh, he was good. How many centuries of practice must he have had? But Deirdre realized she didn't want to think about that, only wanted to concentrate on the sensation of his strong mouth pressed against hers, the way his longish hair brushed against her cheek. He tasted so good...and he smelled good, too, something subtle and warm, like sandalwood.

She opened her mouth to his, allowing the kiss to deepen, while her entire body seemed to come more and more alive, aching for him, aching for more from him than just lips locked with lips. And yet, she also knew she shouldn't allow herself to let go that completely...not yet, anyway. She still needed time before she could take that next step.

Some time later, she pulled back a few inches from him. Amaal watched her carefully, even as he raised a hand to brush a wayward lock of hair away from her cheek. "You are not running away," he said quietly.

"No." She took in a breath and then added, "But a kiss is as much as I'm able to give you right now. I hope you understand."

"Of course." To her relief, he smiled at her. "Do you not think I know you are worth waiting for? I understand that this was quite a step for you to take. I can be patient."

Gratitude rushed through her, mixed with something she wasn't quite sure she was ready to acknowledge.   Tenderness...desire...possibly something much deeper than that. But she could give it time. That was all she needed. A little time to understand what she felt for him, this man who wasn't truly a man at all.

"Thank you, Amaal." She leaned forward so she could kiss him, but gently on the cheek. Another kiss like the one they'd just shared would be a bit too dangerous. "And I think I really will go to sleep now." She didn't add, *Alone,* but he seemed to understand.

"Of course. We should all get some rest. I will let Sasha out before I retire—the snow doesn't bother me, and she might need to go."

This prosaic reminder made Deirdre look around for the dog she'd rescued earlier that day. Yes, there was Sasha, curled up off to one side, out of the way but still close enough to enjoy the warmth emanating from the hearth.

"That sounds like a good idea." Deirdre got up from the couch, said, "Good night," and went down the hall toward her room and shut the door behind her.

Whether she'd actually be able to sleep…well, that was a very good question.

Amaal lay in his narrow, somewhat uncomfortable bed and stared up at the ceiling. He supposed he could have blinked himself home so he could sleep in the much more luxurious king-sized bed in the master bedchamber there, or possibly have summoned a larger bed for his use here, but that felt too much like cheating. The next time he slept in a decent bed, he wanted it to be with Deirdre at his side.

She was only a few yards away on the opposite

side of the hall, but that short distance might as well have been a hundred miles. The kisses they had shared had only further enflamed his desire for her, and yet he knew he must abide by her wishes and wait until she was ready. Judging by the heat behind her embrace, Amaal thought it would not be so very long. However, even a few hours seemed excruciating to him now.

With a small grunt, he rolled over onto his side, plumping up the well-used foam pillow as best he could to get it to provide adequate support. At the foot of the bed, Sasha shifted as well, feet pushing against the plump cushion he had conjured for her to sleep on.

Was Deirdre as restless as he? Difficult to say, for she'd closed her door most of the way, just leaving it open wide enough for Sasha to slip through if she so desired, and he hadn't been able to detect any signs of movement from within. And he would not get up to listen—either she was asleep or she was not, but he would not do anything that seemed as if it was impinging on her privacy, difficult as it might feel to him.

He lay there and thought of humans and djinn, and how their fates had been intertwined for millennia. Nothing he had told Deirdre was a lie, although he had left out one very important fact. She still did not know that djinn and humans lived together even now in communities of the elementals and their Chosen. Precisely why he had refrained from telling her about those surviving humans, he wasn't quite sure, except that, while he enjoyed her company and could not wait to savor all the sweetness of her body, he had no intention of making her his Chosen. He had never allowed himself to be tied down to a djinn woman, and had no desire to do so with a mortal, no matter how enticing she might be.

The wind keened outside. He had looked out the window before retiring for the night and saw that the snow was already nearly a foot high. No great matter, for the weather could not affect a djinn all that much. However, if it piled up much more, the big truck Deirdre had been using would need some digging out before it could be driven. Then again, what need did they have for driving? Freed from the yoke of that wretched device, he could travel anywhere he liked, and could bring Deirdre—and even Sasha—with him.

Perhaps that was the angle he should take. He had done what he could to make this place more habitable, but it was still a poor substitute for his large, comfortable home. Better to convince Deirdre that all of them would be safer there if the weather took much of a turn for the worse. Although the research station clearly had been updated somewhat, its bones were still those of a structure built early in the previous century.

They'd be much better off in his newer, larger house.

This all sounded perfectly reasonable to him. Unfortunately, Deirdre often managed to come up with arguments countering his proposals, arguments he sometimes had difficulty countering. Even though she had wished to work with animals, he wondered whether she might not have done better as an attorney.

All that was in the past, however. No matter what her dreams and ambitions might have been back before the world changed forever, she had to adapt to live in this world now. And he hoped she would learn to live with him…if only for a little while.

Bacon. That was definitely bacon. Deirdre sat up in bed and sniffed at the air, mouth watering at the miracle of a tantalizing aroma she'd thought she'd never smell again.

Well, that first day, Amaal had enticed her with an offer of bacon, if she'd only turn off the device. Apparently, he was now making good on that offer.

She pushed the bedclothes aside and slipped into her Uggs, then pulled a sweatshirt on over the T-shirt and yoga pants she'd been sleeping in.

As she left her room and began to walk down the hallway toward the kitchen, she wondered if she even needed that sweatshirt. It was noticeably warmer in here than it had been the day before. Had Amaal thrown some of his djinn energy into making the research station a bit more comfortable? It definitely felt that way.

When she entered the kitchen, she found him setting a big bowl of scrambled eggs down on the small table in the alcove off to the side where they'd eaten most of their meals. A plate of crisp bacon already sat there, along with a stack of toast, and a mug of coffee waited beside each place setting.

"Good morning," he said.

"Good morning," she replied. The night before, she'd worried that they might be awkward around one another, thanks to those kisses they'd shared. However, Amaal seemed relaxed and natural enough, and she resolved to be the same way. After all, it was only a few kisses. It wasn't as though they'd....

She let her thoughts end right there. Already she could feel herself beginning to blush. Damn Irish skin that showed off everything.

"I never thought I'd have a breakfast like this again," she said as she hastily sat herself down.

"I'm glad I could provide it for you." He sat down as well, and as soon as he'd put his napkin in his lap, Sasha sidled a bit closer, no doubt to be within easy reach if there were any bits of bacon that turned out to be more suited for dogs than humans…or djinn.

Deirdre wanted to chuckle at the animal's obvious ploy. Not too much bacon, but surely a little bit couldn't hurt. She wondered if Sasha's previous owners had given her any table scraps, or whether they'd been strict with her diet. Well, new world, new rules. The dog looked so hopeful, Deirdre couldn't help breaking off a small piece of bacon before she'd even had any herself. She handed it to Sasha, who took it with delicate care, showing great forbearance, considering what a treat she was being it offered.

"It seems she already has you trained," Amaal remarked with a grin as he picked up his mug of coffee.

"Oh, well, she probably has been wanting it, too," Deirdre replied. "I won't give her too much more. The sodium isn't good for dogs."

He absorbed this information without comment, sipping again at his hot coffee. Then he said, "It's still snowing."

"It is?" She realized she hadn't even pushed aside the blinds in her room so she could take a look outside. Snow had tended to catch her by surprise the few times it had fallen when she was up here; it was so quiet, coming down without the noisy patter of rain, which almost always announced its arrival.

"Look outside."

Taking her mug of coffee with her, Deirdre got up from the table to get a peek outside. What she saw almost took her breath away. The landscape had turned pure white, its individual features blunted and nearly obscured by a blanket of snow that had to be almost two feet deep. Yes, they sometimes got storms like this up here, but usually in January and February, not a scant week into December.

It was beautiful...but it also frightened her. She knew she wouldn't be going anywhere in that, not even in the Toyota Tundra that had become hers by default. It would take her hours just to dig out its tires.

And no snow plows making sure the roads had been cleared, no one coming around to salt the asphalt. Nothing, no help at all. Just her, alone here on the mountain with a djinn and a dog.

The chill that went over her then had very little to do with the draft leaking in past the poorly hung window. She turned away from the bleak view outside and went to take her seat at the kitchen table once again.

"There's no need to worry," Amaal said, his voice gentle, reassuring. Clearly, he must have seen some of the fear in her face. "I can keep our power going. The pipes will not freeze, and I can get anything we might need to make our stay here comfortable. But…." He stopped there, instead reaching for a piece of bacon while Sasha watched every movement with keen interest.

"But what?" Deirdre asked, that chill returning to her even though the kitchen was almost uncomfortably warm.

"But I think we would be more comfortable still in my home. It is much larger than this research station, and far better appointed. It has four bedrooms, so you would have your own room, and there is also a basement space you could use for your laboratory. I could bring over any equipment you might need."

That all sounded reasonable, and far too enticing. The research station was small enough that it wasn't all that easy to avoid tripping over each other, and being in a larger space would probably solve that problem. However, if she went with Amaal to his house, wouldn't she be putting herself effectively at his mercy? Here, she could pretend she had some measure of autonomy, but to go to his home base, so to speak, he'd have all the power. What if all this charm was just an act, and he turned on her once he knew he had her at his mercy?

"I don't know," she said, doing her best to keep her tone light. The last thing she wanted was for him to notice any of her misgivings. "That sounds like a lot of work for you."

He chuckled. "Deirdre, there is very little that is 'a lot of work' for a djinn. It could all be managed in the blink of an eye...or very nearly so."

So much for that argument. She played with her fork, then ate a mouthful of eggs, more to give herself time to think than for any other reason. All right, might as well look at this logically. They probably would do better in a larger place. There wasn't any real reason for her to stay at the research station. It wasn't as though anyone was going to come along to relieve her of her imagined duties here. She'd stayed at first because she thought someone might come eventually, and then later because she was too frightened to leave. Now she knew that both those excuses didn't make much sense.

Still, even though he'd offered her a room of her own, wasn't proposing that they jump into bed together, Deirdre knew she was being naïve if she tried to tell herself that sex wasn't his ultimate goal here. She had to go into this with a clear head.

Once again, the memory of his lips pressed against hers rose in her mind, and her entire body felt flushed just recalling that moment. No matter what she tried to tell herself otherwise, she knew she responded to him in a way that she'd never experienced with another person. She had to know she might play coy now, but her body was telling herself something entirely different.

Could she live with that?

She looked across the table at Amaal. He seemed intent on spreading plum jam on his toast, and not paying any particular attention to her, but she knew better. His current silence only meant he was waiting for her response. For a moment, all she did was study his face, the blue, blue eyes nearly obscured by the dark sweep of his lashes, the prominent cheekbones and firm chin and sensual mouth. His hair was longer than that of any man she'd ever been with, falling against the collar of the borrowed sweatshirt he wore.

He was perfect. Every inch of him…those she had seen, and those she guessed she would get to see in the near future.

Another of those shudders went through her. Desire. Want. Need. How long was she going to pretend it didn't exist? Maybe it was wrong, but she didn't know if she could continue to fight her attraction to him.

She took a breath and said, "All right, Amaal. We can go to your house."

TWELVE

Amaal blessed the snow, thanking it for helping to drive Deirdre's decision. He still noted some wariness in her, some trepidation at agreeing to his suggestion, but she did not try to back out of her commitment to go to his house. She only said she needed to shower and get dressed, then pack a few things, but that they could go later this morning.

Not a moment too soon, in his own opinion. While she went off to get ready, he used his power over fire to blast an area clear just beyond the research station's porch so Sasha might go out to relieve herself. Visibly cheered by the sight of all that ground free of snow, the dog ran around, sniffing, until she finally took care of her business and came back inside, tracking mud the whole way. A wave of his hand cleaned up the mess;

Amaal had a feeling that Deirdre would want to leave the place that had been her home for the past few months in as good shape as possible. He'd also cleaned up the kitchen, and tidied the room where he'd been sleeping.

She came into the front room, a large duffle-style bag in one hand, her backpack and laptop case in the other. Amaal tried not to give the laptop case any particular attention; the last thing he wanted was for Deirdre to learn that he had discovered where she'd secreted the device.

"Ready?" he asked, his voice neutral.

Her gaze shifted to his empty hands. "You're not bringing anything with you?"

"There is no need. Anything I was using here was only borrowed. All my belongings are at my house."

A nod. Then she inquired, "How does this work? You just snap your fingers and we're gone?"

"Not precisely. I will need to hold you."

She didn't look terribly thrilled by that revelation, but neither did she argue. After she'd taken a few steps in his direction, however, she paused and said, "What about the dog?"

"You will need to hold the dog. Give me your bags, so your arms will be free to carry her."

This suggestion was met with an even more dubious reception. One eyebrow went up, and she glanced down at Sasha, who smiled up at her, tail wagging. Then Deirdre gave a small sigh and handed over the bags she carried. Amaal hung the duffle and backpack over his shoulder, then clutched the laptop case with his left hand.

"Come along," he said, trying not to sound too eager to hold her...although of course he was.

Deirdre moved closer, her lithe body pressed almost directly against his. Oh, God, how he wanted to kiss her.

Time enough for that later. For now, he inclined his head toward her, and she bent and gathered Sasha in her arms, staggering a bit, since the dog was quite large and heavy for someone as slender as Deirdre. She stood, and he put his right arm around her waist, holding her close.

A blink, and the research station was gone, replaced by the much more elegant living room of the home that was now his. The winter landscape dominated the space, thanks to the floor-to-ceiling windows that filled one wall, while a fire crackled and danced in the stacked-stone hearth on the other side of the space. In here, it was warm and cozy, the air ever so faintly scented with cinnamon, thanks to the specially treated pinecones that rested in a basket to one side of the fireplace.

Deirdre shifted her weight, obviously preparing to put her burden down, and Amaal released her, loath as he was to let her go. Then she set Sasha on the wood floor, and the dog bounded away happily, clearly intent on smelling every square inch of her new surroundings. As she straightened, Deirdre looked around at the living room with admiration in her eyes.

"No wonder you wanted to come here," she said. "I can't really blame you."

"It does afford us a bit more space to spread out," he replied, taking care to keep his tone light. He didn't want her to think that he'd brought the two of them here for any reason other than to have a more comfortable place in which to live and work.

"That's for sure." Another glance around, and then she became brisk, businesslike. "Where's the kitchen? We should probably put out Sasha's bowls so she can get familiar with where they're located."

"Of course. This way."

Still carrying her bags, he led Deirdre down a short hall that took them past the dining room and into the kitchen. Once there, he set her bags down on the island and waved a hand. Immediately, a pair of shining stainless steel bowls appeared on the floor, one filled with fresh water, the other with dry dog food.

They'd left Sasha nosing around in the living room, but as soon as those bowls clanked on the tile floor, she was there, hurrying over to drink some water, then start munching on the dog food.

"Looks like she figured it out," Deirdre said with a wry grin.

Amaal was glad to see that she'd allowed herself to relax a little. During that brief time he'd held her while they transported here, he could feel the tension in her body, the way she'd barely allowed herself to breathe as long as she was in his arms. Had her nervousness merely been because of their proximity, or had she already begun second-guessing her decision to come here? "Apparently," he said. "While she's occupied, let me show you your room."

Deirdre's smile faded a bit as she nodded. "Okay."

He gathered up her bags again and led her out of the kitchen and back to the great room, which encompassed both the living and dining areas. From there, they climbed the stairs to the second floor. The master bedroom was at the end of the upstairs hallway, with the other bedrooms and an additional bathroom ranged down that corridor. Amaal took Deirdre into the first bedroom on the left because it was the largest. It had its own fireplace, and a queen-size bed and walk-in closet, with the comforter on the bed in soothing, earthy shades of brown and cream and a smoky teal color.

"This is definitely a lot better than the research station," Deirdre remarked as she glanced around.

"I'm glad you think so." He set her bags on the bench at the foot of the bed. "The bathroom is right across the hallway, but you can get settled in there later. I'll show you the basement space you can use for a lab—if that's something you'd like to do."

"Sure," she said, although she didn't sound terribly enthusiastic. "Let's take a look."

They went back downstairs, and then down another flight of stairs that led to the lower level from the home's laundry room. When Amaal first moved into the house, the basement had been relatively unfinished, except for some half-hearted wine storage under the stairs. Possibly the previous owner had intended to make it a rumpus room or a "man cave," but had run out of either funds or time. Since Amaal hadn't been sure what he wanted to do with it, either, he'd settled for redoing the wine-cellar portion of the basement with fine oak shelving and several wine refrigerators for the more delicate items in his collection, and then put down wood floors throughout. The walls were now a warm terra-cotta shade, but otherwise the place was empty.

"You see?" he said, sweeping his arm to indicate the oversized space. "There's plenty of room to put whatever equipment you'd like in here.

More microscopes, I would suppose, and a refrigerator for samples. You can request anything you like—I will admit that I don't know very much about human technology, but I will do my best to get what you require."

"I—" Deirdre paused for a moment, as though searching for the best response. "I'm not sure what I'd need. Really, I was mostly making busywork for myself back at the research station. I suppose I could ask for an electron microscope and a centrifuge and an autoclave, but the problem is, I don't actually know how to use any of that stuff—not in a way that would be meaningful. I'm just a student pretending to be a scientist."

Amaal wanted to smile at her obvious discomfiture, but he didn't want to offend her, either. "Yes, you've told me that before." He bent and kissed her on the cheek, was gratified to see that she didn't try to flinch away. "You don't have to put anything in here, if you don't want. There are plenty of things you could do to occupy your time —pottery-making, or weaving, or stained glass. All you have to do is ask for the supplies, once you know what it is that you do want."

Even in the dim lighting down in the basement, he could see the way her cheeks flushed. Because he had kissed her? "That's very generous."

Ah, Deirdre, it is very easy for a djinn to be

generous. But you must always ask yourself what it is he wants in return.

Amaal did not utter those words aloud, however, because he did not wish to throw her even further off balance. He knew she had struggled with her decision to come here, was even now clearly uneasy. Because of that, he only shrugged and said, "I want you to be comfortable here. For now, though, I think we had better go upstairs and see what Sasha has been up to. She seems a well-behaved dog, but...."

"You don't want her rampaging through the house. I totally understand."

They went back up to the kitchen and found no sign of the dog. However, she turned out be lying on her side in front of the fireplace, eyes half shut, clearly in bliss thanks to the warmth radiating from the hearth.

"Well, that answers that question," Deirdre said. Her gaze moved to the bank of tall windows on the opposite wall, where the snow still feel ceaselessly outside. "Is it ever going to stop?"

"I cannot forecast the weather," he replied. "That is a talent of the elementals of the air, and my element is fire. But I believe it would be quite unusual for this storm to last more than another day. Even if it does, we are safe here. You have nothing to worry about."

"I know," she said hastily, although something

in her tone made Amaal think she was not quite as sure of his comforting words as she wanted him to think.

"Why don't you go ahead and get settled in?" he suggested. "I will stay down here with Sasha and watch the storm."

This plan seemed to make her relax slightly. No doubt she had been worried about him being nearby while she unpacked her things...especially that unobtrusive little black box now hidden in her laptop case.

"All right. It shouldn't take me very long."

She headed upstairs, while Amaal went over to one of the couches and sat down. The snow seemed to be falling more thickly than ever, which suited him just fine. He thought of being kept inside for days on end, just him and Deirdre, and a smile touched his lips.

How could anything be better than that?

This room looked like something out of a high-end ski resort, with the four-poster bed and carefully coordinated art on the walls. But this had been someone's home.

Well, someone's vacation home. Deirdre had led a fairly sheltered life, and she certainly hadn't known anyone who could maintain a million-dollar house just to come skiing in it for a few weeks out of the year, but at least she'd understood that those kinds of people did exist. And she got the vibe from this place that the owner had paid a designer to furnish the whole house in pieces that would coordinate from room to room and give a unified feel to the space. Certainly no normal person she'd ever known had lived in a home where everything felt thought out, right down to the picture frames and the rustic little decorative touches like the basket filled with orbs of woven twigs that sat on a table off to one side. A mirror hung above that table, giving her a fleeting glimpse of her pale, strained face before she turned away.

She closed the door, even though she knew Amaal could pop in here any time if he liked. He wouldn't, though. He'd already gotten what he wanted by convincing her to come to the house, and so the last thing he would do was jeopardize the situation by barging in where he wasn't invited.

The walk-in closet was laughably large compared to the meager amount of clothing she had to put away there. In a way, she missed the small, cramped closet back at the research station, because at least there it had been easy to hide stuff by shoving it into the farthest corner. When she set the laptop case down on the floor, it looked way too conspicuous.

All right, time for another solution. She pulled the device out from the side pocket of the case where she'd hidden it and set it on top of the built-in drawers that took up one section of the closet. Quickly, she got out all her underwear and put it in one of the drawers, then hid the device in the cup of one of her bras. Surely Amaal wouldn't go poking around in her underwear, even if he thought it might be a good idea to find out where she'd hidden the little gizmo.

No, the underwear drawer suddenly seemed far too obvious. She frowned and glanced back into the bedroom. The device was just big enough that she didn't think it would really fit under the mattress. Besides, she wasn't sure she wanted to subject it to that kind of abuse. Having a queen-size mattress and her on top of it might be too much for the epoxy she'd used to glue the various sides together to make the cube.

Then her gaze traveled to the basket on the dresser and its rustic decoration of balls made of twigs. If she removed a couple of them and then placed the device at the bottom—

She walked over to the dresser, took out most of the little twig orbs, and set the device in the basket. Then she gathered up all the balls she'd removed and put them back in, taking care to make sure that the outlines of the black box in the bottom were completely obscured. Two of the balls wouldn't fit now that the little black box sat in the bottom of the basket, so she took them over to the built-in dresser in the closet and hid them in one of the drawers there.

After walking back a few steps and staring at the basket with a critical eye, she thought her subterfuge should work. Even though she was straining to see it, she really couldn't see the device. She doubted Amaal would ever look for it there, since he would expect her to hide the black box someplace less obvious.

It reminded her of a story she'd read once in school, about hiding something in plain sight. Was it an Edgar Allan Poe story? Maybe, although she couldn't remember the title or much of its details. Not that it really mattered, she supposed.

But she'd spent enough time up here. She got out her small zippered bag of toiletries and took it over to the bathroom across the hall, although she didn't bother to do much with the bag except slide it into the top drawer of the vanity. Since she only had a small bottle of moisturizer, a stick of deodorant, a tube of mascara and some lip gloss, along with her toothbrush and toothpaste, it wasn't as though she'd need very much time to unpack at the end of the day.

A day. A whole day of her being here with

Amaal, no lab to retreat to, no real way to avoid him.

Did she even want to avoid him?

No, not really. Damn it.

She did pause to reapply some lip gloss, just because she realized it was stupid to keep inwardly protesting that she didn't care what Amaal thought of her or her looks when she knew that she really did care. Why bother to keep pretending? As much as she wanted to deny the reality to herself, she thought she had a fairly good idea of where all this was going to end up.

When she came downstairs, she saw no sign of Amaal or Sasha, although the fire was still crackling away happily in the hearth. But then she heard voices drifting in from another space just past the living room, and realized those voices must be coming from a television.

Sure enough, there was a sort of family/TV room just beyond the great room with its living and dining areas. Amaal sat on the sectional at one end of the room, feet up on the coffee table, watching a cooking show. Deirdre had never followed any of those types of programs, since neither she nor her mother had had the time to cook anything remotely gourmet, but at least it was a pleasant-looking woman performing hosting duties and not some of the loudmouthed jerks she'd seen when flipping channels.

Flipping channels. She blinked at the TV, then looked over at Amaal. How could he be watching what was clearly a cable cooking show? Had the owner of the property DVR'd it or something? That seemed like the most reasonable explanation, but....

"I thought I would do some research," Amaal said, apparently just noting her arrival. "We should have something interesting for dinner, yes?"

"I—I suppose so." She came further into the room and looked at the television again. "Was this on a DVR or something?"

"No," Amaal replied. "I thought of the sort of thing I wanted to watch, and it just appeared. All of these shows were digitized, so they still exist as energy somewhere. It wasn't that difficult to get what I needed."

This explanation only made Deirdre's head want to spin that much more. All right, she understood that shows streamed on cable or directly to devices like Apple TV or Roku were somehow just electrons, when you got right down to it, but still, for Amaal to simply pluck what he wanted out of the ether like that was a little disconcerting.

On the other hand, this might be a great chance to get caught up on all the movies she'd skipped seeing because she really couldn't afford to go…or finally be able to binge-watch *Game of Thrones*.

"That's, um…interesting."

"You're surprised that I can do such a thing."

"Sort of. I mean, yes, it's not something I would have imagined a djinn could do. But I guess there isn't much of a limit, is there?"

"Not really, no." He patted the sectional. "Come, sit down."

She went over and took a seat next to him, then, feeling slightly daring, put her feet up on the coffee table as well, although she paused to remove her shoes first so she wouldn't damage the table's wooden surface. It did feel cozy in here— the room had a fireplace of its own, much smaller than the one in the living area, but Amaal had another fire going, and it felt warm and sheltered and intimate.

Maybe she didn't really want to think about "intimate" right now. Clearing her throat, she asked, "So what's for dinner?"

"You seem to like pasta—and bacon—so I'm watching a show on how to make linguine carbonara."

That did sound good. She hadn't had that dish since…forever. And linguine carbonara was creamy and sort of comfort food-ish, and that sounded good for a cold, snowy day like this. Deirdre shifted on the couch so she faced more toward Amaal. "You're going to make me linguine carbonara from scratch?"

He gave her an indulgent smile. "No, of course not. I would run far too much of a risk of ruining something. But since it is a dish I've never had, I thought it better to watch a show that explains how it's made. That way, when I conjure it for the two of us, it will taste the way it's supposed to."

Since she really had no idea how this whole "conjuring" thing even worked, about all she could do was nod. "That sounds like a plan."

His blue eyes seemed almost too intent. Their gazes locked for a moment, and once again Deirdre felt that needy, hungry heat run through her body. She really shouldn't let him affect her like this, and yet it seemed that once they'd kissed, the barriers she'd tried so hard to keep in place somehow managed to break down a little bit more every time he looked at her. It would have been easy to blame her attraction to him on a simple craving for companionship after so much time spent alone, but she knew it was more than that…far more.

Then he said, tone casual, "Are you all settled in?"

"Yes," she replied quickly. At once her thoughts flicked to the way she'd hidden the device, although she didn't think that was what

Amaal had been asking her. Or at least, she hoped not. "Not that I had much to 'settle.' When I went to the research station the weekend before… well, *before*…I hadn't packed all that much. I took a couple of the tops Kate had left behind because I needed something to stretch my wardrobe, and I got a few more things in Running Springs, but…."

"I can get you anything you want, you know," Amaal told her. "You certainly have no need to be limited by what you had with you at the station."

That was a tempting offer. She'd never been anything close to a clothes horse, mostly because she couldn't afford to indulge herself in that way, and yet having to rotate through her meager wardrobe for the past few months had become more and more tedious. The shops in Running Springs offered a few alternatives, but still….

"That's very generous, Amaal, but I'm probably okay for now."

She wasn't even sure why she'd responded to his offer in such a way. After all, he'd told her that it took very little effort for him to reach out and gather to him the items that he wanted. Somehow, though, she didn't want to feel beholden to him. It was better to rely on the things she'd brought with her. That way, if this whole situation didn't work out, it would be easier for her to leave.

A flicker of disappointment passed over his

face, but then his shoulders lifted and he turned his attention back toward the television. "Of course. All you need to do is let me know if you ever change your mind."

Deirdre nodded, feeling vaguely guilty. For what, she wasn't even exactly sure. But since it was clear that Amaal didn't want to talk anymore, she also tried to focus on the television, on a show made by people who didn't even exist any longer, who'd gone down into the dust with the rest of humanity.

And while she watched, she tried to ignore the lump in her throat, the longing for what had once been and was now gone forever. Then she felt Amaal's arms go around her, holding her close, and the gentleness of his touch made the tears that had begun to sting her eyes flow freely. She sobbed into his shoulder while he held her, forgetting for the moment that he was a djinn, thinking only that she'd been alone for too long and she needed this. She needed someone to be there to hold her, to hold back the darkness.

For now, it was enough.

THIRTEEN

Deirdre retreated to the sanctuary of her room after her bout of weeping, and Amaal did not try to stop her. He was not entirely certain why she had disintegrated like that, shivering in his arms, her tears wetting the shoulder of the sweater he wore, but he was glad that she had turned to him for comfort. Perhaps her little breakdown meant she had begun to let down her guard, that the softening he'd seen after he'd kissed her had progressed a little further. He wanted her to feel safe with him, despite everything.

For now, it seemed that she did.

The cooking show ended. Amaal reflected it was a good thing he could use his djinn powers to summon their meals, for otherwise it seemed he might spend half his life in the kitchen. It was one thing to brew one's own cup of coffee, he thought, and quite another to waste what appeared to be hours and hours, cutting and chopping and mixing and sautéing.

He got up from the sectional couch in the television room and went out to the great room. The snow had finally stopped, but the view beyond the floor-to-ceiling windows there showed only a great white expanse where nothing moved. Some might have called the vista beautiful, with the open glade in the center surrounded by white-frosted pine and fir trees, and more snowy mountains in the distance, but he had never been much of one for winter. Again he had to wonder why the elders had seen fit to give him this property, when there were so many other plots of land that would have been eminently more suitable. Someplace in Hawaii, perhaps, or on the beach in Cancun.

But, he reflected, if he had settled in either of those places, then he would never have met Deirdre. She was unlike any other woman he had ever known, although he had to admit that his experience with human females was not precisely vast. Fiercely self-sufficient one moment, and dissolving into his arms the next. He could not say he entirely understood all her reactions, but at the same time he hoped she was not ashamed of the way she had wept while he held her. There was no shame in tears, especially for one who had lost as much as Deirdre had.

This house was so well-equipped that Amaal had no need to summon the items he desired to dress up the dinner table. He moved away from the window and went to a cupboard in the kitchen where the table linens were kept, and got out a cloth of fine white damask, which he used to cover the dining room table. Matching napkins, and then the plates of fine china, simple and elegant with their band of gold around the outer rim. At last came the sterling flatware, and silver candlesticks for the center of the table.

He enjoyed himself more than he thought he would as he went about these simple tasks. True, he could have snapped his fingers and made all these items appear on the table in their designated places, all lined up and just so, but there was something to be said for doing these things for oneself. Of course, that sentiment did not exactly extend to cooking the meal as well, which seemed like far too much work.

But it was not too much work to go down into the wine cellar he had set up in the basement and study the offerings there. The sauce for the carbonara was a bit more delicate than the chicken cacciatore they'd had the night before, so he decided on a rosé. It would need to be chilled further, but he'd put it in the refrigerator for a while. He supposed he could have laid his hands on it to cool down the bottle, although a water or an air elemental would have been better-suited for such a task. And the last thing he wanted was another of his kind anywhere near here. He would have to explain Deirdre, and that would be difficult, especially if her presence here was reported to the elders. No doubt they would issue some kind of ultimatum, and he would have to make a decision as to what to do with her.

An even worse scenario would be having to defend her from an attack by one of those who saw her existence as an abomination. Amaal thought he might be up to such an assault—fire elementals by their very nature had an advantage in djinn-versus-djinn duels—but he would much rather avoid such a confrontation altogether.

The afternoon light waned. He could not see the sun setting, for the room where he stood faced eastward, but he felt it going down, even as he watched a cool purple dusk steal across the world. Time to start thinking about summoning their dinner, and deciding what else they could have with it. They'd eaten garlic bread the night before, so possibly some crusty rolls in its place, and rather than salad, a dish he'd once had of grilled eggplant and zucchini, livened up with olive oil and garlic.

Yes, that should do. He glanced down at

himself, at the sweater and jeans he wore, and wondered if he dared leave off these mundane human garments for some of the luxurious robes he preferred. No, better not—Deirdre would certainly not be dressing for dinner, since she'd refused his offer to expand her wardrobe, and he thought she might be intimidated upon seeing him dressed in such a way. Besides, he did not wish to remind her of his djinn nature. It was unavoidable, he supposed, but no reason to throw it in her face. The last thing he wanted was to make her uncomfortable around him, not when she had finally begun to seem more relaxed lately. She needed to be at ease, or he feared she would only continue to rebuff him.

He went up the stairs to her room. The door was shut, and he knocked softly. "Deirdre? It is about time for dinner."

A long pause, during which he worried that she might not come to answer his knock. And if she refused to see him, what then?

Even as this uneasy thought darted across his mind, however, she opened the door and gazed out at him. Her eyes appeared somewhat red, but otherwise she looked composed enough.

"Is it that late already?"

"Yes," he replied. "The sun has gone down, and the snow has stopped. You should eat something."

She looked down at her feet. "I'm not that hungry."

Had she cried again, here in the solitude of her room? Amaal thought that was entirely possible, and yet he didn't want to call attention to her tears, or the telltales they'd left on her delicate features. "You need to eat something," he said gently. "We had a large breakfast, but you didn't eat anything for lunch."

"Right." A wan smile, and she added, "I suppose I didn't realize that."

"Then please come down for dinner."

He offered her his arm, and although she hesitated, she did end up taking it, sliding her slender arm into the crook of his elbow. They went downstairs, where he'd made sure the fire would be blazing brightly and that candles flickered from not just the dining table, but the sideboard as well. Because it was now full dark outside, the snowy landscape was hidden, and inside all was warmth and comfort.

"It looks beautiful," she said.

"I'm glad you think so. I wanted you to enjoy your first dinner here at my home."

He guided her to her seat and waited while she sat down, then went to take his place at the head of the table. A wave of the hand, and the meal he'd envisioned materialized before them. Sasha, who'd been dozing in front of the fireplace since she'd already had her dinner, got up at once and took her place near Amaal's right elbow, waiting for her chance to take advantage of any table scraps that might come her way.

Deirdre gave a small gasp, then shook her head ruefully. "I suppose sooner or later I'll get used to that."

Amaal allowed himself a small smile. "I'm sure you will."

The rosé sat in a metal chilling sleeve; he extracted it and poured wine for her, then tipped an equal measure into his own glass. When he lifted it, Deirdre awkwardly followed suit.

"Welcome to my home," he said. "I hope you will find a refuge here."

She touched her glass to his. "I hope so, too. It's definitely much more comfortable than the research station."

That was what he'd wanted to hear. He wanted her to be at home here, to feel easy as their relationship became far more intimate than it was now. At the same time, he knew he needed to hold back a little, make sure she didn't think she was being pressured into something for which she wasn't yet ready. "Some might say that was damning with faint praise."

She chuckled, then sipped her wine. "I suppose I can see why you might think that, but I really didn't mean it that way. This place is beautiful." Her gaze moved past the dining area into the living room, where the light from the fire in the hearth danced and moved on the walls. "Did all the djinn get houses as nice as this?"

"As to that, I'm not sure," he replied frankly. "I haven't had the chance to visit many of them. However, the ones that I have seen did appear to be quite luxurious. And the ones that are not, well, if the land is good, that is all which matters. Many djinn would want to knock down the human structures anyway so they could build a palace more to their taste."

Deirdre appeared to absorb this piece of information with a faint frown, although that didn't prevent her from lifting her fork so she could take a bite of the linguine carbonara. At once her eyes closed, apparently in pleasure. When they opened, the expression in them was far more cheerful that it had been a few minutes earlier. "This is incredible. I can't believe you can get something to taste this good, just from watching a cooking show."

"It wasn't that difficult, I assure you. But I am glad you like it."

"Like it? I love it. Thank you."

He smiled at her, and for a moment they ate in silence, Deirdre clearly enjoying every bite. However, it seemed that what he had said to her earlier still occupied her thoughts, for when she spoke again, she picked up the thread of their conversation.

"You haven't changed this house, though."

No, he hadn't, except for the basement—in part because he hadn't quite decided what he wanted to have as a more permanent structure here. A djinn-style palace, with its courtyards and many windows and open, airy spaces that flowed from one to the other, didn't feel quite right for this alpine meadow. "Not yet. I suppose I shall at some point. But I have plenty of time to decide what I wish to do with it."

"Ah." Deirdre ate a few more bites of carbonara and sipped her rosé. "Do the djinn plan to get rid of all the buildings we left behind?"

Amaal thought that was the ultimate goal of his people, although he knew it would take many years. Such an undertaking was an ambitious one, even for djinn. "I believe so. However, I don't believe there is any particular organized effort to return the Earth to its natural state. Each djinn has to decide what he or she wishes to do with his or her territory. Also, this is the sort of work that comes more easily to the earth elementals, and there only so many of them."

"I suppose I hadn't thought of that," Deirdre said, looking thoughtful. "I wonder what it will look like, once they are all done."

That day was probably far enough in the

future, Amaal doubted she would live to see it. However, he knew better than to tell her such a thing. Also, he did not really wish to contemplate her eventual fate, because he wanted to think of her as she was now, lovely and perfect, the candlelight giving her fair skin warmth and adding even more light to her clear, blue-green eyes.

"This world is a beautiful place," he said, his tone neutral, "and it will be even more beautiful once all these blights are removed from its surface. Think of acres and acres of open grassland, of unspoiled forests, of seacoasts without ports, and only clean white sand instead."

"It sounds beautiful." That wasn't just candlelight gleaming in her eyes; Amaal thought he saw the return of her tears, although they didn't fall. She took a jagged little breath and drank some more wine. "I guess it's something good that will come out of all this. Humanity is gone, but the Earth will be better for our absence. Maybe we were just a cancer after all." Abruptly, she pulled the napkin from her lap and set it on the table, then rose from her seat. "I'm sorry, Amaal, but I just can't do this."

Concerned, he got up as well. "Do what?"

"This!" She gestured toward the table, toward their half-eaten meal and the bottle of wine and the tapers flickering in their silver candlesticks. "This whole romantic dinner thing. I can't sit here with you and pretend that everything is normal, because it isn't. The world I knew is gone, and—and you're a *djinn,* for God's sake, and—"

He laid a hand on her arm, could feel her immediately tense at his touch. Keeping his tone gentle, he inquired, "Deirdre, did I ask you to pretend that everything was normal?"

"Not in so many words." With a sharp yank, she wrested her arm from his grasp. He let go because he knew that to hold on would only upset her that much more. "I tried to tell myself to get over it, that I couldn't change what had happened to the world, could only try to be as happy as my situation allowed. I thought I'd convinced myself. But obviously I was wrong." Her eyes met his, wet with tears, pleading. "I'm sorry, Amaal. I know—I know you wanted something more from me this evening. But that isn't going to happen."

He opened his mouth to reply—although he had no clear idea of what he intended to say—but she forestalled him by hurrying away from the table and up the stairs, her footsteps quick and almost panicked in their swiftness as she retreated to the safety of her room. For a long moment, Amaal remained where he was, as unable to move as if he'd been glued to that particular spot on the floor. Perhaps there was something he could have told her, some words of comfort he could have offered, even though nothing particular came to mind. She had lost everything, after all, her people, her world. Perhaps he had been mad to think that the surface comforts he had to offer her could do anything to soften the sort of blow she had suffered.

For now, all he could offer her was time to heal. A frown creasing his brow, Amaal poured himself another glass of wine and returned to his neglected meal.

Alone.

She'd cried so much, she hoped she was all cried out by now. Deirdre rolled over onto her back and stared up at the ceiling. Her body ached from weeping, and her stomach was a knot of misery.

Why now? She hadn't cried like this back at the research station, not even when the import of Miles Odekirk's broadcasts had begun to sink in and she'd realized that no one was coming to rescue her, that there *was* no one. Or rather, there were so few people left that the statistical odds of a survivor coming across her hideout were rather lower than the chances of the Earth being hit by an extinction-level asteroid sometime in the next week. Either way, she'd cried when she realized everyone in her world was gone, but she'd been able to function, for God's sake. She wasn't this bundle of limp misery, huddled under the covers of an all-too-comfortable queen-sized bed.

It must have been that vision of the Earth remade, all traces of humanity gone, that sent her over the edge. As long as those relics of modern civilization remained, Deirdre could fool herself that the situation wasn't quite as bad as she thought, could tell herself that just because she hadn't met any survivors didn't mean they didn't exist somewhere. But once the djinn wiped away all evidence that anyone else had ever lived here, then all hope truly would be gone.

She was an anomaly, a survivor who didn't fit in anywhere. If only she'd had the courage to leave the research station once she'd finished building one of Odekirk's devices. She could have gotten in Sean's big truck and driven east, heading for the sanctuary Miles Odekirk had offered in the mountains of New Mexico. It wouldn't have mattered if the djinn tracked her down, because the device would have protected her. Now, though, she didn't have that luxury, because of Amaal.

Why had she agreed to come here? What was the point? To give in, to let the djinn who had once been her captive now become her lover? Even as those words crossed through her mind, Deirdre wanted to recoil from them. That would be the ultimate betrayal of her own humanity, though, wouldn't it? To surrender, to allow one of the very beings who'd destroyed humankind to enjoy her body?

Jesus.

She'd gotten a paper cup of water from the bathroom earlier. It sat on the nightstand, and she reached for it and took a long swallow. The water was sweet and cool, probably from a well, since the property here was so isolated. It provided some relief for her raw-feeling throat, but not enough. Another swallow, and it would be gone and she'd have to decide whether to suffer without, or to take the risk of going into the hallway and possibly encountering Amaal. She hadn't heard anything from him, not even a squeak from the stairs as he came up here to go to his bedroom.

Most likely, he was still downstairs in the dining room. If she'd been dumped like that in the middle of dinner, after all the work she'd put in to make it a nice meal, she'd probably have stayed sitting at the table so she could finish the open bottle of wine.

But who knew what Amaal would do? After all, he wasn't human. She couldn't expect his reactions and his thoughts to be anything close to hers. He was djinn, alien.

Maybe she should have grabbed that bottle of wine as she'd run away. Right now she could tell she needed something stronger to drink than water.

At last she heard what she'd been dreading— the faintest creak of the floorboards outside her door. Amaal's voice, quiet, hesitant. "Deirdre? Are you all right?"

Of course she wasn't. She wanted to fling the words at him: *No, I'm not all right, you stupid djinn.* But that would have been cruel and child- ish. He hadn't done anything to her, had only tried to make her comfortable here. Sure, he wanted to get her in bed, too, but in that respect he really wasn't much different from a lot of the other men she'd known.

Well, except that he wasn't strictly a man.

With a sigh, she pushed herself out from under the covers and went to the door. She would rather not have faced him in her sleeping attire, but since that ensemble consisted of an oversized T-shirt and a pair of yoga pants, it wasn't as though she was going to give him an eyeful. She opened the door a crack and said, "I'm okay. I just really don't feel like talking right now."

He'd turned on the overhead light in the hall- way. It shone down on his hair, warming the dark brown locks that framed his face. She saw worry there, and a certain confusion. "If I said some- thing that offended you—"

Oh, God. Deirdre shook her head. "No, it's

not that. It's just…I guess a bunch of things hit me all at once. That's all."

From the way his brows drew together, it seemed he had a feeling she wasn't telling him the whole truth. And of course she wasn't. Right now, she didn't even know for sure what that truth was. All she knew was that she wanted him, and was more frightened of that desire than anything else she'd ever encountered in her life. She had no idea what to do with it. The safest thing had been for her to run away, except the only place she could run to was this room. She'd allowed herself to be trapped here in a djinn's house, snowbound, for God only knows how long.

However, he didn't argue with her, didn't attempt to probe further. All he did was hold out a small basket, the one that held the dinner rolls. "You did not eat very much. I brought these for you in case you get hungry later."

That simple act of kindness made fresh tears start to her eyes. Damn him for being so nice, anyhow. If he'd been rude, arrogant, demanded to know what the hell her problem was, then she could have risen up in righteous indignation. She didn't know what to do about him being nice. Djinn weren't supposed to be that way. They were supposed to be relentless killers.

Since she couldn't really refuse, she took the basket from him and murmured a thank-you.

His shoulders lifted. "It is nothing. Only—"

"Only what?"

"Do you mind leaving your door open during the night? It is only that I can tell that Sasha is a little worried, since she is used to coming and going between our rooms while we sleep."

Damn. Deirdre had been so wrapped up in herself, she hadn't even stopped to think how her histrionics might be affecting the dog the two of them had sort of adopted, or how Sasha might feel about being locked out of one of her night-time refuges. She did tend to start off the night in one bedroom and finish it in another. "Right. I forgot about that. Sure, I'll leave it open."

As much as she hated the idea.

"Thank you." Amaal hesitated for a moment, then said, "I do apologize if I said something that upset you. It was certainly not my intention."

"It wasn't anything like that. Really." She drew in a breath and added, "But I really would like to go to sleep now."

"Of course." He inclined his head toward her, almost a bow. "I hope you sleep well, Deirdre. Remember, you are perfectly safe here."

Safe from other djinn, she thought, a little shiver passing over her. *I don't know whether I'm safe from you.*

Which was completely unfair, considering how much forbearance he'd shown her so far. She pushed the ugly thought out of her mind and said, "I know. Good night, Amaal."

Another pause, as though he was reluctant to leave her. But then he replied, "Good night, Deirdre," and disappeared down the hallway, Sasha at his heels. A moment later, the hallway light went out.

There was nothing else to do but go back to bed. As she crawled under the covers, she wondered if Amaal would ever forgive her for ruining their evening.

FOURTEEN

HE SLEPT FITFULLY, BUT AT LEAST HE DID sleep, dropping into the deepest of slumbers in the dark hours of the morning close to dawn. Because of this, he slept later than he had planned, waking to the gray, watery light of a winter morning.

Through his open door, he heard the sound of water running. After a puzzled moment, he realized the water noises must be coming from the bathroom down the hall. Deirdre clearly had risen before him and escaped into the shower.

Amaal did not wish to dwell on this notion for too long, for then he would find himself imagining what Deirdre's naked body might look like, glistening with water, and he was already frustrated enough after their abortive dinner the night before. However, she was out of her room, which meant he now had an opportunity to discover where she'd hidden the device. Not that he planned to do anything with it, of course, but he thought he would feel better if he at least knew where it was.

After slipping out from under the covers, he summoned a T-shirt and sweatpants to himself, along with a pair of socks, so that he was properly covered. It wasn't the risk of exposing himself to Deirdre that bothered him—the second he heard the bathroom door open, he would blink himself away downstairs—but rather that the house felt chillier than usual, probably because of the heavy snowfall from the day before. He sent some of his energy into the furnace in the basement, coaxing it to run a little hotter. That task accomplished, he went on into Deidre's room.

She'd already made the bed, smoothing the comforter and putting the decorative pillows that complemented it back in their respective places. Her hiking boots sat by the bench at the foot of the bed, but she hadn't laid out any clothes. Most likely, she'd brought them with her into the bathroom so there was no chance of him bumping into her before she was fully dressed.

Very well. He went at once to the closet and located her backpack and laptop case, but neither of them contained the item he sought. Neither was it tucked among the clothes she'd put away in the closet's built-in dresser, although he did find several balls of twigs in with her sweaters and sweatshirts. Why on earth had she done such a thing? True, the little balls had a pleasant scent of dried flowers, but....

Amaal made sure he put everything back where he'd found it, even as he fought a mounting sense of frustration. Where in the world could she have put that damnable device? He was running out of places where she could have hidden it. Perhaps in one of the nightstands? But no, those didn't even have drawers, were more glorified tables than anything else.

Just as he was closing the last drawer in the built-in storage in the closet, he heard the bathroom door open. Damn.

A blink, and Amaal was safely in the kitchen, although he kept mentally running through his search of Deirdre's things, making sure he hadn't left behind any telltales that someone had gone through her belongings. He didn't think so, but he couldn't be entirely positive, either.

Well, she had been in an unsettled state of mind the night before. He could only hope that she would attribute anything out of place to her own actions, and not because the person she shared the house with had gone pawing through her personal effects while she was in the shower. Perhaps it was foolish—her trust in him was already so fragile—but he needed to know where that damn thing had been hidden. Not because he truly thought Deirdre would switch it back on, but….

The best thing to do was look occupied. He got Sasha a bowl of fresh water and set out some food for her, then fetched some coffee beans from the pantry and began grinding them. Making coffee from scratch was a ritual he enjoyed, even though he had no interest in being anywhere near so hands-on when it came to actually cooking something.

He was just pouring the freshly ground Turkish roast into the coffeemaker when Deirdre appeared. Her hair was still a little damp, but otherwise she seemed ready to start her day, minimal makeup enhancing her lovely features, her slender form not shown to its best advantage in the baggy jeans and loose sweater she wore. Amaal did his best to avoid imagining what she would look like in djinn clothing, or even in something that fit properly. His need for her was already too strong.

She offered him a hesitant smile as she came into the kitchen. "That was quite the racket."

"Well, I noticed that you were already awake, so I didn't think the noise would trouble you too much."

"No, it was fine." Her gaze moved toward Sasha, who was happily wolfing down the last of her dog food. Still looking at the dog, she said, "I'm sorry about last night."

"Don't be." He busied himself with wiping out the coffee grinder, partly so she wouldn't think he was staring at her. "I did not think how it might have looked, as though I expected something of you. Truly, I only wished to give you a pleasant evening on your first night here."

"I know. I was being an idiot."

"No, you were not." Amaal set down the coffee grinder, then looked over at her. Now Deirdre returned his gaze, clearly ashamed of how she had behaved earlier. Guilt washed over him then, for searching her room. It was not a noble thing to have done, but he could not take his actions back now. "I cannot imagine everything you've had to endure since the world changed. I would say that I have been insensitive as well."

"Stop it," she said. She came closer, although not close enough that he could reach out and take her hand, as he desperately wanted to do. "I'm trying to apologize. I'm the one who should be apologizing. Not you. It's just...." Her words trailed off, and she crossed her arms, hugging herself in a defensive gesture she probably didn't even recognize for what it was. "It's just that it didn't really all come home to me until last night, when you talked about what the world would be like after the djinn were done remaking it. Before,

I was able to focus on my own little corner of that planet, but that's all. I only thought about staying alive, because I didn't know what else to do. But then when I realized everything we'd done, everything we'd created, would be gone, I...." Again she stopped, clearly fumbling for the right words. "I guess it was all too much. We screwed up a lot. I know that. But I still don't think we deserved what happened to us. We didn't deserve to have every last trace of us erased forever. And I hated you for being a djinn, and I hated myself for being attracted to you." After the flow of words ended, she offered him a lopsided smile. "Anyway, I guess that's what happened."

Did he dare take her in his arms? He wanted to, more than anything. And she looked so small and fragile and worried, standing there in front of him, that he decided he had to try. If she rebuffed him, he would immediately back away, but....

He stepped toward her. She didn't move. Another step, and then he was pulling her close to him, his hand running over her still-damp hair. Her body was tense, almost resisting him, but then she relaxed into his embrace, her arms encircling his waist.

She didn't weep, though. She only stood there, hanging on to him as though he was the only solid thing in her world. Perhaps, after so many weeks of solitude, in a way he was.

Her face lifted to him, aquamarine eyes wide, pleading. It seemed the most natural thing in the world for him to bend down and kiss her. Gently, though...very, very gently, as if she was a soap bubble he might break. She tasted faintly of toothpaste and smelled warm and sweet, thanks to that coconut-scented shampoo she used.

When he pulled away, she was the first to speak. "I don't usually blow hot and cold like this."

"That is good to know," he said gravely. "Then again, I doubt you have ever been in a situation like this one before."

She actually chuckled a bit. "Well, that's true enough. I suppose I needed a night to think things through. But now...."

"Now?" he prompted.

A smile. "I think now I'm willing to give it a try."

Deirdre seated herself at the kitchen table and let Amaal bring her a mug of coffee. He suggested pancakes and sausage—she asked for chicken sausage rather than pork, and he smiled at the request but did as she requested. And after they were done with the coffee, they had orange juice while they ate their pancakes and talked of what they might do that day. The snow lay almost impossibly thick on the ground, but Amaal said he'd spotted a snowmobile in the three-car garage, and this seemed the perfect time to try it out.

It all seemed so friendly and normal. Well, not precisely normal; Deirdre didn't know too many other men who could make big fluffy buttermilk pancakes and real maple syrup materialize out of thin air. But still, a great deal of the tension between them appeared to have melted away.

That she was the cause of the tension, she really couldn't deny. After tossing and turning for most of the night—and shedding a few more tears —she'd come to the realization that she could either continue to struggle against her current circumstances, or allow herself to accept her new reality. She didn't have the power to return the world to what it once had been, so she might as well try to live in what it had become. And that meant accepting what she felt for Amaal. Whether caring for him was a betrayal of her humanity or not, she couldn't say. If she looked only at him, at Amaal the man, she saw someone who had treated her kindly, who had shown her tenderness, caring, affection, despite her early treatment of him. All things being equal, she could say without batting an eye that he was certainly a more admirable person than any of the guys she'd ever dated.

Not that they were actually dating. She really

didn't know how to describe their relationship. About all she did know was that if she'd had the chance to bring Amaal home to meet her mother, he would have gotten a warm reception.

Well, except for that long hair of his. Her mother had never been a fan of that sort of thing, just as she'd had a few choice words about the tattoos and earrings of this one artist Deirdre had dated for a few months during her freshman year of college when she was feeling rebellious.

Deirdre guessed that Amaal didn't wear his hair long to annoy his parents or because he thought a djinn should look a certain way. He wore it long because it suited him, and that was the end of the argument.

"Have you ever driven a snowmobile?" she asked as she snagged the last of the sausages.

He looked resigned at that obvious theft, but then said, "No. Have you?"

"Oh, yes—I went snowmobiling on my last trip to Aspen."

"Truly?" he asked, obviously surprised.

"Of course not," she said with a grin. Relenting, she cut the sausage in two pieces and offered him the slightly larger half. He accepted it with a smile as she added, "I've never even been to Colorado."

"Ah, it was a joke."

"Yes."

He chewed his piece of sausage thoughtfully for a moment, then said, "I have driven cars and motorcycles. I do not think a snowmobile will be too difficult to manage."

"Why would a djinn drive a car or a motorcycle?" Deirdre asked, genuinely curious. It seemed sort of silly for them to use human modes of transportation when they could just blink themselves anyplace they wanted.

"Why not?"

"Because you don't need to."

"Ah, that is true enough. But you see, we djinn would come to this world for the experiences, whether those included consuming fine food and wine, or driving fast cars, or climbing the Himalayas. And that is why I know how to drive a car, ride a motorcycle. Because I wanted to try it."

Deirdre supposed his explanation made some sense. At the same time, she couldn't quite understand a race that was entirely okay with coming here to Earth to eat human food and drive human cars, and yet showed no compunction about wiping out the very people who had created that delicious food and designed those fast cars. One would have thought the djinn would have some respect, some admiration for human artists and creators and inventors. Apparently not, though.

Anyway, Amaal wasn't one of the killer djinn.

He'd told her so, and she had to believe him. If he'd been that bloodthirsty, she doubted he could be so tender, so compassionate toward her, and she doubted he would have been as solicitous of Sasha's needs, either. In fact, even as Deirdre watched, he bent down and fed the dog the last bite of his sausage.

No, Amaal definitely wasn't a killer. So how could she look on him as anything except a friend...and probably soon a lover?

Pushing that thought aside, she said, "We'll need some better gear if we're going snowmobiling, though. It's cold out there."

He smiled at her. "You know that isn't a problem for me."

Of course it wasn't. He could snap his fingers and summon them boots, gloves, down-filled jumpsuits, whatever they needed.

"All right," she said. "Let's do this."

Deirdre had been right about one thing—it was bitterly cold out here, even in the insulated jumpsuits they both wore. Amaal's was dark green and hers was pale blue, bringing out the color of her eyes. Their breath came in little white puffs as he got the snowmobile out of the garage, and even beneath the knitted cap that covered his head,

Amaal could feel the tips of his ears getting colder and colder, since he'd pulled his hair back with a leather thong to keep it from whipping in his face. One might have thought that, as a fire elemental, he'd be impervious to cold. Unfortunately, his fiery nature only seemed to make him more sensitive to chilly temperatures.

Why on earth couldn't the elders have sent him to Hawaii, or Fiji? Or, if they had some obscure reason for keeping him in this part of the world, at least Baja or Cozumel?

Oh, well. If he had to be trapped in this frozen hell, at least he was here with Deirdre. And he might as well find a way to have some fun with it. A niggling little voice inside worried that the snowmobiles might be too conspicuous, that they might be attracting too much attention, but Amaal pushed it aside. Neither he nor Deirdre had done much to hide their activities; if no one had noticed so far, he doubted they ever would. Surely if the elders had caught the slightest wind of what he was up to here, of how he had brought a human who was not his Chosen to live with him, they would have appeared immediately and told him that such behavior could not continue.

Resolutely ignoring those misgivings, Amaal climbed on the snowmobile and Deirdre got on behind him, arms wrapped around his waist. As they'd come down to the garage, he'd asked her if she wanted him to summon her a snowmobile of her own, but she'd declined, had said she thought it would be safer if she rode behind him, since she really wouldn't know what she was doing if she tried to drive one by herself. He hadn't pushed the matter, because of course he far preferred this arrangement, with her slender body pressed up against his, her arms clinging to his waist.

In fact, he could almost view it as a kind of foreplay.

The clouds of the day before had disappeared, and the sky was a clear, deep blue, hard and bright as sapphire. With the sun shining so brightly, and no sign of another storm, Amaal wondered how long all this snow would last. If they had another warm spell like the one this region had enjoyed only a few weeks ago, Amaal guessed that a good deal of it would melt, except for the spots shaded by trees and overhangs.

But the snow was here now, and it beckoned to him, urging him out and away from the house. He caught a glimpse of Sasha sitting on the window seat and looking longingly out at them as he turned the snowmobile toward more open ground. The poor dog wanted to get out and run, but she wasn't quite up to that sort of activity at the moment, thanks to her injured leg. Deirdre had said the dog was doing fine, but she still wouldn't be in any shape for running in the snow for a while yet.

Just past the house, the trees thinned somewhat, and that was where he guided the snowmobile, gaining speed as he grew more confident of their course. Deirdre's arms tightened around him further, and he wanted to throw back his head and laugh out loud for the sheer joy of it. Yes, it had been a very long time since he'd felt this way.

Or…had he ever *truly* felt this happy? Perhaps it was only that the woman who held onto him so tightly had all but told him outright that she was ready to accept him for what he was, that she wanted to move on to the next step in their relationship. No, it was more than merely the anticipation of what might come next. Oh, he was relieved beyond measure that it seemed they would no longer have any scenes like the one that had passed between them the night before, but he also realized he could be content here, snow and all. This world was beginning to feel like the place he was meant to be, and he no longer felt so alien in it.

They crested a small rise and dropped a foot or so to the ground below. Deirdre let out a little shriek, but she didn't tell him to slow down or to be careful. He appreciated her restraint; he knew what he was doing, and he was also glad that she seemed to realize he would never do anything to hurt her or put her in jeopardy.

How could he, when he considered her more precious than anything else in his world?

That realization made him tense suddenly, although he never took his attention away from the snowy landscape before them, or the controls of the vehicle they now rode. Of course he enjoyed Deirdre's company, and even now he thrilled at the memory of her kisses, but were those simple pleasures enough to make her more important than anything or anyone else?

Apparently so. He certainly could never remember feeling this way about a woman of his own kind.

They rode for at least an hour, sometimes slowing so they could take in the many breathtaking snowy vistas around them, sometimes speeding up so Amaal could feel the power of the snowmobile that carried them, could let it take them plunging across mountain meadows, snow flying all around them in a mighty wake as they left deep tracks in the heavy snow.

At last, though, he turned them toward home, the snowmobile sounding almost weary as it chugged up the hill toward the house. They got to the garage, and he extended a hand, using his powers to lift the garage door. Deirdre got off the snowmobile and removed her goggles, then brushed at the snow that had accumulated on the sleeves and legs of her jumpsuit.

"That was amazing," she said. "Thank you."

"It's nothing," Amaal replied, absurdly pleased by her response to their ride. "I was glad to be able to take you out riding. It is good to be able to get some fresh air after being trapped inside during a storm."

She gave him a questioning look. "Do you prefer being outdoors?"

That was a good question. Certainly while he was occupying that penthouse in downtown Los Angeles, he hadn't thought much about missing being outside. Then again, he'd still gone out on the deck and used the pool, had lain in the bright sunshine and soaked up the sun's rays like the creature of fire he was. "I am not sure 'prefer' is the correct word," he said. "It is more that I like to have the opportunity to go out when the mood takes me. Being kept inside because of the weather is a bit too much like the life I led in the djinn otherworld, where the conditions were quite harsh, and we tended to stay inside our palaces."

"You didn't like it there?"

Quite the understatement. "No, I did not. I doubt I could name a single one of my race who would say that life in the place of our exile was preferable to an existence here on Earth. But come," he went on, taking her by the hand, "we should go inside. The sun is beginning to slip down the other side of the mountain, and it is only going to get colder."

Deirdre didn't appear inclined to argue with this assessment, for she nodded and allowed him to lead her inside the house. The warm air that greeted them as they came into the entry was a welcome relief from the chill winds that blew across the snow. At once Deirdre pulled off her gloves and unwound the scarf from around her throat, then unzipped the neck of her jumpsuit.

"I guess I'd better get out of this thing," she said. "It feels boiling hot in here compared to outside, but I know that's probably just my fingers and toes unthawing."

"That is a good idea." On an impulse, he added, "And I thought of what we should have for our *après ski* meal, so to speak. Shall we pretend we're in Switzerland and have fondue?"

Her eyes lit up, but then she seemed to consider and said, "That sounds like fun, but will it be enough for dinner?"

"Oh, I think so," Amaal replied, somewhat amused. Clearly, Deirdre did not know all that much about fondue. "We will have bread and vegetables and cheese, and meat and oil, and then for dessert, strawberries and pound cake dipped in melted chocolate."

"Ah, okay. I didn't realize it was so involved."

"Well, perhaps it would be if I had to create everything from scratch. As it is—" He stopped there, and shrugged. "You know it is not so very much work for me."

"True." She glanced up the low flight of stairs that separated the entryway from the main level of the house. Sasha sat there, tail wagging furiously now that they were home. She could manage the stairs on her own, but she preferred to wait for them to come up and join her, and save her energy for the climb to the bedrooms upstairs when they retired for the night. "And I'm sure Sasha will be more than happy to beg little bits of meat from us."

"Along with bites of bread and cheese, I have no doubt."

Deirdre flashed him a smile. "You're probably right. But I need to go change before I die of heat prostration."

"We can't have that," he said, giving her an answering smile. "I have provided a little surprise for you. I hope you don't mind."

"'A surprise'?" she echoed, looking puzzled.

"You'll see when you go to your room. I think you will like it."

She paused for a moment, then came over and kissed him on the cheek. "I'm sure I will. And I'm looking forward to our fondue."

Then she was hurrying up the stairs, stopping

briefly to bend down and ruffle Sasha's ears before she continued on her way.

The warmth of her kiss still lingered on his skin. Amaal put a hand to his cheek, touching the place where her lips had brushed against him.

He hoped she would like what he had left for her.

FIFTEEN

A SURPRISE. AMAAL HAD SAID HE'D GOTTEN her a surprise. In general, Deirdre had never been a fan of surprises, just because she'd suffered a nasty one when her father walked out all those years ago, but she doubted that was the sort of surprise Amaal was referring to.

When she got to her room and went inside, nothing looked materially different. She glanced around, but all seemed to be in order. Okay, then.

She unzipped her insulated jumpsuit the rest of the way and let it fall to the floor. Underneath, she wore only a T-shirt and a pair of yoga pants, mostly because nothing else would fit under the slim-fitting protective garment. The T-shirt and yoga pants would need to go in the hamper, since she'd perspired underneath the jumpsuit, despite how cold it was outside.

Now stripped down to her underthings, she went to the closet to get herself something clean to wear. But when she opened the closet door, at first she couldn't believe what she was seeing.

Every rack was now full, where this morning when she'd gotten dressed, her pitiful little wardrobe hadn't been enough to fill even half of one. Absent-mindedly, she stuffed her dirty clothes in the hamper next to the door and then went further into the closet, trying to absorb everything she saw. Sweaters and jackets and shirts and even a few dresses off to one side. Shoes in the built-in shelves—flats and boots and pretty sandals for when warm weather arrived, even though right now those summer days felt impossibly far away.

Everything in the closet looked expensive and brand new, but these garments were definitely human clothes. Amaal wasn't trying to get her to dress like a djinn woman; he clearly only wanted her wear things that were more flattering than the clothes she'd brought with her. Deirdre couldn't really argue with that, since she always packed her slouchiest and most casual clothing when she went to work at the research station on weekends. How could she have known she was going to get stuck wearing that stuff all the way through the apocalypse and beyond?

Her eye went to a wrap sweater in a pale

greenish blue, almost the color of her eyes. It looked like it would work for their fondue date. In one of the drawers, she found a lacy camisole to wear under it. Since she wasn't going outside, flats would do.

And in another drawer she found jewelry, simple, elegant pieces that still had to have cost a fortune. She slid on an aquamarine ring set in white gold and a pendant to match, along with a pair of white gold hoop earrings, then couldn't quite resist preening in front of the mirror set on the wall above the built-in dresser. After all, she'd never worn anything like this before in her life, could never have afforded to.

However, her hair was a mess, and she needed to put on a little makeup. When she went in the bathroom, she was halfway hoping that Amaal might have provided more than the lip gloss and mascara she'd brought with her. Unfortunately, it seemed he didn't have the same expertise with women's cosmetics that he did with clothing, because all that stared back at her was the same tube of Cover Girl 24-Hour mascara and the same container of Burt's Bees gloss she'd been nursing along the past few months, hoping to make it last as long as possible.

Oh, well.

She brushed her hair and tidied it as best she could, then put on another coat of mascara and some fresh lip gloss. At least the snowmobile ride had brought some color to her cheeks, and the shadows under her eyes from her restless night were more or less invisible. It would have to do.

As Deirdre headed out of her room and back down the stairs, she wondered why she should care so much about how she looked. Because this was the night when she and Amaal would at last become intimate?

You don't know that for sure, she told herself. *You thought the same thing last night, and then you had a total meltdown. Just let whatever's going to happen, happen.*

True enough, she supposed. She made herself take a couple of deep breaths, trying to be as relaxed as possible.

Of course, that resolution vanished into thin air when she came into the living room and got an eyeful of Amaal. Although he hadn't given her any djinn clothing to wear, it seemed that he'd finally grown tired of sweaters and jeans for himself, since he was clad in an open robe in a dark wine color edged in gold, with black billowy trousers and thick gold cuffs on both wrists.

"You look absolutely beautiful," he said warmly, coming toward her so he could take her by the hand and lead her back toward the fire-place. She saw that he'd set out three separate stainless steel fondue pots on the coffee table, along with bowls of various items for dipping—cubes of bread and chunks of vegetables for the cheese, thinly sliced meat for the oil, luscious-looking strawberries for the chocolate. To one side were several plates, along with a bottle of wine and a pair of glasses with impressively large bowls.

"You're looking pretty magnificent yourself," Deirdre replied. "Now I feel positively under-dressed."

"You shouldn't," Amaal told her. "I've returned to wearing these clothes because they are what I am used to, and far more comfortable than human clothing. But I would not expect you to dress as a djinn."

"When it's warmer, I might give it a try." Those baggy trousers did look comfortable. Of course a woman couldn't wear one of those open robes, but.... Looking at the flow of that sump-tuous silk, Deirdre was feeling a bit of fabric envy.

"Something else to look forward to." He smiled, then indicated that she should sit on the rug next to the coffee table, rather than the couch. "We will eat the way my people do, if you don't mind. There won't be nearly as much bending over."

"That sounds like fun." She sat down on the floor, glad for the thick rug that protected her from the hardwood beneath—and also for the warmth from the fire which blazed in the hearth, since she could feel a few drafts making their way in here.

Amaal followed suit, gracefully lowering himself to the floor so that he sat next to her. He reached for the bottle of wine, which he must have already opened to aerate, since he poured wine for them right away instead of pausing to extricate the cork.

"To an afternoon in the sun," he said, raising his glass in a toast.

"To warmer weather ahead," she replied, and clinked her glass against his.

"A good ways ahead, I fear. But I agree with the sentiment."

They both drank. Deirdre hadn't looked at the label on the wine bottle, and she certainly didn't know enough to begin to guess what was in her glass, but it was light for a red wine, a clear garnet color when held up against the fireplace. The taste, too, was light, without some of the bitterness she'd experienced in other red wines.

"This is good," she commented as she set her glass down on a coaster.

"I hoped you would like it. A pinot noir from Washington State—they grow very good pinot grapes up there. Or rather," he added with a tinge of sadness, "they used to."

Even though she knew that such a topic could be fraught, she had to ask. "What's going to happen to the vineyards, to all the crops? Are they just going to die away?"

"Not all of them," Amaal said. "For of course we djinn need to eat, just as humans do. Some fields will be allowed to go fallow, for that only makes the earth richer for future plantings, but I am sure that many of the vines will be tended and nurtured, for we djinn like our wine."

"I hadn't noticed," Deirdre remarked, then took another sip of her pinot noir.

"I believe you are teasing me."

"Possibly."

He held up his glass, studying the color of the wine within. "There is a certain alchemy in wine-making, a special magic of its own. A poetry of sun and earth and sky. We would never let such treasures go to waste."

Those words, spoken by any of the men Deirdre had known, would have probably sounded pretentious. But on Amaal's lips, they only seemed to be the truth, a truth she'd never considered before now but which seemed so obvious, she wondered why she'd overlooked it before.

"Well, that's good to know," she said. "Not that I was ever into wine, but I think I'd like to learn."

His deep blue eyes met hers. "I think I would like to teach you."

A shiver went through her that didn't have

much to do with wine tasting. What else could she learn from him, this being—this man—who must have already lived many human lifetimes and yet looked only a few years older than she?

Not sure how to respond, she forced a chuckle and said, "I guess right now you can teach me about fondue. Is there an order to eat these in?"

"I would leave the strawberries and the cake until last," Amaal replied. A smile still played around his lips, but he appeared slightly taken aback, as if he had hoped their conversation might have gone in other channels. "Otherwise, it is fine to go back and forth between the bread and meat and vegetables."

"Good." Deirdre was also aware of a moment lost, but she told herself it was for the best. Even though having him this near made her pulse race and her entire body feel tingly and alive, she had a feeling that she'd be more relaxed about falling into his arms after she'd had a glass of wine. Or two or three.

She picked up one of the metal skewers and speared a cube of bread, then dipped it in the cheese. The mixture was hot and tangy—some type of white cheeses blended together, although she wasn't sure what kind. It didn't taste exactly like Swiss, but it was good, as was the piece of cauliflower she dipped in next.

"You like it?"

"It's wonderful," Deirdre said, then reached for a napkin so she could dab some of the drippy cheese off her bottom lip. "Aren't you going to have any?"

"Of course," he replied. "But I wanted to see your reaction to it first."

Not quite sure what to make of that, she managed a small smile, then decided to try some of the meat and oil. It, too, was delicious, the hot oil cooking the thin strip of beef and rendering it savory and extremely tender.

So much for avoiding red meat, but she'd broken that rule several times already.

As she ate, Amaal had several pieces of bread and cheese, then a piece of bell pepper. He switched over to the meat next, while Deirdre took several large swallows of the pinot noir. Yes, that was better. She could feel herself beginning to relax…although she still experienced a little quiver of nerves in the pit of her stomach every time she looked over at Amaal's exposed torso. So many muscles….

"I guess you've had fondue before," she commented as she went back for some more bread and cheese.

"Yes, in Switzerland, and here as well. You had entire restaurants devoted to it, after all."

She supposed they had existed, back in the world before, although fondue restaurants were the sorts of place that hadn't exactly been on her radar. Dinner out with friends had usually involved pizza, since it was cheap, and on dates she'd gone to burger places or out for Chinese or Italian food, again because it generally didn't break the bank. A few of her girlfriends had dated guys with money, and so Deirdre occasionally got treated to stories about steak and lobster consumed at expensive hillside restaurants, but she'd never experienced anything like that.

Well, until now. She supposed that consuming fondue with a gorgeous djinn in a million-dollar getaway in Running Springs might qualify as a fancy dinner.

Amaal refilled both their glasses. Was he, too, trying to work himself up to seducing her? No, that was ridiculous. He'd already made it pretty clear that the only reason he'd been holding back was her own reticence. Also, she'd noticed that wine didn't seem to affect him as much as it did her. Deirdre reminded herself not to even try to keep up, because she was certain to make herself extremely drunk. Tipsy was one thing—tipsy was fun—but the few times she'd gotten downright drunk, she'd basically passed out and woken up the next morning with a raging headache and a vow never to do that again.

"Right," she said. "I forgot about those fondue places, since I'd never eaten at one. I don't think there were any out where I lived, though. My area was pretty working-class."

He was quiet then for a moment, watching her as she lifted her wine glass to her lips and took another sip. "Was it very difficult for you?"

"Not having fondue?"

"That is not what I meant."

Deirdre set down her glass and considered his question. She'd known exactly what he was asking. "I don't know. It was probably harder on my brother, since he was older. He got stuck watching me after school or during vacations—my mother couldn't really afford to pay someone to babysit. She was the one it was hardest for, though. She worked fifty, sixty hours a week sometimes. I didn't get to see her very much. About all I could do was try to stay out of trouble and get good grades so I could go to college and have a career of my own."

Amaal didn't say anything at first. Again he was watching her carefully, although Deirdre didn't know what he expected to see. Was it difficult for him to comprehend the struggles of ordinary humans when, as a djinn, he could have anything he wanted with the snap of a finger?

When he spoke, the question he asked was not one she had been expecting.

"You had no wish to get married?"

"I—" She floundered for a second, then frowned at him. "Why would you ask that?"

"I was just curious. You are twenty-four, yes?"

Deirdre nodded.

"It seemed to me that many of your kind began thinking of marriage around that time, even if they didn't actually make a commitment to such an arrangement until a few years later. You have spoken of no one close to you, only of your family. There was no one in your life?"

Tristan's face flashed into her mind then, smiling Tristan who made her feel as though she was the only woman in the world…right up until the moment when he decided he didn't want her anymore. Voice hard, Deirdre said, "I was seeing someone for a while. It didn't work out. I guess I was just trying to be focused on school—I was in my final year—when everything…well, when it all ended."

"If it didn't work out, then it must have been his fault."

That was Deirdre's opinion as well, but she found herself protesting, "I don't know. Sometimes things just don't work, for whatever reason."

"Hmm." Amaal had his fingers resting on the base of his wine glass, but he didn't seem in any hurry to pick it up. "I am inclined to believe, based on my time with you, that it had to be a fault on his end. No man in his right mind would wish to end a relationship with you."

Hot blood rushed to her cheeks. "Amaal—"

She didn't get any further than that, because he abandoned his wine glass and moved closer to her, pressed his lips against hers. Such warm, strong lips, tasting of wine. It was much better to let herself get lost in that kiss, to let the world spin around her, rather than think about Tristan anymore...or anyone else. In that moment, there was no one else, never had been.

Amaal pushed a strand of hair away from her face. "You are so beautiful, so perfect. Surely the hand of God must have guided me to you."

It was strange, because usually when someone mentioned God, Deirdre got uncomfortable, worried that she was about to get proselytized or something. But when Amaal spoke of God, he did so in an oddly personal way, as if he somehow knew that he wasn't referring to some impersonal deity, but a being who had true influence over his life.

"I don't know about God," Deirdre murmured. "But I am happy we were able to find one another."

"As am I."

He kissed her again, strong arms holding her close, and suddenly they were lying on the rug in front of the carpet, his weight on top of her as he kissed her over and over and her body thrilled at his caresses. She could feel his arousal, too, and for some reason it didn't worry or frighten her. No, she was glad to know how much he wanted her, because she wanted him just as badly. His hands were moving under her sweater, warm against her bare skin, moving upward, going to close on her breasts....

And then there was a terrible crash of a noise, and both Deirdre and Amaal sat upright, shocked for the moment out of their sensual daze. She didn't have to look far to see the source of the sound—Sasha, who'd been lurking nearby and watched every morsel they'd put in their mouths, had apparently decided to take advantage of their distraction and make a run for the bowl of meat they'd left sitting on the table. In the process, she'd also knocked over the fondue pot of hot oil, which had splashed everywhere, although not, fortunately on the dog or either Deirdre or Amaal.

Gathering herself, Deirdre got to her feet, followed by Amaal, whose brow was furrowed in a fearsome frown. "That dog," he growled, but she put a hand on his arm.

"Don't," she said. "The poor thing is scared out of her wits."

It was true—obviously startled by the noise, Sasha had immediately backed away from the coffee table and was now hunkered down a few feet away, shaking. Deirdre, concerned that the dog might have harmed her leg further in her hasty flight from the scene of the crime, knelt down next to her and petted her on the head, then reached for Sasha's injured hind leg to make sure it hadn't suffered any additional trauma. Everything seemed all right, luckily.

Standing next to the coffee table, Amaal cursed under his breath. Or at least, Deirdre thought it had to be cursing, although she couldn't understand the words he used. Then he waved his hand, and the mess disappeared, right down to the oil stains on the sofa.

Yes, having a djinn around could be handy... especially if he wasn't trying to kill you.

"She is unhurt?" he asked, coming toward Deirdre.

"As far as I can tell," she replied, getting back to her feet. "I think she just scared herself. I suppose all that meat just sitting there was too much of a temptation."

"Apparently." He reached out and took her by the hand. "I would like to take you upstairs so we might finish what we started."

Deirdre swallowed. It was one thing to start getting down and dirty in the heat of the moment, but Sasha's little escapade had been like having a bucket of cold water dumped on her head. However, Deirdre also knew she'd wanted to be with Amaal. Her body still thrummed with need, hadn't apparently gotten the memo that her brain had disengaged.

For now, it was probably better to let her body take over for a while. Her brain always seemed to get her in trouble. "That sounds like a good idea."

His deep blue eyes warmed with desire, and he took both her hands in his. However, rather than take her up the stairs, he blinked them away into his bedroom. Deirdre gasped, even though of course she'd traveled this way before, when he brought her and Sasha here to his house.

"I didn't want to waste a moment," he said.

Then his arms were going around her, lifting her from the ground. She had a brief impression of a large room with candles that flickered from the top of the dresser and the nightstand, and a fire going in the double-sided hearth on the other side of the space, and that was all she had time for, because now she was on the bed, and Amaal was once again on top of her, kissing her down her throat to the low opening of her wrap sweater. A gasp escaped her lips, and she writhed against him, reveling in the strength of his body even as she wished they didn't have so many clothes separating them.

Obviously, he had the same idea, because he undid the tie of her sweater and pulled it away from her body, followed by the camisole she wore underneath, then unzipped her jeans. Her shoes, she realized, must have fallen off her feet when Amaal lifted her from the ground, because she was now barefoot. Good—that made it easier for her to wriggle out of her pants, which ended up on the floor with her sweater and camisole. Now she lay before him in only her bra and panties. His eyes gleamed with reflected reddish light from the fire as he ran his hands over her, fingers trailing against the bare skin of her stomach.

"Deirdre," he whispered. "My Deirdre."

Then he bent and kissed her again, mouth moving from her mouth along the curve of her throat, and then to her breast. He undid the front hook of her bra and removed it all in one smooth motion, and in the next moment his tongue swept over her nipple and she gasped, body coming alive more than ever at the sensation.

His hands tugged at her panties, pulling them down. She kicked them off to the side, and then he was touching her as he suckled on her breast, fingers slipping into her, stroking. This time it wasn't a gasp that left her lips, but a cry of primal need. She clung to him, let him pleasure her, until the orgasm came out of nowhere and hit her with the force of a hurricane.

Even as she lay against the pillows and felt the ripples of her climax flood through her body, Amaal sat up and pulled off the heavy silk robe he wore, followed by his trousers. She'd already thought him perfect, but now, his body sculpted by firelight and candlelight, she realized she'd never seen a man this exquisite before.

Her fingers reached for him, closed on his shaft, hard and heavy in her hand. He moaned, moving closer to her, so close, his mouth touching hers again, strong, insistent, his tongue meeting hers, still tasting of wine.

Deirdre wanted to taste *him,* though. She pushed him down onto the pillows and bent so she could take him in her mouth, tongue moving over the silky softness of his flesh, the richness of his salty flavor better than she'd imagined.

He groaned, hips moving in concert with the movement of her tongue, taking him deeper into her mouth, deeper than she ever had with anyone else. A certain tension in his body, a shift in his rhythm, and she knew he was going to come. Good. She wanted him to fill her mouth, to know that she'd had this effect on him.

His hips bucked up off the bed, and the heat of his seed flowed over her tongue, rich and salty. She moaned along with him, kept licking him until he was done shuddering. Then she sat up and wiped her mouth, and moved to lie next to him, her body snugged against his from chest to hip.

A long moment, and then he said, "I did not expect you to do that."

"I wanted to." And she had. She'd always enjoyed oral, and refused to be ashamed about it. Besides, he had tasted so good, better than anyone else she'd ever been with.

"You should have some of this." He sat up, but gently, one arm curving around her waist so that she moved with him. In his hand appeared a wine glass filled with red wine. He gave it to her, and she took it from him gratefully and drank, glad to have something to wet her throat.

"Thank you," she said, then handed it to him so he might have a sip as well.

More than a sip—a long swallow, followed by another. He said quietly, "You need have no fear of becoming with child. We djinn can control when that happens, and now is certainly not the time."

She'd been so overwhelmed by him, she hadn't even stopped to think about birth control. The biology student in her wanted to ask how it was possible for the djinn to suppress their fertility at will, but she put that question aside for later. "Well, that's good to know."

Amaal set the wine glass down on the night-stand next to him and turned back toward her. Even in the firelight, Deirdre could see the glint in his eyes. "I hope you don't think we're finished."

And he pushed her down into the pillows, his mouth leaving kisses from her stomach down to her inner thighs…and then moving closer, his tongue touching her, slow, lingering. She cried out and held on to him, his long hair slipping over her fingers. It was good. Better than good. Better than the best —

The orgasm exploded through her, all heat and honey and delicious tingles that made her limbs so weak, she wasn't sure whether she'd ever be able to stand upright again. Not to worry, since now Amaal was on top of her, pressing her down into the mattress. One thrust, and he was inside, moving in and out of her, filling her so wonderfully that Deirdre could only cling to him and move with his rhythm, every push and pull magnifying the effects of her climax from only moments before, those wonderful ebbs and flows bringing her closer and closer and….

She couldn't tell which one of them came first. Amaal groaned, and she gasped, and they were both hanging on to the other as spirals of ecstasy bound them together, breathing as one, moving as one, until they slowly came back to themselves, becoming two people once more.

Very slowly, Amaal slid out of her, then held her close, his lips pressed against her forehead. Deirdre could feel the heavy beat of his heart, faster than she'd expected, but gradually slowing down. His skin was warm and damp, and she never wanted to let go, even as her mind began to wake up and she realized what she had done.

Did I just have sex with a djinn?

No, her mind corrected her. *You and a djinn just made love.*

Love. Yes, that was what this felt like, this warm and happy and contented feeling, this sense that the only place in the world she belonged was his arms.

And that scared the living hell out of her.

SIXTEEN

THEY SLEPT. AT SOME POINT IN THE NIGHT, Sasha had must have decided she was no longer in the doghouse, so to speak, and had come up to sleep in the bed he'd placed up against one wall for her, but Amaal had slumbered so deeply, he hadn't heard her at all.

At last morning light began to filter its way through the bedroom's slightly sheer curtains. He stirred and looked over at the pillow next to him. Deirdre still slept, her long hair scattered across her shoulders like a remembrance of summer sunshine, with its warm brown tints highlighted in streaks of pale gold.

This was a moment he had been looking forward to for quite some time—to awaken in his bed, and to have Deirdre there next to him. He stared down at her for a long moment, remembering the sweetness of her flesh, the bold way she'd taken him in her mouth with no coaxing. Indeed, his body shuddered slightly now, just recalling how skillful she had been. He had hoped that making love to her would be magnificent, but he hadn't expected it to be quite as amazing as the reality proved to be.

She moved then, eyes opening to meet his. Her sweet mouth curved into a lazy smile. "Morning. What time is it?"

"What does it matter?" he inquired, his tone teasing. "Do you have someplace to go?"

The smile transformed into a serious glance. "No. I'm right where I want to be."

That was what he wanted to hear. Because now that he had had her, Amaal couldn't imagine a morning where she wouldn't wake up next to him. She already felt more real to him than anyone else he'd ever known. "As am I. So I don't see what difference the hour makes."

Deirdre sat up, her hair slipping over her shoulders. It partially concealed the sensual curve of her full breasts...very partially. A hint of color touched her cheeks, and she grasped the sheet and pulled it up to cover herself. "Maybe not to you or me, but in case you haven't noticed, our dog is pretty particular about her schedule. I'm sure she needs to go out, and wants her breakfast."

Her gaze moved toward the door where Sasha

sat, tail beating against the floor in a hopeful way. The dog's expression was so pleading, Amaal couldn't help but laugh. "I think you're right. I had no idea we would have such a tyrant under our roof when we adopted her."

"Comes with the territory," Deirdre said. "At least, that's what I saw with my friend's dogs, even though I never had one of my own."

"Until now."

"Until now." She was smiling a little, but the intensity of her gaze told him how much this mattered to her as well—waking up beside him, sharing their morning, sharing their affection for this animal who had entered their lives. "Do you suppose you could conjure me something to wear? I don't have much that's fit for lounging around the house."

As much as he would have liked to see her in lacy lingerie, that probably wouldn't have been very practical. This was a fine enough house in its way, but it was still rather drafty. "Of course," he said, and in the next moment, a pair of underwear and some loose knit pants and a T-shirt, along with a fleece robe, had appeared at the foot of the bed.

"You're amazing."

"I am a djinn. These sorts of things come easily enough."

"I suppose. But still."

With a shake of her head, she got out from under the covers and got dressed, then finger-combed her hair and fluffed it out over her shoulders. Since it appeared that any further intimacies would have to wait, Amaal got out of bed as well and put on the equivalent of what Deirdre was wearing, only with flannel pajama bottoms instead of the yoga pants she wore.

As soon as they were both clothed, Sasha gave a happy little yip, then turned and made her laborious way down the stairs. The two of them followed her, with Deirdre reaching out to take Amaal's hand as they descended to the first floor. Just the touch of her fingers against his was enough to send a little thrill through him. Perhaps that was her way of saying that she, too, had wanted to make love again. Well, possibly after breakfast. The shower in the master bedroom was quite large, and presented all sorts of interesting possibilities.

Pleased by this prospect, he went into the kitchen and fetched some dog food for Sasha, and also freshened the water in her bowl. At the same time, Deirdre was getting out the bag of coffee beans, which she set on the counter by the grinder.

"You'd better do it," she said with a slightly apologetic smile. "I've never used one of these things before."

"It's fairly simple." He poured the proper measure of beans into the grinder and added, "But it is quite loud."

Deirdre said, "I know," then backed away, wincing a bit as he turned the device on. Luckily, this procedure only took about thirty seconds, after which time he took the freshly ground coffee and put it in the coffeemaker. A wave of his hand, and the carafe was filled with water, which he poured in as well.

"Didn't want to walk three feet to the sink?" Deirdre asked with a grin.

"I see nothing wrong with saving time when it suits me," he replied.

"I guess not." She leaned against the counter. "What's on the agenda for today?"

"Whatever you would like. I saw some skis stored in the garage."

At once she shook her head. "No, I think I'll pass. Snowmobiling was one thing, but I've always been scared of skiing. I've made it this far in life without breaking any bones, and I don't really want to start now."

Wise of her, he supposed. "Well, with all this snow around, our options are somewhat limited." He'd already peeked out the kitchen window and had seen that the ground was still blanketed in white, although today promised to be warmer. Despite that, he did not think conditions were good for going hiking or other similar outdoor pursuits.

"Sounds like it's time for Netflix and chill," Deirdre remarked, and Amaal lifted an eyebrow.

"What a curious expression."

She laughed, and came over and kissed him, warm and full, on the lips. "It just means hanging around the house and watching TV…and maybe indulging in a few extracurricular activities between episodes, if you know what I mean."

Oh, he knew exactly what she meant. Her kiss had already aroused him, and now the thought of being lazy and indulgent, of spending half the day making love…if not more than half the day… sounded like an excellent idea. "You will have to help me choose the television shows."

"I think I can manage that. As long you're able to conjure what I ask for as easily as you do everything else."

"It will not be a problem."

She smiled at him, a small, almost wicked smile, one that brought out a flash of a dimple in her cheek. Amaal thought he liked this side of her very much. Up until last night, she had kept some part of her locked away, guarded, and now he was beginning to see how she might be when not struggling with her feelings for him, or worried about her future.

Well, she had nothing to worry about now.

He would keep her safe, and they would stay here and explore all the intricacies of lovemaking, and then....

And then...what? Amaal did not particularly wish for his mind to go in that direction, not when he was feeling so contented, not when Deirdre was smiling at him like that, and yet he could not quite prevent himself from wondering precisely what he intended to do as the days and weeks stretched into months...if his and Deirdre's relationship even continued for that span of time. His liaisons with djinn women had never lasted particularly long, for they had always been based on purely physical attraction and nothing more. He had enjoyed sleeping with those women, but he was not sure whether he had ever particularly *liked* any of them.

He thought he liked Deirdre, liked her very much. Even now, as he watched her bend down and scratch behind Sasha's ears, and then gravely run her fingers over the dog's hind leg, assessing the improvement in her injury, Amaal experienced another of those odd rushes of tenderness. Yes, he wanted to take Deirdre upstairs and make love to her again, or possibly sink down with her in front of the fire once more and explore her luscious body then and there...once the dog was safely distracted by a bone.

At the same time, though, he wanted to watch

over this young woman he had found, make sure that she was kept safe from all harm. He wanted to know that she would never suffer hurt again, would never sob into his arms as she had the day before, buried in the world's sorrows. She should be bright and joyous, laughing the way she had as they rode a snowmobile across the pristine, snow-covered landscape. Everything about her should be free of the pain she'd carried for so long.

Curious. He had never felt this way about anyone before.

Perhaps this was more than merely liking her. Perhaps....

His mind stuttered away from the thought. He did not want to acknowledge it yet, did not want to admit it even to himself. For that would mean a connection far more lasting than the one he had envisioned, and he did not know how such a thing could even happen, not with the way the world was structured now. There were two roles humans could play in such a world, victim or Chosen. He would not allow Deirdre to become a victim, and yet....

"Amaal?" Now she had gotten up from looking after the dog, had sent a quizzical glance in his direction. "Are you okay?"

"I'm fine," he replied at once, pushing away those unwanted thoughts. "I was just wondering what you would like to have for breakfast."

Her expression grew faintly speculative, as if she guessed he had been thinking about something other than their morning meal. But then she appeared to push her worry aside, because she smiled and said, "I had an omelette with brie and caramelized onions once. It was amazing." A twinkle in her eyes, and she asked, "You think you can manage that?"

"Without a doubt," he replied, glad that he could now focus on something so mundane. "And perhaps some champagne to go with it?"

This suggestion was rewarded with a grin. "That sounds divine."

"Your wish is my command," he said with a little mock bow. She chuckled, and he proceeded to make their elegant breakfast appear on the kitchen table.

As Deirdre sat down, and Sasha took up her usual position off to one side so she might keep a careful eye out for any scraps that might come her way, Amaal let out a mental sigh of relief, glad of the chance to focus on something other than his thoughts.

Like it or not, he had come dangerously close to admitting to himself that he might just be in love with Deirdre Graves.

Breakfast was wonderful. She and Amaal had toasted one another with the champagne he'd conjured, and then they'd both dug in to the omelettes he'd made appear from nowhere, as well as the home fries and fruit he'd added to round out their meal. Probably some of her enjoyment of the food came from the afterglow of their love-making from the night before, and a wicked hope that there would be much more of the same in the near future. If she closed her eyes, even for an instant, she could immediately recall the warmth of his skin against hers, those strong fingers of his stroking her, the way their bodies had fitted so well together.

Who knew that sex with a djinn could be so mind-blowingly good?

Also, the sun was out today, bright and cheer-ful, and she could already see bare patches appearing in the snow outside the kitchen window. If the weather kept up like this, most traces of the storm would be gone within a few days. That thought relieved Deirdre a good deal. No, it wasn't as though she had to worry about being trapped here, not when Amaal could blink her away whenever he felt like it, but....

His gaze seemed to track where she'd been looking. "It appears it's a good thing that we went for our snowmobile ride yesterday. Already the snow is growing too slushy for such activities."

She nodded. "I know. But it was early in the year for that kind of storm, so I'm not too surprised that it's already starting to melt. We'll probably get another warm spell before the real winter weather shows up. It's usually wetter after the first of the year."

"Well, then, I shall hope for the sunshine to continue." He reached for his mug of coffee and took a sip. "Since riding the snowmobile appears to be out of the question, what else would you like to do today...if we get tired of watching this Netflix of yours?"

Deirdre shocked herself by saying, "You mean after you and I get in that huge shower in the master suite and do unspeakable things to each other?"

The question made him actually laugh out loud, even as he shot her a look that seemed to indicate he was wondering what she'd done with the real Deirdre Graves. "Yes, after that," he replied. "Although I am glad to know that you were thinking the same thing I was."

Good to know she wasn't the only one with a dirty mind. But sex with him was so amazing, she wanted to make sure she got as much of it as she wanted...as much as she needed. "Well, there's only so much TV we can watch. It's fun to relax for a little while, but I always start to get antsy. But we obviously can't really go hiking or anything like that, not with all that mud and melting snow."

"We don't have to stay in the house."

Deirdre could feel her eyebrows lift. "I thought you couldn't really leave your territory."

Another short laugh, and Amaal reached for his mug of coffee. "That's not precisely accurate. I can't *live* anywhere else, true, but I'm certainly free to find amusements nearby. I know for a fact that no other djinn are settled anywhere near here, so as long as we stay within a fifty-mile radius or so, we will be fine." He settled back in his chair and asked, "If you could go anywhere within a fifty-mile radius, where would you go?"

There was a good question. Deirdre thought of the modest rented house she'd shared with her mother in San Bernardino. She supposed she could go there, but why? Her mother was dead, and Deirdre couldn't think of anything there that she desperately needed or wanted. Family photos would only make her sad, would be constant reminders of everything she'd lost. Right now, she didn't want to look back—she wanted to look forward to a future with Amaal.

All right, so what else? He'd just given her a new wardrobe, so it wasn't as though she needed him to take her to the mall or something. All right, she could use a bit more makeup and personal items, but none of those needs were terribly pressing.

However, thinking about shopping at the mall gave her an idea. There was a mall they could go to, but the shopping part of it was only secondary.

"Let's go to Ontario Mills," she suggested.

"What is that?"

"It is—it *was* a shopping center. But it also has a Dave & Buster's. It would be fun to hang out there for a while."

Amaal's expression was a study in confusion. "What is a Dave & Buster's?"

"A kind of arcade. With games." Deirdre paused before adding, "You can use your djinn power to get the electricity running, right?"

"Yes," he replied.

"Well, then. Have you ever played skeeball?"

Now he looked even more puzzled. "I don't believe so."

"You'll like it." She thought of how he'd reverted to wearing djinn attire, and realized it might not be the best choice for that kind of activity. "You should probably wear human clothes, though."

"Why is that?"

"Because those sleeves will definitely get in the way."

It was a good morning. After breakfast, Amaal blinked himself and Deirdre into the shower in the master bath, conveniently discarding their clothing along the way. She startled a little at her sudden naked state, but then came to him at once, arms going around him, bare breasts pressing into his chest. Warm water began to beat down on them as they kissed, her hand going to stroke him even as he slipped his fingers between her legs.

Oh, yes, she was very ready. He tried to do his best to focus on her, on the pleasure he was giving her, because he didn't want to spill his seed so soon. And as she gasped and cried out, he lifted her, holding her up against the wall so he could enter her, feel all her heat and womanly wetness surround him. She clung to him, her legs wrapped around his waist, and they moved together, the warmth of the shower only increasing the fever he felt in his blood.

He spent in her just as she climaxed. She cried out his name, fingers digging into his hair. A moment passed, and then he lowered her gently.

Once again she offered him a wicked smile. "I don't know about 'unspeakable,' but that was pretty damn good."

"I am glad you think so."

She went up on tiptoe and kissed him on the mouth, her lithe, wet body pushing against him. Almost at once he could feel himself begin to harden again. A glance down, and she grinned. "Looks like I'd better take care of that."

Before he could respond, she had knelt down and taken him in her mouth, licking him in such a lascivious way that he was fully hard again within seconds. His fingers tangled in her wet hair, and he held on to her as the water beat down on them both. Ah, God, she was good. He'd fantasized about Deirdre doing this to him, but he had never expected reality to be so much better than fantasy.

The orgasm shocked him, not just its intensity, but by how quickly it arrived. Usually he would need a decent span of time to recover when he'd already climaxed so recently, but that didn't seem to be an issue when Deirdre was involved. She stood up, wiping her mouth, then raised her face to the shower's spray, letting it rinse her skin.

"All right," she said, "now we can get clean."

As he reached for the bottle of shampoo, he wondered what he had done to deserve a woman like her. He could only hope that he would prove himself worthy…but feared very much that he might not.

SEVENTEEN

Because Amaal had never visited Ontario Mills, they had to travel there in short blinks once they were past the territory he knew. Even so, they arrived at the vast, empty mall within ten minutes of leaving the house, still a much shorter span of time than driving there would have required.

They landed in the parking lot, which was still filled with more cars than Deirdre had expected. She'd missed the onset of the Heat, had only seen what it did to her companions at the research station, and so she supposed she hadn't realized how quickly it could overtake a person, could strike them down while they were shopping or driving or stopped at a red light. Off to one side, she saw two cars actually crashed into each other, a Ford Explorer neatly T-boning a much smaller Toyota Corolla. Even at low speeds, that kind of accident had caused a lot of damage, but she guessed that the drivers of those cars had had much more important things to worry about.

Resolutely, she turned away from the mess in the parking lot and took Amaal by the hand. "This way," she said, guiding him to the nearest entrance, which she realized was on the opposite side of the mall from where they wanted to be. Still, that shouldn't matter so much. They could just cut through the mall to get to Dave & Buster's.

He gamely tagged along, although Deirdre noticed how he paused for a second to glance up at the clear blue sky before he followed her. Was he worried that the other djinn would see them here, even though this was no one's territory, basically a no-man's-land?

She hadn't thought about that possibility. Well, judging by several things Amaal had said, it sounded as though the djinn who were killing off humanity's survivors had already swept through this area, so she didn't see any reason why they would be hanging around now.

Even so, she couldn't help letting out a little breath of relief as he opened one of the glass doors for her and they entered the mall. It hadn't been locked—who would even be left here to secure the mall? With the Heat, looting really wasn't an issue.

Amaal paused again, except this time it was

only to touch a hand to the wall nearest them. At once, the lights overhead flared into life, illuminating the open areas between the rows of shops, although the stores themselves remained dark.

"To light everything would require a large amount of my energy," he said. "I hope you don't mind that I will only illuminate the places we are actually going."

"No, I don't mind," Deirdre replied at once. So there were limits to his power. She had started to wonder. "We need to go down this hallway to get to Dave & Buster's."

"Lead on."

Still holding his hand, she began to walk in the direction of their destination. It was impossible to ignore the little gray piles of dust she saw here and there, but she told herself things could have been worse. At least those weren't actual bodies lying there. You could almost forget those insignificant piles of dust had once been human beings.

The air in here was stale, and smelled worse than she'd expected. But then, even if you didn't have to contend with the corpses of the people who'd died from the Heat, there were still all the restaurants at the mall and all the snacky places like Cinnabon and Wetzel's Pretzels. They'd had refrigerators stocked with food, and of course it had all spoiled once the power went out for good.

Deirdre waved a hand under her nose. "Sorry about this," she told Amaal. "I'd forgotten about the restaurants here and how there would be spoiled food."

"It's fine," he said, then added, "Or rather, once we are at our destination, I can clear the air in the immediate vicinity. You won't notice anything."

That was a relief. She shot him a grateful smile and tightened her grasp on his hand. Luckily, they were almost to Dave & Buster's. Just a minute more out in the open, and then they were ducking inside.

Damn, it was dark in here. She'd never really hung out at the place, since in general arcades weren't really her thing, but she'd been here a few times on dates. The lighting had always been a little on the dim side, and she supposed she hadn't noticed at the time because the games had been all lit up, providing their own illumination. However, Amaal lifted a hand, and at once the lights on the high, high ceilings came alive, as did the faux Tiffany-style fixtures over the bar.

"Better?" he asked her.

"Yes," she replied. Although she hadn't noticed him do anything except raise his hand, she realized that it smelled better in here, too. She even got a faint sense of air circulating around them, as if he'd turned on the facility's air processing units. "What do you want to do first?"

He lifted an eyebrow. "Well, we are standing next to the bar."

So they were. At this point it was past noon, which meant Deirdre felt as though it was safe to drink. No one was around to judge whether she drank at nine a.m. or nine p.m., but some habits were hard to break.

"Okay, we can start with a drink," she said. "But not wine. We need something sillier than that in a place like this."

"Very well," he replied, apparently not too put off by her suggestion. A glance over at the bar, and he went there to retrieve one of the menus that still lay there, now lightly coated with dust. He used the sleeve of his sweater to wipe the dust away, then handed her the menu. "What would you like?"

Something fruity and fun sounded best. "A piña colada," she said. "Do you know how to make one of those?"

"I am acquainted with the recipes for a number of alcoholic drinks," he said gravely.

Even as he spoke, her requested beverage appeared on the bar. Next to it was a tall, slightly rosy-hued drink. Deirdre glanced up at Amaal. "What's that?"

"A zombie," he replied. "If I am going to be

foolish with my drinks, I might as well get serious about it."

She grinned and retrieved her piña colada, then handed him his zombie. "Okay, now that's settled, it's time to play."

He didn't quite shake his head, but Deirdre could tell Amaal was amused by this expedition and her enthusiasm for it. Well, she wasn't quite sure if she could completely explain herself, but after spending those months at the research station, cooped up with not very much to do, it felt amazingly good to be out anywhere, even a defunct arcade in an abandoned mall.

The skeeball courts were near the back of the building, away from the flashier games. She'd always preferred skeeball because it didn't involve shooting anything or blowing things up, and also because you could get a lot more bang for your buck than with the more expensive shoot-em-up games.

They didn't have a card loaded with credits, but that didn't matter. Amaal touched a finger to the card reader next to the lane Deirdre had selected, and immediately a row of eight balls came pouring down the chute.

"You will show me how this works?"

She bent and picked up a ball, held it in the palm of her hand for a moment. Kind of crazy how good it felt, how normal…reassuring.

Standing back here, with the lights of the game activated and twinkling away, she could almost believe the world hadn't ended.

Almost.

"It's pretty self-explanatory," she said. "You just roll the ball down the lane and try to get it in one of those little circles up there. The smaller the circle, the more points you earn."

"Still, I would like to watch."

Acutely aware of his eyes on her, Deirdre stood in front of the lane she'd chosen and hefted the ball in her hand. She used to be pretty good at this, but it had been a while.

It's not a competition, she told herself. *Just roll the damn ball.*

Which she did. To her surprise, it jumped over the barrier and went in the 250-point circle. Immediately, the dispenser next to her belched out a healthy stream of tickets.

Amaal looked at them in some astonishment. "What are those?"

"Tickets," she replied. "You collected them, then redeemed them for prizes at that little shop over there." She pointed to the redemption center, which was off to their right about ten yards away. At the moment, you couldn't see much of what was inside, since Amaal hadn't turned on the lights in there. "Most of the stuff was just junk, but it was still kind of fun to see what you could get."

"How very peculiar."

She stuck her tongue out at him, and he laughed as she coaxed him, "Just try it."

He touched the card reader on the lane next to hers, then picked up one of the balls. Like her, he weighed it in his hand for a moment, clearly familiarizing himself with its weight and feel. Then he rolled it down it the lane.

It went right down the center without wavering, and flew up and into the 500-point circle.

Deirdre shot him a sideways look. "You're sure you've never done this before?"

His shoulders lifted. "I am a djinn. These sorts of things come somewhat naturally to us."

Of course they did. She had a feeling this was going to be a very lopsided match. Still, she wasn't about to admit defeat this early in the game. After taking a sip from her piña colada, which she'd set on a nearby table provided exactly for that purpose, she picked up another ball and sighted it carefully. Aim was everything—or almost everything. The amount of force she put into the throw was also important. If she threw it too hard, she knew she'd overshoot that all-important 500-point target.

The ball rolled down the lane, dead in the center. It skipped over the little curb at the end, went airborne…and landed in the 100-point circle.

Goddamn it.

Amaal didn't quite smile, but Deirdre thought she could see his mouth twitching as he took a long pull at the straw in his zombie, then went over to retrieve the next ball in his own lane. A smooth, graceful throw…and there it went in the tiny 500-point target. More tickets came pouring out of the machine.

Irritation flared, but Deirdre did her best to set her annoyance aside. They'd come here to have fun, after all. She'd never really considered herself the competitive type, so why should she be upset about her djinn companion beating her?

Because, she thought as she went without speaking to pick up her next ball, *he's got a built-in advantage. It's like going up against someone pumped full of human growth hormone or something.*

Well, maybe that was true, but she couldn't do much about it. This time she made herself relax and not worry so much about how many points she might score. Already Amaal had an almost insurmountable lead, so why stress about something she couldn't change?

Especially when it was really so minor, in the grand scheme of things.

The ball went spinning down the lane. To her surprise, it popped neatly into the 500-point cup.

"Very good," Amaal said. Zombie in hand, he came over to her and kissed her on the cheek. "I knew you had it in you."

"Probably just a lucky throw," she replied, absurdly pleased despite her earlier admonition to herself that the final score really didn't matter.

"Perhaps." He bent and kissed her again, this time on the mouth. It was a good kiss, fruity and sweet and faintly alcoholic, one that sent happy tingles all through her body. "Or perhaps you just didn't want to get beaten."

The next ball he rolled only went into the 100-point circle. Had he done that on purpose, or had he actually blown the shot? Deirdre couldn't tell for sure; his expression was so neutral that it was impossible to know what he was thinking. Either way, she realized she enjoyed watching him play. There was a lot to be said for djinn robes and the stomach and chest they displayed, but right now it was better to get an eyeful of his fine ass in the faded 501s he was wearing.

Their next few shots evened the game further, but in the end, Amaal beat her by 225 points. They gathered up their tickets, and he said, "Well, you can show me how to redeem these now."

"We don't really need to do that," she replied. "Like I said, it's mostly just junk."

"I'd still like to do it."

She shook her head but led him over to the redemption center. The door wasn't locked, although Deirdre was relieved to note that there weren't any telltale piles of gray dust in here. Had Amaal quietly whisked them away when she wasn't looking, or had the clerk who'd been working in here fled before the disease could fully take hold?

Better not to ask. She watched as Amaal waved a hand to turn on the lights overhead, illuminating shelves stocked with everything from pencil erasers to battery-operated drones.

"What can we get with all these?" he asked, waving the bunch of tickets in his hand.

"Just read the signs. They say how many tickets each item is worth."

"Ah."

He went from shelf to shelf, studying each of the items and its accompanying label, his expression quite serious. Looking at him, Deirdre thought she'd never seen anything quite so adorable. That warm feeling was back in her chest, the one that told her this was a lot more than physical attraction or mind-blowing sex. She never would have believed it if someone had told her the same thing a week ago, but she really liked this djinn.

No, that wasn't quite right. She *loved* him,

loved the sound of his voice and the light in his blue eyes when he smiled. She loved the way he teased her, and the way he was so tender and careful with Sasha. And yes, sex with him positively made her toes curl, but that was just the icing on an already delicious cake.

"These tickets don't get you very much, even with a high score," he said, sounding offended. "I would have to win the same game at least ten more times to afford anything remotely interesting, like that radio-controlled car."

"That's how it works," she told him, coming over so she could slide an arm around his waist. "They wanted you to get hooked so you'd keep playing and spending more money. I guess it's just another kind of gambling, really. The house always wins, you know?"

A nod, although his gaze was still fixed on the shelf before him. "I suppose I can see that. Well, I think I shall have to settle for something not quite so interesting, like that plastic kaleidoscope over there." He picked up the object in question, then went and put his tickets on the countertop. After he was done, he turned back toward her. "What now?"

She extended an arm toward the rest of the arcade. "Whatever you like. We have all day, after all."

They wandered from game to game, spending some time shooting at zombies in one, or going head to head on an imaginary racetrack in another. After they'd unceremoniously crashed into each other—causing Deirdre to start giggling, thanks to the second piña colada she'd consumed —they decided it was time to take a break and have a late lunch.

She slid one of the restaurant's menus across the table to him. "We should have something from this. You know, just to make things more authentic."

That sounded like a good idea. Amaal perused the offerings, which were numerous, and seemed calculated to be as unhealthy as possible. Still, djinn didn't have to worry about weight gain or clogged arteries, and certainly Deirdre was too young and slender for such things to be much of a concern for her, either.

They decided on burgers and chili cheese fries, and switched over from the fruity tropical beverages they'd been drinking to something a bit lighter—hard cider for her, a German lager for him. All it required was a wave of the hand to make their food appear.

Deirdre reached for a french fry, then paused, an expression of concern passing over her features.

"What is it?" Amaal asked. "Did they not come out correctly?"

"No," she replied at once, and picked up the fry and bit into it, as if to prove to him that there was nothing wrong with the food. "They're fine. It's just...." The sentence trailed off, and she glanced around them, at the lights blinking on the games, at the empty booths in the restaurant area where they sat. Voice lowering, although of course there was no chance of being overheard, she went on, "Do you think it's disrespectful, what we're doing here? I guess it just hit me as I was looking across the way there, at all those games that should have people playing them. But they can't play those games, because they're all gone. They died here."

Amaal reached across the table and laid a hand on hers, hoping to send some reassurance to her through his touch. "No, I don't think it's disrespectful. This place was built so people could come here and enjoy themselves, just as we've been doing this afternoon. I have to believe that this facility's designers would be glad to know that someone was still able to use it. And those who are gone...." He stopped himself there, unsure as to whether he really wanted the conversation to go in that direction.

However, Deirdre seized on those words,

prompting, "'Those who are gone'? What about them?"

There didn't seem to be much use in trying to avoid her questions. "They've gone on to the next world. Their bodies are dead, but their spirits are not extinguished. And because they are occupied in a new existence, they have little thought for what they've left behind. They would not begrudge you the small enjoyment you have had here."

She sat back against the booth, eyes wide. "You say that like you know it for a fact."

"I do," he said calmly. "I still cannot justify what my people did to yours, but I have had some measure of peace knowing that those deaths were only a transition, not an end."

Tears gleamed bright in her eyes. She reached up to wipe them away, blotting at them with the paper napkin that had lain in her lap. "Thank you, Amaal," she said, her voice tremulous. "That's—it just really helps to hear that."

"I should have said something earlier."

"It's all right." She smiled at him, a smile that appeared somewhat wavery but was still luminous. "I suppose the subject didn't really come up. But now—now I can feel a little better about everything that's happened." A deep breath, and she reached for another fry. "And I think I can eat now."

They finished their meal and then went to play some more skeeball afterward. That seemed the safest activity—Amaal didn't think that one of the shooting games they'd dabbled in earlier was a very good idea, given what they'd discussed during their late lunch. And when they both decided they'd had enough, he blinked them back to the house in Running Springs.

Sasha came toward them, tail wagging, bounding about happily despite the bandage on her back leg. Amaal patted her on the head and told her she was a good girl, and went to get her a treat out of the pantry.

Smiling, Deirdre watched them, then ran a hand across the back of her neck. "Ugh—I got all sweaty during that last round of skeeball. I think I'm going to run upstairs and take a quick shower."

"Should I join you?"

That request earned him a roll of her eyes. "Amaal, I said a *quick* shower. Why don't you take Sasha out—I'll bet she needs to go after holding it in all afternoon."

She was probably right. At least the sun had remained bright all day, with no clouds to block it from working on the snow that had piled up around the house. A quick glance outside told Amaal that bare patches had already begun to appear in the area just beyond the porch.

"Yes, of course," he said. "Come along, Sasha —do you want to go out?"

This question earned him some ferocious tail wagging. Deirdre smiled and headed upstairs, while he took the dog outside. She immediately relieved herself, then went around and sniffed the bare ground for a moment before returning to the porch stairs. He praised her, then blinked the two of them back inside so she wouldn't have to try to climb the steps. A wave of his hand cleaned the mud from her paws, and she was off to the kitchen to slurp noisily at her water.

Amaal paused in the living room, listening to the sound of the shower running upstairs. A rather unwelcome thought crossed his mind, that he still hadn't located where Deirdre had hidden the device. But surely that didn't matter now? They were together, and happy. She would have no reason to use it on him.

Still, he hated not knowing where it had been secreted. Surely it couldn't hurt for him to find it and put it back. Then his mind would be at ease, and Deirdre would never have to know.

That seemed to settle things. He blinked himself into her bedroom and glanced around. Everything appeared neat and tidy and undisturbed. Then again, why wouldn't it be? She had slept at his side last night and hadn't even come in here, except to retrieve some clothes.

Well, he'd already checked the closet top to bottom, so he would ignore it for now. Going to the bed, he lifted the pillows and looked underneath but found nothing. Likewise with the mattress. There really was no place else she could have hidden it, since all her underthings and other foldable items of clothing had been stored in the built-in cabinets in the closet.

Then his gaze fell on the low, round basket that sat on top of the dresser. It was filled with whimsical little balls of twigs, clearly a designer's idea of a rustic accent. He'd never paid any particular attention to it before now, except to enjoy the faint floral scent that seemed to cling to the twigs. And as he recalled finding two of the little orbs in one of the closet drawers, he realized that those balls of twigs were approximately the same size as the device Deirdre had constructed.

He paused, then glanced out into the hallway. The sound of running water came clearly from the bathroom, and did not seem as though it would be stopping anytime soon. Apparently Deirdre had decided that something more than a "short" shower was in order.

Good. He scooped the balls out of the basket one by one and set them aside. At the very bottom was an object that shouldn't be there, one which was square and shining and somehow alien.

For a long moment, Amaal could only stare at

it. An impulse came over him, one that told him to take the device and hide it away, just to be safe. Somehow, though, he managed to ignore the inner voice that told him to steal the thing. If Deirdre noticed it missing, she would know he had to be the one who had taken it. He was already violating her trust by searching her room in the first place; if he took this thing from her, he knew she would never forgive him.

A breath escaped his lips, and he began to put the balls of twigs in the basket, hoping that he was getting them back in the correct orientation. Just as he was setting the last two balls on top of the pile, the water in the bathroom shut off.

Panic lanced through him, but he was done. Everything was back in order. At once he blinked himself downstairs, even while he worried that he had overlooked a single detail, had left behind some trace of what he had done. No, he was fine. Deirdre would never find out.

Good thing, because he was not sure he would ever be able to explain himself if she did.

EIGHTEEN

THE SUN CONTINUED TO SHINE FOR DAYS AND days, and the snow melted so much that the only bits left were in the deep shade, or on the north side of the house. Deirdre was glad of the friendly weather, even though she knew it couldn't last. Still, now she and Amaal could go hiking around the property, could take Sasha with them, her leg healed to the point where she had all her old mobility, even though there was still a ragged bare patch in her fur that would probably take months to truly disappear.

Christmas was now only two weeks away, although Deirdre wasn't quite sure what the holiday would even mean, now that the world had changed so much. It wasn't as though she and Amaal needed to exchange presents; gift-giving lost a good deal of its significance when you were with someone who could basically summon anything you needed.

Still, it was good to have these times in the sun, even if the weather was chilly enough that she needed a jacket to go outside. Besides their hikes, they went back to Ontario Mills several times, went to a bowling alley, even headed out to Big Bear Lake so Amaal could expertly pilot them around in a speedboat he found there, the cold wind blowing through their hair as they cut across the serene blue water.

All in all, she had to admit that they'd fallen into a comfortable existence. Deirdre slept in Amaal's room every night, with Sasha curled up in the bed he'd provided. They made love, sometimes in bed, sometimes in the shower, or the couch downstairs, or…well, probably the laundry room was the only room they hadn't used for that particular purpose.

During this whole time, however, she couldn't help wondering where all this was going to end up. She knew she loved Amaal, but she was afraid to say those words to him, afraid that once they were uttered out loud, they would change everything. And she knew he must care for her, too, although he'd never given any sign of wanting to say the L-word, either.

Then again, it had only been a few weeks. Deirdre had to remind herself that she'd spent far longer alone in the research station than she had here at Amaal's house, although she found that hard to believe. He was so entwined with her life now, and those days and weeks at the station had been so tedious, that it felt as though he'd always dominated her existence.

One afternoon, he seemed to have disappeared. Panicked, she hurried outside, worrying that he'd left the property for some reason, although he'd always been conscientious about telling her when he was taking Sasha out, which was generally his only reason for leaving her alone.

She found him in a small clearing amongst some tall fir trees. They'd passed by the little meadow, which was located upslope from the house a few hundred yards or so, several times when they went out walking, but they'd actually never gone in among the trees. He stood there now next to a tall granite stone that stood chest high, a spear of rock which clearly had been brought here from somewhere else.

Amaal looked up as she approached and offered her a sad little smile. It was so unlike his usual expressions that she glanced from him to the stone and then back, comprehension dawning.

She went to him and took his hand in hers. Although the air was chilly, his fingers were warm. They were always warm, actually. The only time they'd been cold was when she'd used the device on him.

Pushing that thought away, she asked quietly, "Is this where your brother is buried?"

"Yes," he replied. His gaze was still directed downward at the earth beneath their feet. "Despite his crimes, the elders said he could be lain to rest here where he would be near family."

"The elders?" Deirdre had never heard him mention them before. Then again, they hadn't spent much time talking about djinn society; she could tell Amaal preferred to avoid that subject.

A lift of the shoulders, and he raised his head and looked at her. The smile wasn't sad any longer, or at least, it was more the lopsided, slightly ironic smile that had become so familiar to her. "The djinn don't precisely have a government, at least not anything like what you were used to in the world before. We are more tribal than anything. But when there are disputes that can't be settled among individuals or clans, then the elders step in. Or when a crime has been committed, they are the ones who mete out punishment."

"That's what happened with your brother?"

"Not precisely. As I told you, he fought another djinn, and lost. But because Omar had broken the rules that govern such things, they did have the final say as to whether he should be allowed a peaceful burial." Amaal's mouth twisted, and he went on, "I rather think they allowed it because it forced me to bring him here, and to stay where I was told."

Deirdre looked back at him, somewhat confused by this statement. "You mean you weren't here before?"

A sigh. He ran his hand through his hair and said, "No, I was not. These were my lands, and I was supposed to dwell here, but this house and this climate are not exactly to my taste. I would have preferred something much warmer."

Well, she couldn't really fault him for feeling that way. Trying to sound encouraging, she said, "It's not so bad. At least it's beautiful up here, and it's not as though you had to live in Siberia or something."

"No, I suppose not. But I had taken a very nice penthouse for myself in the downtown area of Los Angeles, and I would have much preferred to stay there. The elders, unfortunately, had a different idea. Back here I was sent, and back here I must stay."

The frustration in his voice was obvious. Deirdre couldn't really even blame him, because she had to admit, as beautiful as this house was, it didn't seem to suit Amaal very well. She could picture him in a penthouse atop a high-rise, with views all the way to the ocean, maybe a rooftop swimming pool. It was much warmer down in Los Angeles than up here in the mountains. What had the elders been thinking when they gave him this land? You'd think they'd be a little more careful when determining where someone was supposed to live for eternity.

Eternity. She'd danced around the subject in her mind as best she could, but she couldn't quite ignore the reality of their differences. Amaal was a djinn, and supposedly would live, if not forever, then for a very, very long time. She was mortal. Right now it didn't matter, but if she stayed with him, she'd begin to age. He'd be perpetually twenty-eight or twenty-nine in appearance, while she sure as hell wasn't going to be twenty-four forever.

Once again she shoved the thought out of her head. It wasn't anything she could do much about anyway.

"Well," she said, knowing that she sounded a little too forcibly cheerful, "look at it this way. If you hadn't been given these lands, we would never have met. Maybe the elders really did know what they were doing."

He smiled at her then—a real smile—and his fingers tightened on hers. "You are right, of course," he replied. "I have often wondered whether they have the gift of the Sight, although I am sure they would deny it if asked. It is worth the snow and the cold if I have you here with me to keep me warm at night."

That comment made her warm as well, and she went up on her tiptoes so she could kiss him, could feel the heat spread through her once again at the sensation of his lips touching hers. Amazing how it didn't seem to matter how often they kissed, how often they made love. Each time felt like the first time, a wondering exploration of the overwhelming attraction she felt for him.

"Let's go inside," she said, tugging gently on his fingers. "It's starting to get downright cold out here, with the sun going down the other side of the mountain."

He didn't protest, only allowed her to lead him back toward the house. Even so, she couldn't help but notice how he glanced over his shoulder as he walked away, as though saying goodbye once again to the brother he had lost.

Amaal smiled as he left the bedroom, listening to Deirdre humming to herself in a happy, tuneless sort of way from within the shower. They often took their showers together, but today she needed to wash her hair, and he'd learned it was better to let her perform that particular task on her own. He had already bathed, and thought he would take Sasha for a walk. Once again it was a fine day, the sun shining brightly overhead.

Yesterday his feet had guided him to the clearing where Omar had been laid to rest, but Amaal saw no reason to go that way now. Sasha at his side, he strolled in a leisurely fashion slightly north and eastward, toward the road that connected this property with several of the others in the general vicinity. Those homes were, of course, unoccupied, but the going in this direction was a bit easier, since the land had already been tamed.

He was just cresting the final rise before he got to the road when he found his way blocked quite unexpectedly, and by one of the last people he had expected—or wanted—to see.

Idris, the third, and some said the youngest, of the elders. Because he was an elder, and had no forebears, he bore no patronymic, was known only by his first name.

He stood in the middle of the path, arms crossed. Unlike most djinn, who tended to wear clothing in the colors associated with the element they controlled, Idris was garbed in black from head to toe, relieved only by a narrow silver border along the hem of his long robe. His gaze met Amaal's, unsmiling, regular, handsome features nearly expressionless. A faint breeze caught at his shoulder-length black hair, ruffling it against the silk that covered his broad shoulders.

The presence of an elder here could mean only one thing, but Amaal pushed back at the sudden panic that flared within him and said in cheerful tones, "Well met, Idris. How do you do on this fine winter day? Are you checking on me? I assure you, I have not gone back to my penthouse."

"No, you have not," Idris agreed. "I know this, because I have visited there several times and found it unoccupied."

This statement evoked an unexpected sense of relief. Perhaps Amaal could never return to downtown Los Angeles, but at least no other djinn had taken up residence in the lofty apartment he had been forced to abandon.

"Well, then," Amaal said, as if that solved everything, even though he knew of course it did not.

"That is not why I am here," Idris went on, expression still stony, forbidding. "You are abiding by one rule, Amaal al-Tariq, but you are breaking another, one that is even more serious. You know that you are not allowed to cohabit with a human unless you have taken her as your Chosen, and yet you have been living here for several weeks with the one known as Deirdre Graves."

Damn. Amaal did not ask Idris how he know Deirdre's name, or that she had been living with

Amaal for some time now. Idris was an elder, and it was their responsibility to know such things. It had only been a matter of time, Amaal supposed, and yet he had hoped against hope that somehow this arrangement he had worked out with Deirdre would escape notice.

"I have," he said forthrightly, since he knew there was no point in lying, not when Idris already knew the truth. "I did not wish to leave her alone, as doing so would only put her in danger."

This remark caused Idris to lift an eyebrow. "Indeed?" he responded, disbelief clear in this voice. "So you have sheltered her here only out of the goodness of your heart."

That, of course, was not the truth at all. Amaal had not allowed himself to truly analyze his feelings for Deirdre, but he was forced to admit to himself that he wanted her here because he desired her, and because she filled his lonely days. At the moment, he was not prepared to say anything more than that.

"These are dangerous times for humans on their own."

"True," Idris said. "But it is not your responsibility to care for her. You know the compact all djinn agreed to. It is not something that can be modified to suit your particular needs...or lusts. If you care for this woman, make her your Chosen, and take her with you to a community where others like you abide. Otherwise, you must let her go."

"But the hunters will find her," Amaal protested, a very real fear stirring in his heart. True, she had the device to protect her, but what if it failed somehow? Then she would be utterly defenseless.

"That is no concern of yours. Or rather, if you love her, then it should be simple enough to claim her as your Chosen. Otherwise, why should you care whether or not she lives?"

Good question. Of course Amaal did care, cared very much. He did not want Deirdre to die. On the other hand, how could he possibly allow himself to be tied to her for the rest of his very long life?

"I will speak to her," he said, which of course did not mean anything one way or another.

Idris seemed to see through this ploy, for his dark eyes narrowed slightly. However, he only gave a lift of his shoulders and said, "Yes, you will. And if she is still here by the time the sun sets tomorrow, I will remove her to her former residence. Do you understand?"

Amaal swallowed. "Yes, elder. I understand. I will take care of this."

"Good. I hope your word is worth more than your brother's."

That little barb was apparently the elder's

parting shot, for Idris disappeared immediately afterward. Sasha, who had been nosing around in the dead pine needles under a nearby tree, looked up in surprise and gave a small whine, as though she wasn't quite sure what to make of the other djinn's departure.

For himself, Amaal could only stand there for a long moment, heart heavy and every limb weighted with worry. The moment he had feared had come, could not be avoided any longer. Idris meant what he had said, and so Amaal knew he could not put this off...and yet he could not think of anything he wanted to do less than go and speak with Deirdre. In that moment, he was still not entirely sure what he intended to say to her.

On the surface, the solution seemed easy enough—he would make her his Chosen, and then they would be able to leave this place. Not to the settlement of humans and djinn in Bel-Air, for he doubted that either Malik al-Mazin or his Chosen would be too happy to have the brother of their erstwhile adversary settled among them. But there were other groups not so far away, one in Laguna Beach and another in San Diego, both of which offered far more hospitable climates than the one in which his current home was located.

Whether he had the courage to do such a

thing, to bind himself to Deirdre forever…he could not say.

He supposed he would find out soon enough.

Sasha came bounding through the front door, tail wagging as she headed toward the kitchen in anticipation of receiving a treat. Amaal followed much more slowly, his steps almost dragging.

Deirdre, who had just come downstairs after getting dressed, looked at him in some concern. Had he hurt himself somehow? No, that was impossible; djinn practically had to get run over by a train before they would be truly injured.

"Amaal?" she said, her tone questioning. "Is everything all right?"

In response, he gave her a tight little smile. "I suppose that depends on what you mean by 'all right.' I have had a visit from one of the elders, and so we need to talk."

"'The elders'?" she echoed. What in the world did the elders want with Amaal? He'd been doing as he was told by sticking around the lands he'd been assigned, so why would one come all the way out here? Were they in trouble for their jaunts to Ontario Mills and Big Bear Lake, even though Amaal had assured her such outings were allowed?

"Yes, one of the elders," he said. With one

hand, he gestured toward the living room. "Come, Deirdre, let us sit."

Unease growing, she followed Amaal into the living room, then sat down on the couch next to him. Usually he would reach out to take her hand in his when they were seated this close, but now he only sat there with his hands resting on his knees, his entire body practically radiating tension.

"What's wrong?" she asked.

He let out a breath. Gaze fixed on the tall windows just past her rather than on her face, he said, "I fear I have not been entirely truthful with you."

Fear shot through her, fierce and painful as a bolt of lightning, but she forced herself to say calmly, "Truthful about what?"

"About humans and djinn." He breathed in, fingers digging into the silky fabric of the pants he wore. "You see, while there are a great many of my people who are dedicated to erasing the last of humanity, there are also a small number who have done what they could to make sure some humans survived."

"Like you have?"

That question only elicited a thin smile. Those blue eyes, such an echo of the sky, still wouldn't meet hers. "Not precisely. Those djinn were allowed to choose one human each to be saved, to be their partner for the rest of their lives. And because those djinn had sided with humanity, they now dwell apart in their own settlements, away from the rest of my people."

Deirdre sat quietly for a moment, doing her best to let Amaal's words sink in. The one thing which stood out the most clearly to her at first was that there were other survivors. She wasn't quite as alone as she'd thought she was. The knowledge sent a rush of warmth through her, a relief so deep, at first she didn't even quite recognize it for what it was.

But then....

She tilted her head at Amaal. "You said those djinn chose humans to be with? Isn't that what you've done with me? Why aren't we living with the rest of those djinn and their humans?"

With a sigh, he turned toward her. For the first time, his gaze met hers...although she wasn't sure she liked what she saw in his face. A good measure of guilt, coupled with the expression of a man who wished he could be anyplace but where he was.

"That's not exactly true for the two of us," he said, after a noticeable moment of hesitation. "We've been living with one another, but I haven't formally chosen you."

Despite this reply, she was still more confused than anything else. "Why not?"

"Because—" Amaal broke off there and got to his feet, took a few steps away from her so he stood by the window. Staring out at the muddy yard, he said, "Because I know what that means, and you do not. To be Chosen is to be bound to the djinn who selects you for all eternity. It is not something done casually."

"Oh." Deirdre could see why such a decision might require some forethought, but the more she thought about it, the more she felt anger start to rise in her, slow-moving and terrible as an avalanche. She rose from the couch as well, but she didn't try to approach Amaal, only remained where she was, arms crossed. "So that's all I am to you? A casual fuck?"

He turned around, handsome features tight and strained. "No, of course not."

"Then what?"

"I…." The words trailed off, and he shook his head. "I care for you, Deirdre. Truly, I do. But to make you my Chosen—I had never thought I would do such a thing. Not with anyone. It requires a certain temperament, one I was not sure I possessed. That doesn't mean I do not have feelings for you."

Tears began to burn in her eyes, and she could feel a lump forming in her throat. Somehow she managed to choke her way past it. "Feelings you were just fine with as long as they didn't require any kind of commitment, right?"

"Deirdre — "

He began to move toward her, and she held up a hand. No, she didn't want him to try to hold her, because she feared that if she allowed him to touch her, this anger would melt away. She needed it. She needed to stay angry, or she worried she wouldn't be able to do what she knew she must.

"Don't, Amaal." She gulped in a breath. "I need—I need to go think about this. All right?"

"I think it would be better if we talked—"

"Well, I don't. Not now. If you do care for me, then you'll respect me enough to let me be alone for a little while."

A nod. He stood a few paces from her, hands knotted into fists at his sides. Deirdre could tell he hated having to stand there and let her walk away.

But he didn't argue. He only remained where he was while she went to the stairs and slowly climbed them, one foot after the other, each one of those steps as painful and labored as though she was walking through quicksand.

At last she got to her room, though—the room Amaal had given her when she'd first come here, not the master suite they'd been sharing for the past few weeks. She'd moved most of her clothes into the master bedroom closet, but the stuff she'd been wearing when she'd first come to the house was still here, along with her backpack.

Good. She was going to need it.

Off with the designer jeans and the pretty green cashmere sweater Amaal had provided, the low expensive boots. She got back into her faded Levi's and bulky sweater and hiking boots, pulled her hair back in a scrunchie. At least this confrontation had taken place early in the day; she was pretty sure she'd be able to walk back to the research station before nightfall without too much effort.

Then she went to the decorative bowl where she'd hidden the device and took it out. For the longest moment she stood there next to the dresser, holding the small black box in the palm of her hand and staring down at it. Would she have the courage to switch it on?

She knew she had to. Otherwise, Amaal would surely use his djinn powers to keep her from walking away. He might not want to make her his Chosen, but he wanted her here…at least for now. Sooner or later he would have gotten tired of her and sent her away, but she had no doubt that he wanted to control the timing of their separation, wanted it to be on his terms.

Amaal might be a djinn, but deep down he was just as big an asshole as her ex-boyfriend Tristan.

That thought wrenched something deep inside, and at last the tears began to trail their way down her cheeks. How could she have been so stupid as to let herself fall in love with a djinn?

Because she'd thought he would be different.

Mouth set, she heaved her backpack over her shoulder. She realized she would be leaving her meager toiletries behind, but she could always scrounge some more, especially now that she knew the device worked and she could drive the truck she'd left behind at the research station without worrying about any djinn coming after her.

Right now, she just wanted to get the hell out of here.

As she zipped up her backpack, she caught a glimpse of herself in the mirror that hung above the dresser. Gone was the happy bloom she'd worn for the past few weeks—now she looked just as pale and hunted as she had back when she'd been living alone at the station, certain that at any moment the djinn were going to descend on her hiding place and murder her, just as they had every other survivor.

Well, every survivor who wasn't Chosen, apparently.

Deirdre opened the door to her room, half expecting to see Amaal standing out in the hallway. Her right hand hovered over the touchscreen of the device, just in case.

But he wasn't there. Had he been worried that he might upset her further if he didn't allow her as much distance as possible?

Maybe. She wasn't about to give him the benefit of the doubt, though.

She came down the stairs and saw Amaal sitting on the couch. Sasha was leaning against his knee as he scratched her behind the ears. Seeing the two of them, a pang went through her, followed by a wave of doubt. Was she being too hasty here?

No, she told herself. *Don't be a wimp. He's had you here for two weeks and has known the whole time that he wasn't supposed to do that without making you his Chosen. He* lied *to you.*

She could tell when he noticed the backpack, the device she held in her left hand, because he immediately leaped to his feet, consternation clear on his face. "Deirdre, please—"

"Don't bother, Amaal."

"Leaving isn't going to solve anything."

That remark only made her shake her head. "Neither is staying. Actually, I can't stay, can I? Because your djinn rules won't let me, and you're too much of a chickenshit to do the right thing and make me your Chosen."

He took a step toward her. "Deirdre—"

With one swipe of her finger, she switched on the device. At a low setting, nothing that would hurt him. It would only drain his powers, make him weak enough that he couldn't prevent her from walking out the door.

The effect was immediate. All the color drained from his face, and he staggered a bit before regaining his balance. When he spoke, his voice was ragged. "That was a wretched thing to do."

She shrugged. "Maybe. But I needed to make sure you wouldn't stop me, or follow me. I'm going to keep it turned on the whole way back to the research station, and I'm not going to shut it off. You need to stay away from me. Got it?"

"Deirdre, I know you're upset, but please—"

"Of course I'm upset," she cut in. "That doesn't mean I'm not thinking clearly. We had some fun, and it's over. It's fine. I'm sure you'll forget all about me once the right djinn woman comes along."

A fine sheen of perspiration coated his forehead. "You don't mean that."

"I do."

Voice tight with strain—and maybe more than a little desperation—he asked, "What about Sasha?"

Deirdre looked over at the dog, who now lay on the floor, chin on her paws. It seemed clear enough that she was troubled by the angry exchange her people had just shared. Guilt flowed over her, but Deirdre knew she couldn't let concern for Sasha prevent her from going.

Besides, she'd always had a sneaking suspicion that the dog liked Amaal best.

"You can keep her," she said, her voice hard. "This is a better place for her."

"But you'll be alone!"

"So what?" Deliberately, Deirdre descended the short flight of steps to the entryway, paused before the front door, and then opened it, letting in a cool gust of air. "Haven't I always been?"

And she slammed the door behind her.

NINETEEN

THIS WASN'T HAPPENING, WAS IT? HAD Deirdre really just left him?

Since she'd walked out of the house several minutes ago and appeared to have no intention of returning, it seemed she had.

Amaal sat on the couch because he wasn't sure he had the energy to remain standing any longer. Sasha came and put her muzzle on his knee, golden eyes staring up at him imploringly.

"I'm sorry," he said, although he wasn't sure who he was apologizing to, the dog or the now-absent Deirdre.

Damn it, he should have taken the device once he'd found it and hidden it somewhere. The thought had crossed his mind, but he'd pushed it away, telling himself that there was no need to do such a thing, that he was only risking Deirdre's anger if she should ever find out.

Well, she was angry...but not about the device.

He leaned against the back of the couch. His energy was still sapped, his powers gone, which meant she must still be in range. She'd never really explained how far the field of effect extended; perhaps she didn't know for sure, either. And of course she was being forced to walk back to the research station, as they hadn't brought any vehicles here. No need, when he could blink them from place to place. The garage here had been empty except for the snowmobile when he arrived, and so he'd assumed that the owners of the house had been away when the Heat struck. Too bad, because if there were a car, he could have gotten in it and followed Deirdre that way. He felt too weak to walk any distance, and certainly not as far as the research station, but he thought he might have been able to drive a car.

As soon as that thought crossed his mind, he wanted to rebuke himself for it. Deirdre had made her feelings exceedingly clear. What would be the point in chasing after her when she'd all but told him that she wanted nothing to do with someone who couldn't commit to making her his Chosen?

And that was just ridiculous. The djinn who had taken humans as their partners had had more than a year to observe those they had selected, to make sure that their Chosen would be compatible with them. He and Deirdre had only known one another for a few weeks. Surely she couldn't think that such a short acquaintance was a reasonable basis for an eternity together?

As far as he could tell, that was exactly what she thought.

With a groan, he pushed himself up from the couch and went into the kitchen. He needed a drink. Luckily, there were several bottles of white wine in the refrigerator, so he would not be forced to make a laborious descent into the cellar to fetch something.

It was excruciating to have to uncork the wine the human way, without using any of his powers, but at last he managed to get the bottle open. He fetched a glass and poured a healthy measure of wine into it, then took several swallows. Thanks to the effects of the device, even that small amount of alcohol hit him with all the force of a ton of bricks, but he welcomed the sensation. If he drank enough, he might forget what Deirdre looked like, the low music of her voice. The way she snuggled up to him in the cold early morning hours, when even their plentiful bedcovers didn't feel like quite enough.

Damn, this was going to be harder than he'd thought.

And then, without warning, the crushing sensation that weighted his limbs and stole his powers away was suddenly gone. Amaal blinked in surprise as his energy flowed back to him, even as he realized what must have just happened.

Deirdre had gone out of range. However, that didn't mean he could safely pursue her, for of course the moment he got close enough, the device would begin to work on him again.

Besides, hadn't he resolved to let her go? He had enjoyed her company, but the good times they had shared were certainly not enough inducement to allow him to be shackled to her for eternity. Really, he thought as he poured himself some more wine, he was well rid of her. She had saved him from the difficulty of extricating himself from their relationship, which was bound to have happened sooner or later.

Perhaps he should take her advice and go seek out a djinn woman. He knew—because Omar had mentioned it once in passing—that Dima al-Dawud, a very comely air elemental, had settled in a palatial desert estate in Palm Springs. It would be much warmer there, that was for certain.

Yes, that seemed like the best plan. If he drank enough, and lost himself in another woman's arms, he would soon forget all about Deirdre Graves.

It was a good thing the world was so empty. That way, no one was around to see the tears that stained Deirdre's cheeks as she laboriously made her way to the south and east, back toward the research station. Luckily, it wasn't as though this was all trackless wilderness; only a few minutes after leaving the house, she came across a road with a mile marker that told her she was three miles from Running Springs, which meant she probably had no more than a five-mile walk to reach her destination. She'd be there a little after noon, most likely.

Habit ingrained during her months alone made her continually look up at the sky as she walked, although she saw nothing except hawks and crows, and a large bird she thought might have been an eagle. Anyway, she knew the device worked, and so there was no chance of a djinn descending on her. Any air elemental that even tried to get close would fall out of the sky like a plane shot down by a rocket-propelled grenade.

That thought didn't reassure her quite as much as she'd hoped it would, however. Even though she'd told herself that she didn't want Amaal to pursue her, she knew he wouldn't even bother, not when he had no chance of coming anywhere near without having his powers stripped once more.

She'd been walking about an hour before the tears stopped. It was stupid to cry so much over losing him, when she'd lost far more in the recent past, thanks to the disease his people had invented. He wasn't worth it. The only thing she could do now was look forward to the future.

What that future would be, she really wasn't sure.

Another sob, one of relief, rose in her throat when the research station finally came into view, looking none the worse for wear despite being abandoned for nearly two weeks. Deirdre hastened her pace, glad of the chance to get inside. No, there hadn't been any signs of pursuit, but she couldn't help but experience a wave of relief as she let herself in and then locked the door behind her.

The opulent front room Amaal had called into being was still there. It hadn't disappeared when they left, and so she realized anything he brought into existence was real, wasn't some kind of elaborate illusion.

Well, except the affection he had professed for her.

Scowling, she slung the backpack off her shoulders and set it down on the kitchen counter. The refrigerator was still humming away, thanks to the solar panels on the station's roof. Deirdre had no doubt that everything still worked the way it should, which was good. She wouldn't have to do much to get herself back up and running, just as though nothing had happened.

The question was...did she really want to do that? Settle back in here and pretend that the whole interlude with Amaal had never occurred?

No. That couldn't happen. She wouldn't let it.

After all, she had the device to protect her now. She'd just walked across more than five miles of empty country, and nothing had happened to her. There was no reason in the world for her to keep on hiding here.

She needed to leave, to go be with her own kind. It would be a journey of a thousand miles, but with the device protecting her, she should be able to make it to Los Alamos. Better to make the attempt, and possibly die trying, than to skulk at the research station until at last the supplies from the surrounding countryside gave out and she was forced to move on anyway.

All right. Now that she had a plan in mind, Deirdre knew she had to figure out the best way to implement it. She had only a hazy idea of where Los Alamos was even located, but she knew she'd need to head east until she got to New Mexico and then go north. That meant she could take the 10 Freeway for a good chunk of the route. She'd siphon the gas out of the other two vehicles on the property, get the Toyota truck as filled up as possible. There were rubber hoses in the lab that should work for that particular task. And she could continue to siphon gas as she traveled. She'd seen a section of the 10 Freeway off in the distance when she and Amaal had gone to Ontario Mills, and although it had its share of abandoned vehicles blocking the lanes, it wasn't so jammed that she couldn't get through. True, she'd probably only be able to drive around forty miles an hour or so, at least until she got into the more wide open spaces out beyond Palm Springs, but if she left in the early morning, she should still be able to make it to Phoenix by nightfall. Then she could hole up there and continue on to New Mexico the next day. Somewhere along the way, she'd get a map from a gas station or truck stop, since she couldn't rely on the map application on her phone the way she used to, and she'd need real directions once she was past the territory she knew.

Yes, that sounded as though it would work. Why, then, did the prospect of leaving make her feel so desolate?

Because some part of her still cared. She was angry at Amaal for lying to her, for concealing some difficult truths about this new world, but despite all that, she couldn't quite hate him.

It would have been easier if she could.

With a sigh, she went to the pantry and began

gathering the items she thought she would need for her road trip.

Amaal had fed Sasha, though he had no appetite himself, and now she lay curled up in front of the hearth. A fire flickered there, the only light in the house. He watched the flames moodily, feeling now more than ever Deirdre's absence. How could she have made such a hole in his world? It should have been easy to forget her—after all, he had lost count of the women he'd been with over the centuries, just as he'd forgotten their names. But it seemed the more he tried to push Deirdre out of his thoughts, the more she crowded in.

It was now quite late, nearly midnight. He lingered here in front of the fire because he had no wish to go upstairs to an empty bed. Unfortunately, he knew he could stay here all night, and it would change nothing. That bed would remain empty, because Deirdre was gone.

He should get some sleep. Two wine bottles drained, and he'd contemplated opening another. However, he'd held off. Becoming drunk might blunt the pain for a while, but it would only return once the alcohol wore off.

What was she doing now? Probably asleep, he guessed, in one of the narrow beds that had been provided for the student researchers at the station. Her slumber would be untroubled, for she had done the right thing, had she not? She had made herself walk away when she realized there was no future for her with him.

Deirdre was much stronger than he.

Amaal ran a hand through his hair, then pushed himself up from the couch. Sasha opened a sleepy eye to see what he was doing, but when she realized he was not doing much of anything except standing there and staring at the fire, she shifted slightly and went back to sleep.

This was ridiculous. He should not allow one human woman to rob him of his rest. Oh, how Omar would laugh if he were still alive, laugh at the power Amaal had given Deirdre. She had only been gone for twelve hours, and yet each of those hours had been a torment, an eternity. How was he supposed to function when deprived of the woman he loved?

The woman he loved....

Those words brought him up short. He had avoided acknowledging them for some time now. Something within him had prevented him from recognizing what these feelings truly were, perhaps because he had never experienced them before.

But he realized now, as he stood there in the fire-lit darkness, that he did love her. Somehow she had managed to creep inside his soul, to take up residence in the empty spaces there. Would he throw that away simply because he feared a lifetime shared with her?

Especially when these hours without her already felt like an eternity.

A resolve formed within him. He must go to her and tell her he loved her, beg her to come back. She would be his Chosen, and they would never have to suffer another parting.

That sounded very simple, but he worried what her response would be. Perhaps she had already convinced herself that she was better off without him.

One way or another, he needed to know. And it could not wait until morning. He would go as far as he could using his djinn power and crawl the rest of the way if he must, once he was back within range of the device.

If she turned him away…well, he must make sure that would not happen.

Deirdre stared up at the ceiling. She'd gone to bed more than an hour earlier, knowing she needed to be up and moving by dawn, but sleep was proving elusive.

The reasons for that sleeplessness were easy enough to pinpoint. The bed was hard, very unlike the memory foam splendor she'd slept on at Amaal's house. More than that, though, was his absence. She kept wanting to reach out with her hand to feel him sleeping next to her, but she knew he wasn't there, would never be there.

Forget about him, she told herself. *Think about going to Los Alamos, meeting a human guy.*

Surely not everyone there would be paired up already. There had to be single survivors like her.

Problem was, she didn't want to think about being with someone else. How could anyone ever be better than Amaal, more passionate and tender in bed, more ready to indulge in foolish fun, just to pass the time? He'd made her laugh when she'd thought she would never laugh again.

Damn it.

She pushed back the covers, thinking she would get up and make herself some chamomile tea. There was a box in the cupboard, one she'd procured some months earlier when anxiety had prevented her from sleeping. It wasn't quite the same thing as taking sleeping pills, but the tea did help a little. She just couldn't get on the road tomorrow with only four or five hours of sleep under her belt.

After pulling a sweatshirt on over her long-sleeved T-shirt and yoga pants, and pausing to slip her feet into her Uggs, she headed for the kitchen.

She'd done this in the dark so many times that she didn't bother to turn on the light in the hallway, even though she knew she had no reason to fear a djinn attack now. Neither was there any reason to worry about conserving electricity, not when she was leaving tomorrow morning and never coming back, but old habits died hard.

She did turn on the light in the kitchen, however, just so she could see what she was doing. There was the kettle, sitting on top of the stove where she'd left it. She filled it partway with water, then went to the small pantry to get out the box of chamomile tea.

Just as she was going to fetch a mug from the cupboard, a sharp sound from the front of the station made Deirdre stop short. She paused, one hand resting on the cupboard door, a surge of adrenaline spiking through her.

There it was again. A knock on the door.

No, that was impossible. She tried to imagine what it could be. Raccoons throwing pinecones at the front of the building? Hardly. That was ridiculous. But....

Another knock. This time she could have sworn she heard someone say her name, but that was impossible. It was probably just the wind moaning through the pine trees that surrounded the research station. She should ignore it.

And yet....

Shaking her head at herself, she turned away from the cupboard and walked resolutely toward the front door. As she went, she wondered whether she should have detoured to get the shotgun, which now lay on the kitchen table next to her backpack and the other items she'd gathered in preparation for her trip east the next morning.

Well, if it was raccoons, they should be easy enough to scare off without the shotgun.

She hoped.

Deirdre turned on the porch light. Maybe that would be sufficient to chase away any animals.

But there was another knock, and she heard it very clearly this time.

"Deirdre…."

She flung open the door and saw Amaal kneeling there on the porch, face pale and drawn, bright blue eyes shadowed in pain.

Oh, God, he had followed her here. Had come to her through the dark, through the device beating on him, taking away his energy. For all she knew, he'd had to crawl up the porch steps, strength utterly spent.

"Amaal—"

"Please," he said, an echo of the same entreaty from their first meeting. "Please, Deirdre…let me come inside."

Without speaking, she knelt and wrapped an arm around his waist, helped him get to his feet.

He was shivering violently, no doubt from the freezing night air. She had to get him inside.

They went into the station, and she closed the door behind them. At least the comfortable furniture he'd conjured was still there, so she helped him over to one of the couches. He fell onto it, his head flopping against the high back, eyelids closed.

"Amaal, what are you doing here?"

He opened his eyes and gave her a weak smile. "I should think that would be obvious."

A perilous warmth seemed to awaken inside her, but she did her best to ignore it. She couldn't let him give her any hope. Not now, when she'd done her best to harden her heart against him.

"Well, explain it to me anyway."

With a faint moan, he pushed himself upright. Just getting inside and away from the icy night air seemed to have helped him a little, although he still looked very pale. "Because I realized I could not live without you, Deirdre. I was a fool and a liar. I know you have no reason to forgive me, but I hope you can."

Hearing him state the truth so baldly, with no attempt to make his part in the situation sound better, made Deirdre's knees feel a little shaky. She went and sat down on the other sofa before her legs failed her completely. But...was he really telling her the truth, or only what she wanted to hear so she would come back to him? Not quite looking at him, she said, "Yes, you were a world-class jerk."

"I know that." He paused, then went on, "And I know you may be thinking that I am only uttering pretty words now so I can convince you to return. But that is not the situation at all. I want to be with you now and forever, Deirdre. I want you to be my Chosen."

The tight, angry knot of hurt within her began to slowly loosen. He couldn't possibly be telling her something like that if he didn't mean it. She didn't know much about djinn, but she knew they didn't mess around. They had their own rules, rules that were supposed to be obeyed. Amaal wouldn't dare ask her to be his Chosen if he didn't mean it. That was not the sort of commitment to be taken lightly.

But because she'd been hurt before, she wasn't about to jump right in and say yes. "What, twelve hours without me, and you suddenly realized I was the one for you?"

A sad smile touched his lips. "I would not say it was sudden. Rather, I realized what I'd been trying to ignore for too long. Your soul speaks to mine, Deirdre, just as I hope my soul speaks to yours. I tried to contemplate going on without you, and I realized that was impossible. All I can do is tell you the truth of my heart, and hope you recognize that truth for what it is."

For a long moment, she could only sit there and watch him, look for some sign that he wasn't being sincere. But she couldn't see anything except a terrible need in his eyes, even stronger than the weariness the device had brought on.

And she knew what she had to do.

She got up from the couch and walked past him, doing her best to ignore the confusion and sudden fear in his expression. She went to her room and retrieved the device from where it rested on the nightstand, and brought it back with her to the front room. Then she sat down next to Amaal, and took his hand in her free one.

"This is how you shut it off," she said, and moved his fingers over the touchscreen.

Awareness dawned, and he smiled. Almost at once the color returned to his face, the light to his eyes. He took the device and set it down on the low table before them. "Does this mean…?" he began, and trailed off, as though he wasn't sure he wanted to ask the question after all.

"Yes," Deirdre replied, then bent and kissed him on the cheek. "It means that I believe you. It means that I want to be with you. Because your soul does speak to mine, and I never want another day to pass without being able to hear it."

He reached over and touched her hair, then

moved his fingers down to cup her cheek. "Because I love you, Deirdre Graves, and I want to spend eternity with you."

The knot inside her was finally undone. She moved closer to him and whispered, "I love you, too, Amaal."

He kissed her, and though the room was chilly, she no longer noticed, because he'd rekindled the fire inside her. For a long moment, they embraced, and then he said, "Let me take you back to my house. I cannot say our home, for we will need to decide where to go after this."

"To one of the communities of djinn and Chosen."

"Yes. There is one in Bel-Air, but I advise against that, for that is where the man who killed my brother resides. I fear it might be somewhat awkward."

That comment, accompanied by an ironic curl of his lip, was more like the Amaal she knew and loved. "No, probably not there," she agreed. "Where else can we go?"

"There is a settlement in Laguna Beach, and another in La Jolla, just north of San Diego."

Both of those prospects sounded wonderful. To live near the beach, enjoy the mild weather, and never have to endure another snowstorm? She thought she could gladly spend an eternity that way.

"I like Laguna," she said. "I've been there a few times. It's a beautiful little town."

He smiled. "Then that is where we will go."

"And we can bring Sasha with us?"

"I see no reason why not."

She snuggled against him, felt the warmth of his body, the reassurance of his presence. After a brief pause, she said, "Thank God you came here tonight. I was going to leave tomorrow, head for Los Alamos. I didn't know what else to do."

For a long moment, he was quiet. He kissed the top of her head, then said quietly, "I would have gone to find you. Once I knew I could not live without you, I would have gone to the ends of the earth to get you back. Never doubt that, Deirdre."

The quiet conviction in his voice was clear. Yes, she thought, he would have gone looking for her, would have dragged himself into Los Alamos if he must, if that was what he needed to do to get her back.

"I don't doubt it," she said. "Just as I'll never doubt you again."

"Good," he replied. "Because you will never have any need to."

And he kissed her again, over and over, right before his arms went tight around her and he blinked them away, back to the house which was supposed to be his, but which he intended to give up so they could start a new life together.

A life in the sun. A life with Amaal, the djinn who loved her.

Yes, she thought, she would be happy with an eternity of that.

The End